'This engaging novel retells the prodigal. A medieval pilgrimage i pilgrims, each carrying a burd about, and each meets with Go along the way. This is a book for those who go on pilgrimage and for those who pilgrim in their chairs! A beautiful book that had me gripped by the story; it made me long to go on pilgrimage again, to meet with God as I walk and to experience even more of His mercy and grace.'
Penelope Swithinbank, chaplain at Bath Abbey, spiritual counsellor, author and pilgrimage leader

'A timeless journey of love, loss and redemption played out across a compelling medieval landscape.'
Anne E Bailey, Historian, Oxford University

'*The Pilgrim* is the story of not one but many journeys. It's a wise and engaging tale, full of the bitter-sweet truths of life. Ambitious young warrior Hal discovers that actions are important and sin has consequences. As Brother Hywel, he joins a band of pilgrims, each of whom comes with their own hopes and frailties, and as they travel together, their desires and secrets are gradually revealed. *The Pilgrim* is a beautifully set novel, crafted with real compassion, revealing the truth that true pilgrimage happens in the soul, amidst tragedy, miracles and the gift of the peace of God.'
Andrew J Chamberlain, writer, presenter of The Creative Writer's Toolbelt Podcast

'With a real sense of place and time, and characters that pop from the page, this novel is a masterpiece of historical fiction.'
Wendy H Jones, author and writing coach

'*The Pilgrim* is a beautifully told tale of encountering friendship, faith and forgiveness. A young man with so much promise is introduced to the ways of the world and soon falls foul of his foolish lust. Filled with shame and remorse, he yet remains determined to prove himself. He enters a monastic community, full of ambition, but his pride leads to another fall. Now a broken man, he is instructed to accompany a diverse group of people on pilgrimage. As he begrudgingly joins them, we begin to wonder – will he find his own redemption on this journey?

'Joy has a marvellous gift of storytelling. This is an easy-to-read book that drew me in, and I enjoyed spending time with the characters, especially Hywel. At the same time, *The Pilgrim* has depth that made me think and reflect. I found myself making my own spiritual pilgrimage as I joined Hywel and his companions travelling across the stunning countryside of Wales.'
Rev Peter Goodridge, Rector, St John's Elmswell

'Joy Margetts has done it again: a gripping historical novel which entertains and engages from start to finish, with wise spiritual insights every bit as relevant to twenty-first-century readers as to the thirteenth-century characters who are learning and living them. I was hooked from page 1, and stole any moment I could to read the next piece of the tale, which is full of unexpected twists and turns. The whole thing is beautifully written, with characters you can't help but warm to, and gorgeous descriptions of the stunning Welsh scenery providing a backdrop to the unfolding drama. Like a modern-day *Pilgrim's Progress*, *The Pilgrim* tells a story rich with drama, suspense and deep truths for any disciple of Christ. Read it if you want to walk closer with Jesus. Read it if you love a good novel. Whatever your motives, you'll come away challenged and inspired.'
Lucy Rycroft, author and founder of thehopefilledfamily.com

The Pilgrim

Joy Margetts

For Emily

instant apostle

Be blessed!

Joy x

First published in Great Britain in 2022

Instant Apostle
The Barn
1 Watford House Lane
Watford
Herts
WD17 1BJ

British Library Cataloguing-in-Publication Data

A catalogue record for this book is available from the British Library.

This book and all other Instant Apostle books are available from Instant Apostle:

Website: www.instantapostle.com

Email: info@instantapostle.com

ISBN 978-1-912726-61-5

Printed in Great Britain.

For Mum and Dad,
who have lived lives of pilgrimage,
and faithfully been a guide to so many others

Contents

For more information about Joy and her writing, go to
www.joymargetts.com

Author's Note

My debut novel *The Healing* was such a personal book on so many levels. When I began to write *The Pilgrim*, it didn't feel so personal. I wanted to write another book, and I wanted to write about Hywel. I wanted him to have his own story, as he had become so dear to so many of my readers. I knew the basics of his backstory – I'd written those into *The Healing* – and so I had my starting point. Although there are similarities between the books – there are monks and abbeys, and horses and journeys, and grins and laughter, and tears and words of wisdom – it is a different book. The spiritual journey it describes is different and not based so much on my own.

But the more of it I wrote, the more I realised that my experiences are all over it. I know what it means to carry guilt and shame, to be reckless with the feelings of others. I know how destructive pride can be, and how painful it can be when God humbles us. I know that God can use the unlikeliest of people and situations to teach us how much we need Him, and need others. I have had to learn what true leadership in serving others looks like. I have had to kneel in repentance at the foot of the cross and plead for God's mercy, time and again.

I have also experienced the overwhelming peace of His presence, the bubbling up of His joy within me, the reassurance of His love for me in the words and actions of others, and the wonder of deeply encountering Him in worship.

All of these things are in the book. All of these are Hywel's lessons to learn and experiences to encounter. So I am in there, perhaps inevitably.

The Pilgrim Route

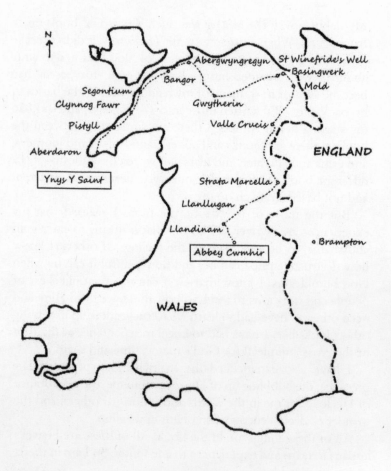

Part One
Hal

1
Brampton Barre

Late summer 1202
England

The sound of clanging swords echoed around the stone walls of the castle, punctuated by grunts and yells and, incongruously, laughter. Hal wandered up the path from the bailey below and paused, leaning on a gatepost, to watch his brother, Robert, and four others taking turns to spar with one another on a small, flat patch of ground at the foot of the motte. He grinned. Robert was pouring with sweat but laughing as he broke away and approached him, brandishing his practice weapon threateningly at his younger brother.

'Hal!' Robert's grin matched his own. 'Where were you? We were down a man and could have used you, even if you are of little use with a sword!'

Hal backed off slightly, holding his hands up to ward off his brother's rank smell and flying perspiration as much as to avoid the sword he was swinging around.

'You know full well I could have held my own against you, or anyone else wanting to give me a try!'

'So where were you, then?' Robert threw himself down on the grass slope of the motte, and wiped his sweaty brow with his tunic sleeve. 'Get me a drink, will you?' he nodded imperiously in the direction of the well below them in the courtyard.

Hal glared good-naturedly at his brother, but walked down to the well and grabbed the pail that a servant had just wound up from the fresh water depths. It was a warm afternoon, and the sky had been clear all day. Hal took a large swallow of water himself, and then wandered back up to where Robert now lay with his hands behind his head and his eyes closed. Taking aim, Hal threw the remains of the water pail over his brother, who jumped to his feet, spluttering and shaking his drenched head.

'You deserved that! Ordering me about like some wench in your favoured tavern! And you were in need of a wash as much as a drink.'

Robert stood with his hands on his hips. For a moment it looked like he would explode with anger, but then just as quickly, his eyes crinkled and his lips twitched, and before long he was laughing loudly as he tackled Hal to the ground and shook his wet hair in his face. Both now were well soaked, and breathing heavily, they flopped side by side on the grass.

'I was with Cenred in the stables, if you must know. I wanted to watch him examining your horse. You know, the horse you ran into the ground yesterday?' Hal elbowed Robert in the ribs.

'I was a bit careless with him, I admit.'

'I know you aren't intentionally cruel, brother, but getting your thrills riding hard over difficult terrain was a bit rough on your poor horse.'

'I am sorry for it. Is he recovered?'

'A strain and swelling to his right rear fetlock. Cenred wasn't very happy with you, but says Flight will recover if you let him rest for a few days. He showed me a poultice he uses. Stank to high heaven. Almost as bad as you stink now.'

'Well, you stink of horse muck, so I think we are even,' Robert quipped back.

They laid beside each other companionably, allowing the warmth of the slowly setting sun to dry them. Hal was three years younger than his brother but already taller and broader. Both were dark-haired and dark-eyed, but Hal was the image of his father, with his wide face and square jaw, while Robert had his mother's high cheekbones and finer features.

Hal knew his brother had many female admirers and could see why. At twenty-one, Robert was every bit the image of a fine Norman lord, and his reported prowess with the ladies was almost as impressive as his handling of a weapon. As firstborn and heir, he would in time succeed his father as Lord of the Manor, and undoubtedly make his family proud. He was promised in marriage to a daughter of a wealthy family, a good match that had been long arranged. Hal was well-built and strong and no less able than his brother to handle himself when faced with an armed opponent. He was no less handsome, either, but had much less experience of the fairer sex than his brother; he was destined for the Church.

Hal's stomach rumbled loudly.

'You hungry again, little brother? I swear you have hollow legs, the amount you eat.' Robert lifted himself up onto his elbows. 'It's not long until supper. We had both better go and clean ourselves up. Father won't appreciate either of us appearing at the table stinking.'

Robert rose effortlessly to his feet and reached out his hand to help Hal up. Hal grabbed his hand and Robert tugged, but much harder than Hal was expecting, so that he went sprawling forward onto his knees, his hands landing in the muddy puddle his emptied water pail had made.

Robert was already running. Hal levered himself up and ruefully wiped his filthy hands on his tunic. 'Well played, brother!' He grinned as he watched Robert's hastily retreating back.

Hal followed Robert in the direction of the cluster of substantial wooden buildings that were home. They offered them comfortable enough accommodation, within the safety of Brampton Barre's curtain walls. The stone keep tower, built by their grandfather, loomed above them, but it was rarely used, apart from to accommodate a handful of guards on sentry rotation. Life had, thankfully, been peaceable at Brampton for some years now, not least owing to the protection of Roger de Mortimer of Wigmore, their more powerful neighbour. Hal's father, Sir Robert de Brampton, held the lands all around Brampton and had vassals aplenty but, as a *mesne*[1] lord, was a vassal himself to Mortimer. It was a mutually beneficial relationship, and their little household had wealth enough from the produce of the land, and sheep and wool sales.

There were just the three of them bearing the Brampton name living in the castle now. Hal had been too young to really remember his mother, who had died bringing their sister into the world, a weak child who had lived barely a few weeks. For Robert de Brampton, the loss of his wife and his daughter had focused his affection on his remaining children. He had lavished attention on his sons, but with wisdom, good sense and enough discipline to produce young men of good character. He had ensured they had the best of education – in letters, accounting, land management and the normal physical pursuits – but in return he expected much of his sons.

For Hal's future, his father has chosen the Cistercians. Hal knew he had high expectations for him to rise through the ranks and gain position for himself within the Order, perhaps as his own brother, Jerome, had done. The abbey at Cwmhir was where he would enter into his novitiate, partly because it was under Roger de Mortimer's benefice, and also in memory of Hal's Welsh mother and her family connections. Hal was content with his lot. He knew his only hope for any position of status or influence for himself was within the Church. He was confident in his ability to do well and secure a place of prominence, in time, just as his brother would do well when he

---

[1] Within the feudal system a *mesne* lord held land and vassals, but was also vassal himself to a higher-ranking lord.

took his father's place. They had both been prepared well for greatness, and both owed their father their best.

The smell of roasted meat made Hal salivate as he hurried from his hasty ablutions into the hall where the table was already laid, heaving with its bounty. His father was in his place at the head of the table, and Robert was sat to his right.

'Nice of you to join us, lad. Sit, Henry, so we can all eat.' His father tried to give him a stern look, but Hal could see that his eyes were twinkling.

'We should have started before he got here. He'll likely clear the table by himself if we hesitate much longer,' Robert quipped.

'You might be right there, son. The boy must still be growing, which is a bit alarming! I've not seen a young man put so much food away at every meal placed in front of him, and not put on any belly flesh.' Sir Robert patted his own slightly rounded belly ruefully.

The three of them set to, making a fair-sized dent in the food laid before them, drinking a fine ale and sharing their stories of the day. Hal loved these times around the table. His father's hair was more grey than brown, and his face lined and wrinkled around the eyes, but he was still a formidable and charismatic figure. Hal watched him as he listened to Robert's account of his swordplay and smiled at the way his father looked tenderly at his older son and laughed with him. Hal knew he would receive the same look when the conversation turned his way. His father's affection for both his sons was never in doubt.

Hal realised then that his brother had spoken directly to him, and was looking at him with a bemused expression on his face, waiting for a response.

'Sorry?' he grinned back at him.

'Away with the horses again, I presume? You are obsessed with those four-legged beings. It is definitely time to widen your experience, my brother, perhaps with beings of the two-legged variety. I was just saying to our father that I thought it time you joined me in the village tonight.' He looked knowingly at Hal, one eyebrow raised.

Hal knew exactly what 'going into the village' with Robert meant. There were local ladies aplenty who welcomed his brother's body into their beds, and his coin into their purses. Hal knew Robert well enough, that once he married his betrothed he would remain faithful to his wife, but while he was yet free, then… well, he would make the most of what was on offer to one of his rank and position.

Hal had thought long and hard about whether he should follow his brother's example, while he still had his own freedom. It definitely held an attraction for him. His vow of celibacy loomed large in the not too distant future.

Hal looked to his father.

'Henry,' his father's face was kind, 'I know you are serious about taking your vows, but until that day I believe you are free to experience all that the world offers. I would expect it to help any young man meant for the Church to get certain things out of his system, and I think it would be good for you too. You are a man now. Robert is right. And you can trust him to guide you in the honourable way to "widen your experience", as he put it. My only advice is the same as I gave him when he began his night-time trips out. *Be careful, and be kind.* The good reputation of our family depends on it.'

Hal looked back at Robert and smiled sheepishly. 'I must admit I've watched you sneaking out, with not a little envy at times. I thought you would never lower yourself to take your little brother along with you.'

'Well, it is a hardship, but I am willing to endure it for your sake. Tonight is your night, little brother.' He held his cup up. 'I'll drink to that.'

Hal clinked it with his own, smiling to hide the sudden and unexpected twist in his stomach. *Nerves, that's all,* he thought to himself.

The night was moonlit and the sky clear, but that meant it was chilly too. Hal was glad of the cloak he had put on. Glad both for added warmth and that he could hide himself from prying eyes as they walked down the hill towards the village. He pulled his hood up, feeling very exposed all of a sudden. Robert, in contrast, walked tall and proud, his head uncovered, but Hal noticed he also walked with his hand resting on the hilt of his sheathed sword, watchful of his surroundings.

'You have to be alert at night, even in the village here. There are some unsavoury sorts around, who will soon as stab you in the back for the purse on your belt as wish you good evening.'

Hal felt for his own sword and quickened his pace to walk in step with Robert. They were heading for a simply built wooden cottage at the far edge of the village.

'Not the tavern for you tonight, brother. I want you alert enough to enjoy your first time, without the fuzzed brain of drink,' Robert was saying. 'And you will be well looked after by Mae. She is a little older, but experienced, and she won't tease you for your innocence.' Robert put his hand reassuringly on Hal's arm, as if sensing his unease. 'Don't be nervous, brother, I'm sure you'll do well enough. You are a de Brampton, after all!'

The knot in Hal's stomach twisted even more painfully. The urge to run in the opposite direction was almost overwhelming.

Robert rapped softly on the low door three times. He stepped back as the door opened, and pre-empting Hal's inclination to fly, grabbed his brother's sleeve to pull him forward. An extremely curvaceous woman stood in the open doorway, a lit candle in her hand. Hal tried not to focus on her barely clothed breasts, concentrating instead on her face, which was as round as her frame. She was pleasant enough to look at, her light brown hair curling around her face, and her smile warm. He took a deep breath and stepped forward, as she stepped back to make way for him to enter. The door closed softly behind him.

Hal adjusted remarkably easily to his new way of life. There had been no further talk as yet of him leaving to go to Abbey Cwmhir, and so he purposed to make the most of whatever time he had left. As the weeks wore on, he filled his days as he had before, preferring to spend the majority of his time with Cenred and the horses, in stable or paddocks, or on horseback, riding the hills, or hunting wildly through the forests with Robert. Come night-time, at least twice a week, he would make his way down into the village, or sometimes to the neighbouring villages, usually with Robert for company. Sometimes they went to the tavern to meet their consorts, sometimes to small, humble homes, sometimes to haylofts, occasionally to forest glades.

As he gained in confidence and experience, Hal had begun to select his own favoured companions. Mae had been kind enough to him, but there were plenty of others younger and more appealing. Susannah was one. A petite woman, with mouse-brown hair and twinkling hazel eyes, who laughed easily and made him laugh too. He found, surprisingly, that he appreciated her feminine company and listening ear as much as he enjoyed the more carnal pleasures, and so sought her out more than any other. He didn't delude himself that it was love, and although he paid her enough to be exclusive to him, he wasn't naïve enough to believe that she was.

He was enjoying life immensely – his night adventures had opened up a whole new world to him – but his days with Cenred were just as rewarding. Hal couldn't remember a time when Cenred hadn't been around, in the castle or in the stables. A faithful retainer at Brampton, he had been a constant, dependable presence in Hal's young life. The older man was known the whole region around for his natural gift with horses, and for his skill in handling, caring for and breeding them. Hal found himself drawn to the man even more as he grew older; they spent hours together talking horses, tending horses, exercising horses. Cenred had called Hal himself a 'natural' when he displayed his own aptitude with the beasts, and seemed pleased to willingly share his horse expertise with him. Hal didn't know if he would be able to continue to work with horses once he joined the Cistercians, but like his night-time exploits with the ladies, he was determined to enjoy the pleasure it gave him while he could.

Cenred's home was a small, one-roomed wooden cottage, close to the stables. He had once lived among the other servants, sleeping and eating in the great hall with them, but had long since earned the privilege of his own living space through his years of faithful service. It was a simply furnished but comfortable home, and Hal had found himself visiting often as a boy. Even as a young man he would find occasion to sit with Cenred by his small fire, and just listen to his horse stories. Hal had always felt safe and comfortable in the man's company. Cenred was strong and solidly built, with an almost bald head and thick arms and legs. His face was not handsome. In fact, he had the look of a toughened fighter, a man perhaps not to be trifled with. In Cenred's case, however, looks were deceiving. The words that came from his mouth were usually softly spoken, his manner quiet and calming, and his generosity and kindness well known to all. Hal loved and trusted him for it.

When the older man suddenly took a wife for himself, it was a surprise to everyone. He went away to Ludlow, for a day and night, and came back with a young woman astride a fine bay horse. The woman was stunningly beautiful, to Hal at least. Her red hair flowed down her back beyond her waist, and her eyes, when she turned them on him, were mesmerising, green, like forest moss in the sunlight. She was small and fine-boned, with alabaster pale skin, but held herself with an almost regal aspect. Cenred introduced her to them as Hild, but never gave any other explanation as to who she was, where she had come from or why he had married her.

It made just appearing at Cenred's threshold a little more awkward for Hal. When he did visit their home, Hild would treat him with respect, but keep her distance, offering him food and drink, but leaving them to sit at table without her. Hal could not have even described what her voice sounded like, he had heard it so rarely. But her face he could describe to the minutest detail. He had seen it many times in his dreams.

When Hild had first come to Brampton, Hal had been content to admire her only in his dreams. But, his fleshly passions having been well and truly aroused by his visits to the village, he unwittingly began to see his friend's wife in a different light. Sitting at Cenred's table, he would find himself watching her as she moved gracefully about the room, entranced by her pale skin, or by the way her glorious hair fell in waves. He began to avoid Cenred's home even more, worried that he might give himself away. The internal struggle was real. She was so young and beautiful and Cenred was so old in comparison. And yet to any onlooker they seemed happy enough together. Hal found himself daydreaming about what it would be like to be married to such a woman. And in the night his dreams became yet more vivid.

He came across her one day on the riverbank. Winter was fast approaching and there was a biting wind. She was bent over, cutting reeds, and as he approached, drawn like a moth to a flame, he could see that she had injured her hand, the crimson blood stark against her pale skin. He stepped forward and unthinkingly took hold of her hand to examine her wound. It was a clean cut, likely made as she ran her hand down the sharp edge of a half-frozen reed.

He looked up to find her watching him. He also caught the look of unguarded admiration, and as their eyes met there was a moment of connection, before she quickly dipped her head. He still had firm hold of her hand and she didn't pull it away, standing patiently as he used his clean sleeve to wipe the blood and his fingers to apply pressure to her palm. He realised she was trembling.

'Hild, are you well? Do you need to sit?' He was concerned that she might fall into a dead faint.

'No, no. Do not concern yourself,' she answered breathlessly. 'I must go. Cenred will be expecting me.'

She spoke and he heard the words, and registered the music of her voice, but neither of them moved. She made no attempt to release her hand from his, and he would have given the world to hold on to her hand forever. He kept watching her as she took a deep breath and then turned her face back to him. Her beautiful eyes sought his and he could read them plainly. She felt as he did. It was palpable in the air between them. Yet it was not right, not possible, not theirs to explore further. She was not free.

Hal reluctantly released her. She looked down at her hand and touched her fingers momentarily to where his had touched her palm. She seemed to come to an awareness then and moved quickly, glancing around to check they had not been observed, picking up her basket of reeds and walking swiftly away from him without glancing back.

Hal watched her walk away, until she disappeared out of his sight. He knew in that moment, as she walked away, that she took a part of his heart with her.

How can a young man stay pure?

Only by living in the Word of God and walking in

its truth.

Psalm 119:9, TPT

2
Hild

Spring 1203

It was early spring and the rain was lashing down outside. Hal stood in the open doorway watching the rivers of rainwater flowing past the door, frustrated that the weather had prevented his planned visit to Susannah the night before, and also delayed his ride with Robert today. He sighed noisily.

'Oh, go find something to occupy yourself and use up some energy, brother!' Robert growled at him from where he was sat, with parchments and pen, and lists of figures sprawled across the tabletop in front of him. 'I can't think straight, with your moaning and sighing!'

Hal glanced back at him. Robert didn't much enjoy the book-keeping tasks his father had delegated to him to do, although he was well capable of them. He too was likely frustrated at being cooped up inside.

Hal grabbed a cloak and, pulling it up over his head, made a dash for the stables. He would find Cenred, and see if there was anything they could do inside.

A few moments later he staggered into the stable, soaked through, and found horses, but no Cenred. He spent a few moments checking around; clean water, hay and oats had been provided for the horses. They all stood calmly watching him, unperturbed by his presence, as he wandered around the stable.

Hal waited a few more minutes, and still there was no sign of Cenred. Feeling yet more frustrated, he made a decision. He would go to the cottage and find out where he was. He had not been to Cenred's home for months, not since that encounter with Hild on the riverbank. She had avoided him also, which, though it pierced him like a dagger to the heart, he knew was her way of protecting them both. He would not linger, not go in, he promised himself. He'd just find out where Cenred was, and go to him, wherever that was.

He steeled himself to knock on the door, his wet cloak dripping, his heart pounding in his chest. Before he lifted his fist, the door opened and she was standing there. She took one look at him and her eyes clouded with concern.

'Come in, Hal. You will catch your death.' She stepped back, and he stepped forward into the warmth of her home.

The fire was well alight, and a pan hung above it. He stood just inside the door, still dripping, while she dipped a ladle into the pan and poured some warm milk into a cup, stirring a spoonful of honey into it. She turned to hand it to him, but he hadn't even stepped fully into the room. She said nothing, put the cup down on the table, walked over to him and took the heavy wet cloak from his shoulders. He let her take his arm and lead him over to the table, where he sat down on the bench closest to the fire.

'Drink,' was all she said.

He took up the cup and put it to his mouth, tipping it back to take a deep swallow. It was creamy and sweet and warming, taking him back to his childhood and the kind ministrations of his long-suffering nurse. Hild sat down quietly, facing him, and watched him drink.

'I came looking for Cenred,' he said eventually, his voice sounding odd, even to his own ears.

She looked intently at him, and nodded. 'Yes, I guessed so,' she said quietly.

'Is he here?' Stupid question. He could see every corner of the small abode from where he sat. It was obvious Cenred wasn't there, but his nerves at her closeness flustered him.

'He left early this morning and won't be back until late. Summoned to Wigmore, to help with a difficult foaling, or some such thing…' She was seemingly on edge too.

'Do you love him?' He could not believe that the thought that had ceaselessly swirled around in his head for months had inadvertently left his mouth. Now that it had, he wanted her answer to his question more than anything.

She looked surprised, but she did not take her eyes from him. 'I care for him deeply. He is a good man, and a kind husband. He treats me well, shows me affection, gifts me things.' She glanced up towards a bunch of dried wild flowers hanging from a nail in the wall.

'Are you happy, then, with him?' The door had been opened a crack now and he dared to push it further. Although something told him to stop with his questioning, he needed her answer, for his own heart's sake.

'I am content.' She stood abruptly then, and walked over to the window, looking out at the rain as it continued to fall relentlessly. Her arms were clasped across her front, and her knuckles were white where she gripped her elbows.

Hal steeled himself to ask the next question. This was a dangerous path he was heading down, but he could not step off it now. Like a stray leaf, carried against its will by the rainwater river flowing rapidly downhill outside, it seemed he was unable to stop where his heart was taking his mouth.

'You have been married some time, and yet there is no child?'

He heard the sharp intake of breath and saw her sway slightly and grab the windowsill. Was that a cruel question? Had he hurt her unwittingly? He felt a stab of pain at the thought. He stood and moved over to her, close but not touching. Willing her to turn to him.

'Cenred doesn't demand of me. He is content to share my bed and not my body.' She was angry. 'You had no right to ask that! You should leave now.'

He didn't leave. He couldn't. He stepped forward and lifted his hand to brush her cheek, surprised to find it wet with tears. She gasped at his touch and her eyes flew to his. They flashed with something – rage, passion – was there a difference? He could not tell, but as he bent his head to kiss her lips, she did not flinch. She hesitated slightly, then stepped into his embrace, and her own long-denied passion matched his, kiss for kiss, touch for touch.

He woke to find her gone from his side. She was standing by the bed, fully clothed, her back to him, braiding her glorious hair. 'You are so beautiful,' he said, resting his head on his hand, watching her.

'You should go.' She spoke without turning, her voice barely a whisper.

'I love you, Hild.' He meant it, with every fibre of his being. He loved her. It was not just lust. She had captivated him heart, body and soul.

She paused in her hair-braiding momentarily. 'I know.' She still did not turn, but walked over to pick up her veil from where he had pulled it from her head, not so very long ago. He watched as she stood clutching the veil, worrying the fine fabric in trembling hands.

'I love you too. But it is not enough, and never will be. If you really, truly love me, Hal, please, you must leave now, and never look back.' She turned to him, her eyes wet with tears. 'What we did, it was wrong and it must never happen again.'

He sat up then, still watching her, his heart and mind in turmoil.

'Hild?' One last appeal. His voice was breaking, as was his heart. She shook her head and turned away again as he leant over to grab his clothes and hastily dress himself. He stepped over to her but she moved, turning to hand him his still-damp cloak.

'Go, Hal,' she whispered. It took everything within him to not pull her back into his arms, but she turned her back and buried her face in her now crumpled veil.

Hal pulled the door open and lifted his hood to cover his head. He glanced about outside but the relentless rain ensured there was no one to witness his departure. Just in case, he faked a jovial voice and called back as he stepped through the door, 'My thanks, Mistress Hild, for your hospitality. I will call on Cenred again tomorrow.'

She closed the door firmly behind him.

Hal made his way blindly to the stables. He could not go home. The day was drawing on, and dusk approaching. He stumbled across the threshold and one or two of the horses snickered with alarm as he threw himself heavily down on a pile of hay. He sat like that, his head in his hands, for what seemed an eternity. He had been through a whole maelstrom of emotions, from unbridled joy to searing pain in the matter of a few short hours, and he felt utterly spent. He could not make any sense of what had just happened and he didn't want to think of anything, only of his own pain and loss.

He felt the warm nudge of a horse's nose on the side of his face. He wasn't sure if the horse meant to comfort him, or if he just wanted access to the pile of hay he was sitting on. Hal got to his feet and turned his face into the horse's neck for a brief moment, before stepping away. He turned and looked around his stable refuge, and a thought struck him that stole the breath from his body. Cenred! Everything in that stable reminded him of the man, of the time he had spent with him there, the shared laughter, the wisdom, the friendship. He felt the bile rise to the back of his throat and he retched violently, as guilt descended on him like a lead-weighted cloak, and he dropped to his knees on the stable floor. *Betrayer!* His conscience screamed at him.

'Oh, God! What have I done?' Hal groaned.

He stayed in that attitude of prayer with his head on his knees, but didn't expect God to answer him, to even hear him. The realisation hit him that in those few short hours everything had changed, because of his recklessness. He had betrayed his friend, betrayed his family, betrayed Hild. He was no longer the man he had been, nor the man he had hoped to be, and he would have to live the rest of his life with the knowledge of what he done.

But Cenred doesn't need to know. The same voice inside his head whispered.

Hal glanced up then. He was in pitch dark, the sun having set, and Cenred could return at any moment. Hal jumped to his feet and forced his legs to run, knowing that he could never truly outrun what he had done. And knowing that he did not have the courage to face it.

Hal didn't see Cenred that night, or the following day, or for many days after, finding excuses to avoid being where he knew the older man would be. He missed his company, and missed being with the horses, but the guilt he carried was so intense, he felt sure that it was written all over his face. He couldn't risk seeing Hild, either; just a glimpse of her would twist the knife in his heart. He was miserable and wretched. He would sneak into the stable and saddle up his horse before daybreak, and ride until both he and the horse were exhausted, staying out overnight many times. He found other places and other women to distract himself. When he did return, he would watch to see that Cenred had left the stables for the night, before returning his horse and rubbing it down himself. Until on one occasion, he mistimed it and Cenred emerged from the stable just as Hal was leading his horse into the yard.

'Hal!' Cenred sauntered towards him, beaming. 'Good to see you, my boy! You have been a stranger lately. Anyone would think you were avoiding me!' He was all smiles, with no sign of malice or suspicion in his tone.

Hal felt his face redden, and said nothing, allowing Cenred to advance and clap him warmly on the back, and then take the reins from him. Cenred was talking softly to the horse as he led him back to the stables, chuckling to himself about the state of him – he was filthy from Hal's ride through forests and muddy fields.

'You got him well and truly mud-splattered there, Hal. He'll take some brushing to get him clean, but I'll put him to rights,' he said amiably.

Hal was stunned into silence still. Cenred was just as he had always been with him. Gentle, kind, teasing, smiling. How could that be when something so momentous had changed in their relationship? Only... Cenred did not know! For him, nothing had changed. That he had noticed Hal's absence was plain, but he didn't seem to be reading anything into it. Perhaps Hal could do this, could be with Cenred, work with him as before and not give himself away? He followed Cenred into the stable where the older man had already secured the horse and removed his saddle and bridle.

'I'll help,' he said, amazed at how normal his voice sounded, as he gave Cenred a small smile. He picked up a brush and began to methodically brush the flank of the horse. Cenred joined him with another brush on the other side, and they worked together in silence. It felt normal, easy even, and Hal allowed himself to relax.

Cenred began a conversation about the horse fair he wanted to attend at Ludlow, and Hal soon found himself joining in, helping to plan the trip, and what purchases they might look to make. Once the horse was groomed, fed and watered, they wandered side by side out into the dim evening light.

'Thanks for your company tonight, Hal. Don't be a stranger again,' Cenred called back to him as they parted ways. Hal smiled, genuinely, in response, but as he watched Cenred amble towards his home, to his wife, he felt the knife twist again inside him and he knew deep down that while he could pretend that nothing had changed between him and Cenred, everything had.

He continued in his pretence with his dealings with Cenred, and he tried hard to act his old self with his family, but the strain didn't wear well on him. He escaped his messed-up emotions with the oblivion of drink and the company of willing ladies. More often than not his nights ended up in the village tavern, where there was wine, ale and female company all under one roof. He would drink until he felt nothing, and then sleep it off in some obliging lady's bed.

This night he had gone to the tavern as usual, and drank too much; not enough to pass out fully, but enough to get himself involved in a brawl with two locals. The landlord stepped in, and Hal turned on him wildly, pulling back his fist to land a punch. He was desperately trying to focus his swimming eyes to take aim, when a hand grabbed hold of his wrist from behind in a vice-like grip.

'Enough, brother!' Robert had Hal's wrist in one hand and had wrapped his other arm around his chest from behind, forcing him to step back from his advancement on the bemused-looking landlord. They staggered back together, Hal leaning his full weight on his brother, who manoeuvred himself around so that he could hold Hal up, pinned to his side.

'I doubt he could have landed a strike on me if he had tried, my lord,' the burly landlord smirked at Robert. 'He'll have a sore head in the morning, I dare say. It's not the first time I've had to step in to break up a fight he has started. He's been feeding my coffers well and I've no complaints about that, but he needs to learn to handle his drink a bit better, methinks.'

Hal had gone limp in Roberts' arms, half-conscious now the fight had left him. Robert shifted his position again to take his weight, knowing Hal would likely slump to the ground if he let go of him. He was trying desperately to maintain a little dignity for them both.

'My apologies, landlord,' Robert said curtly, nodding to the man. He wasn't going to make excuses for his brother, but he would definitely have some tough questions for him when he eventually sobered up.

Robert half-dragged Hal down the street. It was thankfully well after dark and the village street was deserted. The fewer villagers that saw Hal like this, the better. They came to a horse trough, and Robert let Hal slip down, so that he was sitting with his back to the rough stone, his legs spread in front of him and his head sagging almost to the ground.

'Oh, Hal! What has got into you, brother? This is not like you.' Robert crouched over him to whisper the question.

'I love her.' It was almost incoherent but Robert caught it. Hal had laid his head back against the cool stone but his neck didn't seem strong enough to hold it up, and his head began to slide to one side, his upper body following it.

Robert grabbed him and sat him upright again, holding on to his tunic as he spoke firmly into his face.

'You can't let a woman do this to you, Hal. It's not love; it's just lust.'

'No… I love her.' Hal's reply was emphatic, if a bit slurred, and he grabbed on to Robert's tunic to steady himself as he looked back at him.

'Hal, half the town think they are in love with Susannah!' Robert was half-bemused at the state of his brother and half-exasperated with him.

'No… not her… Hild.' Hal slumped back, releasing his hold on Robert, obviously exhausted with the effort.

'Whoa, brother!' Robert stood up straight with his hands on his hips. 'Now, that is a whole different matter. Hild is a married woman. I admit she is good to look at…'

'Beautiful,' Hal whispered.

'Yes, well… that may be so, but that is definitely one woman where you must look and not touch, brother.'

'Too late.' Hal's head had sagged to his chest, and his words were so muffled Robert hoped that he had not heard aright. He grabbed a pail sitting idly by the trough and dipped it into the cold, murky water.

'Sorry, brother, but I have to do this. There is no way I am carrying you back to the castle, so I have to sober you up somehow. Look at it as payback,' he said, as he threw the contents of the pail over Hal's head.

It did the trick. Hal sat bolt upright and his eyes flew open.

'Hey!' he spluttered and shook his head, spraying foul water in every direction, before groaning and holding on to his head. Robert watched as his brother's eyes slowly focused on him.

'Robert? What? Where am I?'

'Not where you should be at this hour.' Robert bent down and dragged Hal to his feet, slinging his brother's arm around his shoulder. 'Come on. Let's get you home to bed. We have some serious talking to do, but not here and not now.'

I'm so ashamed.

I feel such pain and anguish within me.

I can't get away from the sting of my sin against

you, Lord!

Everything I did, I did right in front of you, for you

saw it all.

Against you, and you above all, have I sinned.

Psalm 51:3-4, TPT

3

Consequences

A shaft of bright sunlight pierced Hal's half-closed eyelids and he stirred, groaning. His head was throbbing and there was no way he was opening his eyes completely unless somebody put that light out. Mercifully a shadow passed over his face, and he gingerly opened one eye, to find his brother standing over him with his hands folded across his chest.

'Time you were awake. The rest of us broke our fast hours ago. Father asked after you. I said you had had some bad fish yesterday and were paying the consequences. I assumed you wouldn't want to eat this morning?' Hal groaned again and put his arm up over his eyes.

'Could you speak a little quieter?' he whispered pitifully.

'I'm barely speaking above a whisper as it is. Believe me, I don't need anyone else in this household to overhear what I am about to say to you, brother.'

His words made Hal remove his arm from his face and open both eyes to try to read his brother's face. Was he angry? Disappointed? Joking? He couldn't tell. But whatever he wanted to say, it was obvious he was going to say it here and now, despite Hal's fragile state. Hal tried to raise himself up a bit, willing the room to stop spinning and the throbbing to ease.

'Here, drink this.'

Robert handed him a cup of water scented lightly with what smelt like rose petals, and Hal made himself sip the perfumed drink, praying it would help ease his head. His stomach roiled, but was seemingly already empty. He could only imagine the mess he had made of himself. How he had got to his bed and who had removed his soiled clothing was a mystery to him. As was most of what had happened the previous night. He remembered leaving Susannah and heading to the tavern; beyond that it was as much out of focus as his eyes were, as they tried to fix on his brother's face.

'Do you remember what you said to me last night?'

'I don't remember even seeing you last night, let alone what I said,' Hal admitted ruefully. 'Did I insult you? Apologies, brother. Was likely a joke.'

Hal laid his aching head back down on the pillow, but Robert stepped aside and let the sunlight from the window stream across Hal's face again, so that he was forced to sit up to escape it.

'This is important, Hal. I need you to listen well to me. Last night you told me that you loved a woman, a married woman, and that you had…'

Hal's eyes flew open and his hand grabbed out at Robert's sleeve. Panic and pain coursed through him.

'I named her?' He looked pleadingly into Robert's serious face, and fell back in despair as he watched his brother nod. He put his hands over his face and dug his fingernails into his scalp, willing the pain, both head and heart, to go away.

'I don't want to know any details, and I counsel you to not speak of it to anyone else. And it is for that reason that I think your visits to the local drinking houses must end now. You might say something when not in control of your senses, to someone who will make good use of that information to sully your reputation, that of our family and of the lady in question. It is not to be chanced,' Robert continued firmly. 'Added to that, I had to wade in to break up a brawl last night, a brawl that you had instigated. It was not the first time that you have caused disruption in the village, I understand. News reached me first last night, but it could have as easily reached our father's ears and I will not have that, Hal. I will not have my father, or our family name, dragged into your sordid little escapades, all because you cannot control your passions.

'You have a choice, Hal. You promise me that you will stop your loutish behaviour in the village, and I will not let news of what you have been doing reach our father's ears. Or you continue, and find yourself cut off from my protection.'

Hal had listened painfully to his brother's words. He didn't need to feel any more guilty than he already felt, but he knew Robert was justified in saying what he did. He was thankful for his brother's intervention. He knew he had to do something to halt his spiral downwards into self-destruction, but he was at a loss as to what.

'I have a proposition for you, brother. Something to occupy your mind and body and keep you out of trouble.'

So Robert had a solution? Hal eased himself to the side of the bed so that his feet rested on the cool stone floor, grounding himself. His head was mercifully beginning to clear. Robert sat down beside him. Hal glanced over at him and was pleased to see a softening in his brother's features.

'I don't deserve your help, brother. But I am grateful for it. I will do anything, anything to get myself out of this mess.'

He doubted that there was anything Robert could offer that would make the pain inside him go away, lessen the guilt, mend his heart, but if there was something to help him refocus his mind and energy for a time, that would be something.

'Father has charged me with doing a full land survey over the summer months. Now that the weather is improving and the days are lengthening, he wants me to ride to the far boundaries of our holdings and record how the land is being used, record expected yields, and see how his landholders are faring. I could use your help with this. I know you will not have the same interest as I have, as there is another life planned for you away from here, but it will be a good opportunity for us to spend some time together before you leave. What say you? It will take you away from the horses and Cenred, but my guess is that might be a good thing?'

Hal had shifted so that he could rest his heavy head in his hands, but turned to look gratefully up at his brother. 'I would be honoured to help you, brother,' he whispered, swallowing back the emotion that unexpectedly rose in his throat.

Robert kept his word and kept Hal busy. Their days were long and involved; they rode many miles and visited many tenants and farms. When they weren't out on horseback, they were ensconced inside, writing out meticulous records of their findings. Hal rarely had time to think, let alone brood on his troubles. He was grateful to fall exhausted into his bed each night, grateful for Robert's company, grateful to be doing something useful, grateful to be kept away from Hild. Even his visits to Susannah had become few and far between. She was sweet, but she wasn't Hild, and being with her didn't make him forget the woman he loved; rather, it forced him into unhelpful comparisons.

It was after one of those unsatisfying nights with Susannah that Hal found himself back in the meadow down by the river, near the spot where he had first connected with Hild all those months earlier. It was early and barely light, but the late summer day was already warming up. There had been several unseasonably hot days, with the sun high in a cloudless sky, and even being on horseback had become unbearable. Robert had decided on a few days of rest and was off somewhere enjoying his own relaxation with a willing female friend. Hal was unsettled, and wanted to walk, to stretch his legs and clear his mind, before the day got too hot.

He was not expecting to see Hild when he did, although his mind had dreamed her into being many times, and seeing her now, he shook his head to make sure it wasn't an illusion. She was heading for the water's edge, carrying a basket of linens under her arm. Hal did not think she had seen him and he ducked back into a small copse of trees, so that he could watch her unseen. He indulged himself in observing her from a distance, not wanting to inadvertently scare her away and break the moment; the bittersweet joy was worth it.

As he watched, she placed her basket down and stood upright, stretching her back with her hands placed behind her hips. The sun was rising behind her, bathing her with a glorious light that only enhanced her ethereal beauty. And then he saw it, and it made him catch his breath. An unmistakeable rounding of her belly. Not large, but obvious, owing to her slight frame. She was with child! Hal leaned his head hard against the tree he was half-hidden behind, so that the rough bark dug painfully into his scalp. He felt numb. A wave of nausea threatened, and he took some deep breaths to calm his stomach as his mind began to whirl. What would this mean for him? For her? For Cenred?

Cenred! Surely he must know now that his wife had been unfaithful, for the evidence was there to be seen clearly. Unless perhaps they had been intimate? He shook that thought away.

She was still here in Brampton. So if, as was likely, Cenred knew the child was not his, he had not turned her out, not shamed her. Cenred had still kept her as his wife. Hal knew he was a good man... but this was beyond good, saintly even. He was also confident that in Cenred's care, both Hild and their unborn child would be kept safe and provided for. So their guilty secret could stay secret. Hal didn't need to step forward to claim the child, or to support the mother.

But this was Hild, and this was his child! Could he walk away and let another man raise his child, love the woman he loved? Hal knew deep down that he had no choice. Another piece of his heart broke away, as he realised that Hild hadn't come to him with her news, but had gone to her husband. She had known that was her best option, her safest place. She had shown courage, humility and self-sacrifice in doing so. And while it hurt him, he understood. If she could be selfless, then so could he. He wouldn't put her reputation or well-being at risk for the sake of his own longings. He had no right to her, or to her child – much as he longed to hold them both in his arms and surround them with his love and protection.

As he pulled himself upright again, he allowed himself one final glance back at Hild. But she wasn't bent over her wash basket as he expected, she was stood looking in his direction. Hal slowly stepped out into the open. She did not come running to him, but slowly moved a few steps closer until he could see the smile she gave him. She stood with one hand resting lightly on her stomach and then she lifted one hand to her lips, kissed her fingers and then turned them towards him fleetingly, before turning and walking away. She must have heard, as he did, the sound of the group of women approaching from the village with their own washing loads. He pulled his gaze away from her and ducked quickly back into the shelter of the trees, hearing the calls of greetings between Hild and the women.

His mind was whirring as he walked back towards home. She had smiled at him. There had been no anger, no reproof in her demeanour towards him. In fact, Hild had glowed with impending motherhood. Had their careless act unknowingly fulfilled her heart's desire? It was some consolation to his battered heart to see her so happy, so content.

'Hild is with child.'

Hal had returned to find Robert sitting alone, indulging in a huge breakfast.

His brother glanced up from his food as Hal sat down heavily at the table opposite him, but soon turned his attention back to the hunk of bread he was making short work of.

'You heard me?' Hal was expecting a bit more of a reaction from his brother.

Robert swallowed his mouthful, washed it down with a gulp of ale and then glanced around before replying.

'I heard you, brother, but I already knew. It has become common knowledge within the castle in the last few days. Cenred is ecstatic, I understand.'

Hal folded his arms on the table and rested his forehead on them. 'You might have told me.'

Robert did not speak for a few minutes. When he did, his tone was not unkind, but he spoke firmly.

'It is obviously painful for you, brother, but nothing can change here. She is still married to another, and whether it is your child or not...'

'It is mine.' Hal lifted his head to fix a glare at Robert.

'It is Cenred's child, whoever fathered it,' Robert stared back at him just as hard. 'And she is Cenred's wife, not yours, nor ever can be.'

'I know.'

'As I say, Hal, nothing changes.' Robert's voice and face had softened, and he laid his hand lightly on Hal's arm. 'You will have to live with the consequences of your actions, brother, but that does not include harming her or Cenred any further, to satisfy any desires of your own. Not if I have anything to do with it.' He rose from the table then. 'We still have work to do. In fact, I suggest we ride out today and find something to occupy ourselves with. Find a spot to swim, maybe; it's going to be another hot day.'

Hal took the hint. That was the end of any conversation they would have on the subject of Hild and her unborn child. He would have to find his own way to cope with the effect on his heart and mind. Hard work would help. He rose from the table and followed his brother out into the sun.

Autumn came in with storms that stripped the trees bare, and dark, dreary, damp days that mirrored Hal's mood. His misery was hard to hide from those closest to him, and good food and good wine no longer offered him any pleasure. Sitting at table with his father and brother, a time he had once appreciated so much, had become a trial. He tried to engage with the lively conversation and laugh when he was supposed to, but it had become harder and harder to pretend. He was exhausted by it.

The land survey was almost complete, which meant even more time on his hands. Hal was desperate for something to change. He sat staring blindly at the meal in front of him but had barely touched it.

'Henry, my son? Are you sickening? You have lost your appetite for good food, and for life in general, it seems.' His father's eyes were full of concern.

'I am well, Father.' Hal forced a smile. He turned back to his plate, unwilling to let his father scrutinise his face further.

'That may be,' his father continued. 'Yet something is troubling you, I can see it. Is it something I should know about?'

Panic seized Hal and he glanced over to Robert to catch him shaking his head and giving him a warning glare. His father didn't know and mustn't know what really troubled him. He thought quickly.

'I think I just need a change, Father, a new direction for my energies. Now that the land survey is nearly done, I find myself feeling purposeless, that is all.'

'I think, son, it is time we plan for your leaving of us.' His father was watching him still, so Hal schooled his features into a smile.

'I agree. Thank you, Father,' were the words from his mouth, while his mind yelled, *No, not yet!*'

'I would appreciate one last Christmas with us all together, but I think the New Year must mark your time to depart from us and take up your new life with the Cistercian brothers,' his father continued.

Hal breathed. A few more weeks, at least. The chance to see his child born, his Hild happy, perhaps.

'As you desire, Father. I will begin to prepare myself, but yes, I would enjoy one last Christmas celebration at home.' He allowed himself to smile genuinely then. He would miss his family at Brampton and so would try to make the most of his time left here with them. He raised his cup to his father and drank deeply, before purposely turning his attention back to his food.

Christmas came, but it was not the great family celebration they had planned. On the eighth day of Christmas, Hild began her birth pains. On the tenth day she birthed a stillborn son, and then slipped quietly away herself. On the twelfth day of Christmas they buried them both.

It was a small group that mourned them. Many who might have come were otherwise occupied in full-blown festive activities; others were put off by the thick snow on the ground and the biting wind. Sir Robert and his sons stood with their old friend, Cenred, at his wife's graveside. A few other faithful servants stood huddled together in groups, and with the priest wrapped up in his many layers and the two shivering gravediggers, it made for a sorry party.

Sir Robert had placed himself on Cenred's left side to offer his support. Robert stood on his father's other side, looking grim. Hal held back at first, but realised his expected place was beside them and he came to stand by Cenred. His heart was as numb as the frozen fingertips poking through his woollen mitts. As he stood gazing down into the open grave which gaped, dark and threatening, against the stark white of the freshly fallen snow, he felt his whole body sway towards it, and an overwhelming urge to throw himself into the pit overcame him. He felt a strong hand grab his. Cenred. His old friend held fast to him and whispered, 'Hold steady, lad.'

They watched as the simply wrapped bodies were lowered into the ground, the gravediggers' breath coming in great clouds as they huffed and puffed in the freezing air. The priest stepped forward and began to speak the familiar words of committal, rushing through them as they all stood shivering. He nodded then to Cenred who, never letting go of Hal's hand, bent down and grabbed a handful of snow and threw it on top of Hild's shrouded form. It seemed right somehow. Snow and not soil. She was too lovely to be marred with dirt. As Cenred stood upright he pulled Hal closer to him so that they stood shoulder to shoulder, giving strength to one another.

They stood like that until they were the only ones left standing at that graveside.

Cenred spoke softly. 'She was happy, Hal, so happy to have the chance to be a mother. It was all she had ever wanted and I did not know that, not until the child was on the way. These last few months she has been so loving, so content, so happy in herself. I am grateful that she knew such happiness before she left this world. And now she has her son, and they are in heaven together.' He paused. 'She would not stay, you know, once she knew he had gone ahead. Even if she could have fought to live, she did not choose to. Do you understand, Hal?'

Hal turned and could see the trace of tears on the older man's face, shocked that his own cold cheeks were still dry.

Cenred continued, squeezing Hal's hand tightly. 'She wanted to call the boy Moses. Said it reminded her of the child placed in a reed basket in the river.'

Hal groaned, and found himself leaning his weight ever more heavily against the man standing strong by his side. He knew the significance of the name, the images it evoked of her on the riverbank, among the reeds, her bleeding hand held in his... Or stood bathed in early morning sunlight in all her splendour.

Something broke inside him and he crumpled to his knees in the wet snow, oblivious to the cold, and howled his pain into the freezing air. The tears came then as he gripped his arms around himself and swayed backwards and forwards. He cried for his own loss, he cried for Cenred's pain, and he cried for the child he would never see, never hold, never know. He thought he felt Cenred's hand resting warm on his shoulder for a while, but when he finally looked up, he realised he was alone.

He stayed there long enough for the cold snow and frozen air to numb his whole body, while his heart slowly froze over. He vowed to himself: never again would he love like he had

47

loved her. Never again would he hurt like this. And he would find a way to pay for what he had done. Cenred had said that Hild had been happy, and that Hild had *chosen* to leave this world with her son, but Hal knew the truth. He alone had been the reason they had died. His selfish desires had killed them both.

Please bend down and listen to my sobbing,

for my life is riddled with troubles

and death is just around the corner!

Everyone sees my life ebbing out.

They consider me a hopeless case and see me as a

dead man.

They've all left me here to die, helpless,

like one who is doomed for death.

They're convinced you've forsaken me,

certain that you've forgotten me completely ...

I'm drowning beneath the waves of this sorrow,

cut off with no one to help.

Psalm 88:2-5,17, TPT

4

Escape

When Hal finally staggered into the hall, his lips were blue and he was shivering violently. Robert was sprawled on a chair by the fire, a cup in his hand, gazing into the flames. His father was pacing, only coming to a stop as Hal half-fell through the door. He came over to him and flung his own thick, fur-lined cloak around his son's trembling shoulders.

'Get out of those wet things, son, and come sit by the fire. I will speak with you.' His tone did not invite argument.

Hal was so spent, so numb, he moved instinctively, removing his wet clothes and pulling on dry ones. He returned to sink into a chair across the fire from his father. Robert had vacated his seat, but handed his brother a cup of warm ale and then took up position standing behind his father, watching intently as Hal drank the cup dry. He was still shivering, but the colour was coming back into his lips and fingers.

'You have a death wish, it seems?' Sir Robert didn't wait for his son to reply. 'You have exposed yourself today, Henry, and not just to the effects of the weather.

'I observed you in the graveyard and it was obvious that you were grieving deeply, and not just for Cenred's loss. I asked your brother here if there were more to it. He preferred that I ask you direct. So, it must be done. What was your relationship to Cenred's wife and her child?'

Hal slumped forward in the chair, his head and hands hanging low. 'Must I speak of it now?' he whispered painfully.

'The child was yours?'

Hal managed a nod. He felt raw, exposed.

'We have all done things we are ashamed of, been a bit wild in our youthful pursuits, caused people grief unwittingly by our selfishness. But this, Henry? *Another man's wife?* The wife of our friend – a man who trusted you, who treated you like a son of his own? This was not well done, my boy. This was not *careful*, and it was not *kind!*'

Hal listened, his head still bowed. When he did look up, his father was sitting watching him. His face was not angry – Hal could have taken that – but what he saw in his father's eyes was something he had never seen before. He saw disappointment. And that cut him to the bone. He watched as his father sat back and closed his own eyes. Hal saw the age lines deepening on his father's face. It compounded the guilt already lying heavy on him. He felt the crushing weight of it all, but didn't feel he deserved anything less.

And then from deep within him a different emotion rose up, and he found himself gripping the arms of his chair. He was angry now; very, very angry. He was angry at the injustice of it all. At Hild for loving him, giving herself to him and then leaving him. Angry at Cenred for having Hild as his wife, and yet not knowing how to make her happy. And he was angry at God for taking Hild, and for taking their child. Most of all, Hal was angry at himself for being the cause of everyone's pain. It was almost too much to bear. His knuckles were white, his jaw clenched tight. It was taking everything within him to contain himself, willing himself not to let the sudden rage erupt all over his family.

Sir Robert rose awkwardly from his seat. 'I must go to Cenred now,' he said sadly. 'I must offer him some comfort and think of how to make amends for the pain we have caused him.'

'Not *we*, not *you*. I, I caused the pain!'

His father paused at Hal's outburst but did not turn back to his son.

'You bear my name, I share your shame,' he said sadly, and walked away towards the door, bowed like an old man.

Robert appeared in front of Hal. He said nothing, just handed Hal his outdoor cloak and hauled him to his feet. He walked over to where the practice weapons were stored and grabbed two swords, handing one to Hal.

'Come with me,' he ground out, dragging Hal through the door and out into the courtyard.

'Now, fight!' he said, shoving Hal hard, so that he fought to stay on his feet.

Hal hesitated, not trusting himself, knowing if he released his rage into the weapon he held, he could do Robert great harm.

'Fight me!' Robert yelled and stood with his arms outstretched, egging him on. 'What? Are you scared? I thought you were the big man? I thought you could handle yourself. I think now that I trusted you too soon. You are no man. You are a foolish little boy who couldn't control his passions. Fight me, you coward!' He shoved him hard again.

Hal roared then, and flung himself at Robert, pouring all his raw emotion into the fight, swinging his sword and meeting every thrust of his brother's weapon. His anger made him strong and Robert began to fall back under Hal's onslaught, until he lost his footing and lay panting in the snow. Hal raised his sword to strike him a final blow. Something made him check and he suddenly had clarity, seeing his brother lying sprawled, defenceless, before him in the snow. The rage-fuelled mist lifted as quickly as it had descended. Hal dropped his sword arm and staggered backwards. Robert jumped to his feet and grabbed Hal's sleeve to hold on to him, and he had no weapon in his hand any more.

'Hal?' It was softly spoken.

Both were breathing heavily, and sweating, insensible to the cold air and to the freezing snow beneath their feet.

'Hal?' Robert tried again, raising his voice slightly, as Hal stood mutely, trying to slow his breathing and calm his racing heart. He lifted his eyes to meet his brother's, and saw only concern there.

'Sorry,' he sighed and dropped his head, looking down at his sword arm as if it didn't belong to him.

'Did it help?'

Hal looked up quickly to find his brother smiling slightly. He still had hold of him, his hand firmly around his arm.

'You provoked me on purpose?' Hal was confused.

'It seemed the best thing to do. You looked ready to explode. I thought it better I take the brunt of it, rather than anyone else. Father especially.' Robert was ruefully rubbing his side, where Hal had caught his ribs hard. 'I will bruise colourfully, but it was worth it.'

Hal held his brother's gaze and realised in that moment just how much his family cared about him. That had not changed. He had disappointed them, failed them, but they had not turned their backs on him. He dropped his weapon and grabbed Robert. He found himself wrapped in his brother's strong embrace, and he let himself be held. Every last bit of anger melted away, and with it any energy he had left. He felt himself go heavy in Robert's arms, and realised with surprise that his cheeks were wet with tears. Robert adjusted his position so that he took his brother's weight, placing his arm around his shoulders and holding him close, as he helped his brother back inside the hall. He did not let go of him until Hal fell exhausted onto his bed. Hal closed his eyes and felt Robert remove his shoes. Then a thick fur coverlet was drawn up over him to his chin.

'Sleep, brother. There will be time and energy enough tomorrow to resume the fight.'

The next day dawned cold and lifeless, and Hal woke feeling likewise. The warmth of his bed had faded, and the cold inside him permeated his whole being. The energy that had left him the previous night had not returned with sleep. He turned to face the wall, rather than face the day and its reality. He heard people moving about, voices whispering, pans clanging softly. He heard the howling of the wind outside, but he could not engage with any of it. He closed his eyes, willing the world to disappear.

At some point food arrived, and Hal smelt the savoury aroma and glanced over to see a steaming bowl and cup sitting on a small table close to his bed. It did not interest him. He turned his face back to the wall.

'You must drink, Hal.'

He did not know what time it was, it was still light outside, but the shadows in the room had lengthened. Hal turned over and saw that the bowl had gone, but the cup was now in Robert's hand. He was crouching by Hal's head, his face etched with concern.

'Drink, brother.' Robert thrust the cup in Hal's direction. Hal licked his dry lips and reached out instinctively, lifting himself up on to his elbow to take a deep drink. Warmed mead. It burned slightly as it went down his throat, but in a pleasant way. He drank again and as the liquid hit his stomach, he felt it warm and soothe him.

'More,' he whispered, and thrust the cup back at his brother, who walked over to the side table where a flagon stood.

'Just a little, Hal, to help you relax. You don't need to drink much more of this on an empty stomach. It will muddle your senses.'

And that would be a bad thing? Hal thought. Mead-fuelled oblivion sounded just about perfect right now, but as he took another large drink, he felt the exhaustion overwhelm him again, and as he laid back he fell into a fitful sleep.

In the dream he was with Hild, in her bed, her beautiful hair spread out in red waves across the white linen, and her eyes smiling up at him, full of love and desire. He lowered himself to kiss her, but as his lips met hers he felt the cold hardness of

54

bone. He pulled back in horror to see a skull with empty eye sockets where her lovely face had been. He was wide awake then, sweating and trembling. Horrified to dream of her that way. Wanting to close his eyes and see her lovely face smiling up at him, but not wanting to hazard seeing the nightmare image again.

He sat upright. It was dark, and he could hear the snores and heavy breathing of the others, scattered in beds and on pallets around the great hall. The skies had cleared, and the moon shone in through the high window, seeming to highlight the side table still bearing the flagon of mead. Hal slipped out of his bed and moved quietly over to pick up the flagon. He was relieved to find it still heavy with mead. There was no cup so he unstopped it and took a deep swig, wiping his mouth with his sleeve.

Hal glanced around at the room that had once felt a safe place, and the urge to escape overwhelmed him. He had to get out. Placing the flagon carefully back on the table, he grabbed the thick coverlet from his bed and threw it around his shoulders. He found his shoes and forced his feet into them. He was unsteady on his feet from the effects of not eating, and lying down for too long. The mead was also beginning to make him light-headed, but he grabbed it nevertheless, and took another deep draught.

Hal crept towards the door, opening it as quietly as he could, and let himself out into the frozen courtyard beyond. He headed towards the motte and the keep, and entered the gatehouse without being challenged. A quick glance into the guardroom confirmed that both guards were snoring and oblivious to the night-time intruder. Hal allowed himself a sly smirk at that. Useless. They would be punished if found out. Well, he wasn't going to tell anyone; their negligence served his purpose.

He found the stairwell and began the tortuous climb up the spiral stairs, the circular motion adding to the swimming of his head. He still held tightly to the flagon of mead, and had to stop more than once to steady himself, leaning heavily against the stone wall. He was determined, though, and finally emerged on the parapet, the sudden blast of cold air clearing his head. The star-filled winter night sky would have been beautiful at any other time. Romantic, even, in the right circumstances. Hal snorted. Ironic. He slid down to sit leaning back against the castellated wall and took another deep drink of the mead. He didn't want to think, and he didn't want to feel. He just wanted to escape.

As the mead took hold he began to resolve himself to his plan. He let the coverlet fall from his shoulders and felt the cold air penetrate through his tunic. He shivered, so took another swallow of the mead, before placing the flagon carefully to one side. He stood swaying to his feet, holding on to the wall for support. Between the castellations he could step easily over the low wall into oblivion.

He stood, his arms outstretched, holding on to the two stones either side of him, and breathed the cold air deep into his lungs. Did he have the courage to do this? It was just one small step, and then it would be all over. The pain, the grief, the anger, the guilt, his father's disappointment. Gone. He could escape it all. And be with Hild...

No, maybe not, not if he took his own life; wasn't that what the Church taught, anyway? He didn't know what God felt about that, but was he willing to take the chance? But how could he go on living with the knowledge of what he had done, the pain he had caused to the people he loved most in this world? He had failed them all. He closed his eyes and imagined her face again. If only he could ask Hild what to do. Would she want this?

No! She wouldn't. He saw her reach out her hand to grab him.

'No! Hal, no!' It wasn't Hild's voice, nor was it Hild's hands that grabbed hold of him and held on tight. 'Hal. Not this, brother. Step back, Hal. Please!'

The voice was agonised, the hold so tight it almost squeezed the breath out of him. Hal opened his eyes, and saw that he had placed one foot upon the low wall. He shivered then, both with the cold and with the realisation of what he had almost done. He looked down into the dark void below him and stepped back quickly, suddenly feeling sick to the stomach. Robert helped him lower himself to the floor and sat down heavily beside him. He was shaking. Hal put his own hand out to rest on his brother's arm as if to soothe him.

'Robert?'

His brother was quietly sobbing, his face in his hands. Hal had not seen that for many years, not since they were small boys, and not often then. He felt the tears trickle down his own cheeks and drop from his chin. He left his hand on his brother's arm until the sobbing subsided and Robert had leant his head back with his eyes closed, his breath still coming in great heaves.

'Sorry,' Hal whispered. The word sounded so small and insignificant against the hugeness of what had just passed between them.

The next words from his brother's lips were spat out through a clenched jaw.

'Whatever made you think that this was the best thing to do? How could you have imagined this would make things better for anyone other than yourself, Hal?'

He didn't wait for answers that Hal couldn't give. The emotion was palpable in the air around them. Robert leapt up and grabbed Hal roughly by the tunic, pulling him to his feet and snarling into his face.

'Do you have any idea what this would have done to our father? To me? To Cenred? Don't you think there has been enough grief and loss felt here in the last few days? And you would add to it all?'

Hal was still feeling light-headed from the mead, and thinking clearly enough to give any kind of an explanation was impossible. It seemed Robert was actually uninterested in anything he might have to say anyway, as he grabbed the coverlet from where Hal had discarded it, and pulled Hal roughly towards the stairwell, kicking the flagon of mead so hard that it smashed into tiny pieces as it hit the stone wall.

They were more than halfway down the stairs, Robert still holding firmly on to his brother's sleeve, when they were met by a clearly flustered sentry.

'My lords,' he puffed, 'your father is approaching.'

Robert groaned audibly. 'Here, you take him,' he shoved Hal towards the guard, 'and keep him with you. Don't let him out of your sight until I return! I will see to my father.'

Robert continued down the stairwell at double speed and ran past the other guard as he emerged from the guardroom, clearly dishevelled and sleep-dazed. He saw his father painfully climbing the path from the bailey below.

'Father!' He ran to meet him, breathing heavily in the freezing night air.

'Robert? Where is your brother? Is all well?' His father sounded worn and was shivering from the cold. A male servant was loitering nearby.

'Father, all is well.' Robert tried to temper his voice, and his swirling emotions. 'Hal is safe,' he nodded back at the keep. 'You should not be out here; it is very cold tonight. What disturbed your sleep?'

'That man there.' His father waved his hand towards the servant, who was standing jumping from one foot to the other and rubbing his hands up and down his arms trying to ward off the cold. 'He was outside relieving himself and happened to glance up and saw two figures on the parapet. Seemed to him that they were fighting. He came to rouse you, but found you and Hal gone from your beds so woke me instead.'

Robert looked over to the servant and nodded. 'He did right to raise the alarm, and in any other circumstances I would commend him. But you did not need to rise from your bed. As you can see, there is no cause for concern here.'

Robert tried to sound reassuring, but in the moonlight he could see his father's face. Sir Robert was no fool and was staring hard at Robert, his gaze penetrating, his eyes knowing.

'I will return to the warmth, but I will not rest again until you are both back under our roof, Robert. I have my own idea of what has passed here tonight and I will not be denied a full explanation from you. See to your brother, and then bring him back to me.'

He turned then and allowed the servant to take his arm and walk him back down the steep slope. Robert turned back to the keep and to Hal.

Hal was sitting on the floor of the small round guardroom, huddled under the coverlet. The guards had stoked the fire and it was producing some warmth, but he was still visibly quaking. His eyes were wide and bloodshot.

'To your duties,' Robert spoke firmly and the two guards sloped sheepishly out of the room. He was under no illusion that they would likely return to the relative warmth of the guardhouse as soon as they dared.

Robert pulled up a stool and sat opposite his brother. His anger had subsided but the frustration remained. He sat and waited, watching as Hal eventually met his gaze, swallowed hard and forced out the words, 'You saved me.'

Robert sighed deeply and leant forward, his elbows resting on his knees.

'I heard you rise from your bed and saw you move towards the door. I thought perhaps you were going outside to relieve yourself but then noticed the flagon in your hand and that worried me. I threw some clothes on, by which time you were already heading into the gatehouse. I thought perhaps you were looking for some drinking companions. I've no doubt those two useless sops would have obliged.' He glanced around at the evidence of the guards' own insobriety. 'Then I saw you emerge at the top of the stairs and step out onto the parapet. I ran then, Hal. Something made me run, up the motte and up those damned stairs. And then I arrived to see you step up onto the wall and I...' He paused and dropped his head into his hands.

'Hal. It would have killed me to watch you take your own life,' he whispered.

Hal shifted and spoke, his voice barely audible. 'I was not thinking. I can't bear that I have put you through this, Robert. I did not think of the hurt I would have caused you and Father. I thought I wanted to die, but... I don't.' He shivered. 'I'm just not sure I know how to live any more.' Hal reached out for his brother, placing his hand on Robert's. 'But I will resolve to try, with God's help, and yours.'

Robert stood and helped his brother to his feet.

Hal held on to him firmly. 'Take me home, brother,' he said.

My heart is severely pained within me,

And the terrors of death have fallen upon me.

Fearfulness and trembling have come upon me,

And horror has overwhelmed me.

So I said, 'Oh, that I had wings like a dove!

I would fly away and be at rest.

Indeed, I would wander far off,

And remain in the wilderness. Selah

I would hasten my escape

From the windy storm and tempest.'

Psalm 55:4-8, NKJV

5
Cenred

Sir Robert was sat in his chair, beside a newly stoked blazing fire, huddled in his thick cloak and looking older than his years. Robert and Hal stumbled through the door clinging to each other, the fur coverlet thrown over them both. Once inside, Robert released his brother and stepped away, leaving Hal standing alone, a dejected figure, facing his father. Robert found a cup of something and sat himself in a chair opposite, but his father's attention was fully on Hal.

The pitiful figure approached and dropped to his knees at his father's feet. 'Father, forgive me,' he whispered, reaching out for his father's hand lying on the arm of the chair, his eyes turned to his father's face. He found no reproach, only tenderness and concern in his father's eyes.

'My son. Hal.'

He had used his pet name; that much registered in Hal's still clouded brain. Sir Robert turned his own warm hand to clasp his son's cold one. Hal leant forward and rested his head on his father's knees, as he had done many times as a boy needing to feel his father's affection. His father sighed and rested his other hand on his son's head. After a moment he spoke quietly.

'Son, this is probably the worst pain you have ever felt in your life, and I cannot tell you that you will never feel pain like this again. But I can tell you this... your life is worth something. You are worth something. To me, to your brother, to many who care for you, and to God. Your life is not yours to throw away. I will look for ways to help you through this; we all will.

But only God knows if you can come through this and make a better life for yourself. It is my prayer that you will.

'But now, now you must sleep, and I must talk with your brother.' He waited for Hal to nod his acknowledgement. 'Son, do you promise not to try to leave us again? Or do I need to post a guard on the door?'

Hal lifted his head and met his father's gaze. 'I will not leave. Not until you say I must.'

He pulled himself wearily to his feet and made his way back to his now cold bed, clinging for dear life to the fur coverlet that still hung from his shoulders. He curled himself into a ball and sleep came surprisingly quickly. A deep, dreamless sleep.

Robert sat gazing broodingly into the fire. After some time, his father spoke, his voice barely above a whisper.

'He was bent on self-destruction?'

'I believe so.' Robert sighed and leant in towards his father, so that he too could keep his voice low. 'I'm not sure he was in control of himself. I get the sense he was just trying to escape what was going on inside his head. The mead did not help his addled brain.'

'Pain and grief can drive us to do senseless things. I know that only too well. When I lost your mother and sister, a sort of madness descended. It was only the fact I had you, my sons, that kept me from...' Sir Robert paused, and closed his eyes for a moment. 'I fear for him, Robert.'

'I know. I do too. Although I think he scared himself tonight. Do you think he will get through this?'

'I don't know, but I want to believe he will. I honestly do believe there is a future for him, Robert. Our decision to set him aside for the Church was not made lightly. Your mother was a woman of faith and wanted this for him. We need to do something for him now. He needs to get away from here, and he cannot go to Abbey Cwmhir in this state. That would not be fair on him, or right for them.'

They sat in silent contemplation for a few moments. Robert stood and filled his cup again, offering one to his father who shook his head in response. When he had sat down again, Sir Robert continued, 'I have been thinking. Roger de Mortimer has requested of us a dozen armed men. King John is at Westminster for the season and has summoned the Marcher Lords[2] to attend him there, to tackle the question of Prince Llewellyn and his rapidly gaining power. Mortimer is wary of the king and doesn't trust him, so wants to go well-armed. He is raising a small troop from his own retinue and whatever vassals he can persuade to join him. I was going to oblige him with some of our men, but now I think I must include myself within that number, and take Hal with me as another. I can use the opportunity to meet up with some old associates in London, and it will get Hal away from here. Maybe give him time and space to grieve and recover without the constant reminders of his guilt all around him. I expect we will be gone for at least a month, maybe two. I will leave you to oversee things here at Brampton. You are well capable.'

Robert nodded his assent.

'When we return I will write to Abbot Rind at Cwmhir and arrange for Hal's admission,' his father went on. 'I also think that the time has come to finalise your marriage with the Lady Anne. She is of child-bearing age and it would be good to have some new life, some change here. I would like to see you produce me a grandson before I leave this world myself. Life is shorter than we think, Robert.'

'You are not old yet, Father. You are still strong.'

'I don't feel it tonight, son. Only God knows the length of my days,' he sighed heavily. 'You will agree to the marriage taking place in the spring?'

'Yes. I am at your command, Father.'

---

[2] Nobles given land on the border of and into Wales (Welsh Marches) by the king of England, with obligation to defend the Marches on the king's behalf.

Robert was spent of emotion and couldn't argue with his father if he wanted to. Deep inside himself he knew it was the right time for him to grow up and take responsibility for both his family and his inheritance. Hal's actions had only hastened the inevitable.

'Now we must see if we can get some more rest before the dawn comes and we have to face the morrow with whatever it brings.' Sir Robert hauled himself to his feet, and as Robert also stood he found himself drawn into a rough embrace.

'Thank you,' his father whispered into his ear, 'for saving your brother, and for bringing him back to me.'

It was a pale and subdued Hal who appeared and joined his family at the table to break fast. No one was eating although the table was laden with good things. All three looked exhausted. The morning was dark and dreary and a cold wind whistled through the gaps around the door. Hal shivered. The clear skies of the night before had given way to heavy dark clouds, and a light rain was falling that froze as it hit the cold ground, making venturing outside treacherous.

They sat together silently for some moments, each occupied in his own thoughts, or in Hal's case, trying desperately not to think at all.

'Henry!' His father spoke first. 'I have made the decision that you need to get away from Brampton. And as soon as it can be arranged.'

Hal's head shot up. 'Not Cwmhir? I am not sure that I am ready, Father.' Panic coursed through him at the thought. What could he possibly offer the Church in his current state? How could God possibly want him now?

'No. No, you are right. You are not ready for that.' His father's tone soothed him. 'I am leaving as soon as the weather improves to join forces with Roger de Mortimer on a journey south to Westminster. I want you to accompany me. You will be required to ride armed and ready to fight if called upon.' He looked steadily at Hal and waited for a response.

His son let out a small sigh and nodded. 'I can do that.' Hal glanced across at Robert. 'Will you come also?'

'No, Hal. Not this time. Father is entrusting me with the care of the estate in your absence, and there is work to do here. You will do well enough. You can handle yourself in a fight.' He grinned then and rubbed his ribs ruefully. 'I have the bruises to prove it.'

Hal allowed himself a small smile in return.

'And anyway, I have a wedding to plan for, it seems.' Robert reached over for a piece of cheese and some bread, as what looked suspiciously like panic crossed his face. 'I'm suddenly starving.'

It was as if the tension in the room had lifted. Enough had been said. Last night could be forgotten and a plan for the immediate future was in place. Hal watched as his father filled his cup and served himself some food. He licked his dry lips and his stomach let out an audible rumble.

'Eat, Hal, for goodness' sake. Your stomach is disturbing the peace!' His brother threw a hard-boiled egg at him, which hit him full on the chest. Hal grimaced but gathered the remains of the egg and added another to his plate. *If life must go on then I must eat*, he told himself.

They rode out on the third day. The air temperature had risen enough to cause the ground to soften into a mush of mud and ice. Hal had managed to avoid Cenred, seeing him only the once as they rode away from Brampton. His old friend was standing in the open doorway of his cottage and raised a hand as they rode past, a small smile on his face. Hal swallowed hard and turned his face forward, and to what lay ahead. He needed to ride away from his past and embrace whatever the next months held for him. His father had explained that he would be going to Cwmhir when they returned, and Hal had resolved that he would serve his father well for these last few weeks they had together.

It was distraction enough. The long ride south was through new and unfamiliar countryside, the weather and terrain making it a challenging ride at times. Hal used his expertise more than once to care for horses that had become lame or been ridden too hard. He threw himself into every task he was called on to perform.

Westminster was eye-opening, or what he saw of it. The stone-built palace of the Norman kings was breathtakingly ornate, but Hal found himself more often outside in a tent with the other soldiers while his father served Mortimer within. London's bustle and noise was stimulating, as were the women and the taverns, and Hal immersed himself in all of it. He was still numb inside but could pretend as well as the next man to be enjoying all the pleasures on offer.

As the weeks passed, away from Brampton, the pain seemed to ease and he could put the guilt to one side for the most part. There were other things to occupy his mind and senses. They saw little in the way of action. Hal earned a few bruises helping to break up a squabble between groups of retainers. He effectively apprehended a man observed stealing a merchant's purse, for which he received a coin or two in reward, but for the most part, Hal's sword remained sheathed.

It was only as they headed for home that they met a real threat in the guise of a bold Welsh raiding party that had crossed over the border to steal sheep. They had made a mistake in crossing the path of Roger de Mortimer's men and it was a swift, if bloody, fight. Hal took a man down and received a cut to his upper arm in return, but the opportunity to let his guard down and fight with unfettered emotion was a releasing experience. It felt good to have done his bit in ridding the area of at least one lawless rogue.

He rode back to his father after the fight, exhausted but pleased with himself. His father was mounted on his horse alongside Roger de Mortimer himself. He did not return Hal's smile.

'You fought well, young Brampton! Pity we are losing you to the Church,' Mortimer addressed him. 'Your father has had some news from Brampton Barre, so I have agreed you and your own men can leave us here and return direct.'

'Thank you, my lord.' Hal breathed heavily before turning his attention back to his father. 'What news, Father?'

His father pulled his horse closer, his face hard to read. Was it bad news? Not Robert? Hal's smile vanished as his eyes made contact with his father's.

'It is Cenred, Hal. He is sick. Grievously sick. They have called for the priest, but Cenred has been asking for you. Will you ride home with me now? Will you see him?'

Hal closed his eyes and swallowed down the sudden wave of emotion. He raised his head again to meet his father's concerned gaze. He steeled himself then. He could do this. For the sake of Cenred's friendship, for what they had been to each other, he would return to face whatever he needed to face. Hear whatever Cenred needed to say to him. Beg for the man's forgiveness at least. Say one last farewell, if it came to that.

They turned their weary horses in the direction of Brampton and made good progress. Within the hour they made sight of the castle. They slowed the horses as they approached and Sir Robert signalled to Hal to pull back alongside him for the last mile or so.

'I want to talk to you, son,' his father began. 'There are things you don't know about Cenred and Hild, things I think you should know. Cenred never intended to wed. He left for Ludlow that time to meet with a horse dealer, to acquire that bay. He tried to pay a fair price for the horse but the dealer was a greedy man and wanted more than Cenred was willing to pay. Cenred was ready to walk away when the dealer made Cenred another offer. He could have the bay for the price he had offered if he took Hild as well. She was the dealer's orphaned niece and had by all accounts been kept by him as a slave. It turned out that he had found himself a woman he wanted to marry but his new wife would not share the house with Hild.

He saw Cenred as an easy way of disposing of an unwanted burden.

'Although he never intended to marry, he took compassion on Hild. The good man that he was, he knew that he could save her from the situation she was in, but only by marrying her, to protect her reputation. So he did, bringing her back here, offering her a home and his care and protection. And she flourished here. You saw that. He loved her in his own way.'

'But not perhaps how she wanted to be loved?' Hal was hurting at the thought.

'That may be your understanding. It does not justify what you did, though.' His father shot him a hard stare.

'No.' Hal hung his head. 'I think my love for her and carrying our child made her happy. But I also stole so much from her, and from Cenred. They would have done well enough without my unfettered desires interrupting their contentment.'

'God only knows what might have been, son. I am only telling you this now so that you understand things from Cenred's perspective. To see the man he really is. I can only guess at why he wants to see you. But I believe it is for the best, for you both.'

They rode into the courtyard as the sun was beginning to set. Hal dismounted and a servant came out to see to his horse. He walked over to offer his father a hand to dismount but he dismissed him.

'Go, son, don't delay further.'

Hal made his way over to Cenred's cottage. The door stood slightly ajar and a figure was moving around inside. Hal recognised the hunched form of the local midwife, known for her healing herbs. She turned as Hal approached and waved him in.

'He has been waiting only for you. The priest was here but he sent him away. He said he could not receive absolution until he had spoken with you. He said he knew you would come.' She nodded in the direction of the bed.

The large form of Cenred was laid out, unnaturally still, on that bed draped in its familiar coverlet. The man's face was hardly recognisable. He was yellow-skinned and drawn, sweat droplets covering his wide forehead. Hal pulled a stool over and sat by the bedside. He let his eyes wander around the space, and to the dried flowers still hanging, now dusty and limp, from the nail in the wall. She was still here. It was still Hild's home. The pain resurfaced briefly. He turned his attention back to Cenred to find the man had opened his eyes and was watching him.

'I knew you would come.'

Hal had to lean in to hear him, it was so softly spoken. He felt Cenred's hand rest on his. It was cold to the touch although the room was stiflingly warm. Cenred wheezed in another painfully drawn breath before speaking again.

'She loved you.'

Hal closed his eyes, and dropped his head. He felt Cenred squeeze his hand.

'And you loved her?'

Hal nodded once.

'And I loved you both.'

Cenred paused. Hal felt a warm tear drop from his chin.

'Hal, you are like a son to me. She was like a daughter. You gave her what I could not. Do not be sad on my account. I have long forgiven you, forgiven you both.

'It did burn at first, the betrayal, but then I saw how happy she was. And then I saw your grief at her loss, and knew I could not bear to add to it... I forgive you, Hal... as I forgave her.'

Hal was hearing Cenred's words but they didn't quite register. He was offering him forgiveness? Was that possible? He realised Cenred was speaking again.

'I have but one thing to ask you in return.'

Hal lifted his eyes to meet those of his friend. 'Anything! I will do anything. Tell me what I must do.'

The desire to put things right, to somehow negate the pain and grief his actions had caused this man, was so overpowering.

'Forgive yourself.'

Hal was confused, and also disappointed. Was there not something else he could do? What Cenred was asking was impossible.

He felt a squeeze on his hand again. Cenred had closed his eyes, but seemed determined to say more.

'I must commend myself to God's forgiveness soon. You will find God will forgive you also, if you come to Him truly repentant. But, Hal, accepting that you *are* forgiven and forgiving yourself... those are the only ways that you will be able to walk free... of the guilt and pain you are bearing now.

'You are so young, Hal, and there is so much good you can do with the rest of your life. But to do so you must be *free*. It is what I desire most for you. What I long for.' The last was barely a whisper.

Hal felt Cenred's grasp on his hand loosen as the man relaxed, exhausted from the effort of speaking. His breathing was slow and laboured.

Hal felt movement behind him and turned to see the priest standing quietly by. He rose from the stool and allowed space for the minister to do what he had come to do. A familiar hand rested on his shoulder and Hal felt his father's presence at his side.

The customary words spoken and the prayers uttered, the priest stood back and Sir Robert stepped forward and took Cenred's hand in his own.

'Go to your rest, dear friend,' he was saying. 'You are free to leave now. All will be well here. I will see to it.'

Hal watched, paralysed by emotion, as Cenred took a last breath and slipped peacefully into eternity. He could not understand fully what had just passed between them, but he knew it was momentous. He grabbed the priest's sleeve as he passed by him to leave the room.

'Father, I need you to hear my confession,' he whispered.

'Come, son,' was the reply. 'Now is as good a time as ever.'

71

Lord, if you measured us and marked us with our

sins,

who would ever have their prayers answered?

But your forgiving love is what makes you so

wonderful.

No wonder you are loved and worshiped!

This is why I wait upon you, expecting your

breakthrough,

for your Word brings me hope.

Psalm 130:3-5, TPT

Part Two
Hywel

6
Cwmhir

Early spring 1204
Wales

Hal's first sight of Abbey Cwmhir was glimpsed through the trees as they made their way on horseback down a steep wooded path into a lush green valley, with sloping wooded hillsides shielding it all around. The abbey sat proud like a ship in a wide ocean of fields, some ploughed brown ready for sowing, some green with pasture grass. It was impressive enough, the main church and buildings built of well-cut stone, with simple decoration, as was the Cistercian way. The prominent church building, with its tall windows, towered above the cloister and accommodation buildings beside it.

The day was bright but not warm, as winter was still lingering long into what should have been early spring. The first few white-headed snowdrops were appearing under the trees, but Hal imagined these woodlands would be awash with wildflower colour when spring fully came. New life, new beginnings. Hal mused to himself, would Cwmhir offer him that? He hoped so. There was no turning back now.

It had been good to have his father's company on the ride here, along with the necessary retainers. It had taken them three days and the weather hadn't always been as kind as it was today. True to his word, within a week of being back home, Sir Robert had written to Abbot Rind to forewarn him of Hal's arrival and they had set off soon after. Burying Cenred had been hard and they were not the only ones to feel his loss. Brampton Barre had felt a different place without his presence, duller somehow, and Hal was not sorry to leave. He was glad of it, glad of the opportunity to move on with his life, to leave behind his memories and everything that triggered them.

Hal had dwelt briefly on what Cenred had said to him, but was not sure he had accepted what had been offered to him by way of absolution. He had made his confession to the priest and done the required penance, but still the guilt lay heavy on his heart, and his pain was only buried shallow, so that it broke to the surface easily enough whenever he went looking for it. He had resolved therefore to not think any more of Cenred, of Hild, of any of what had happened. He resolved to start his life afresh from this point. He had a duty to his father, his family and to God to make his commitment to the Church a wholehearted one. He would make his father and brother proud of him again. He would restore their good name. He would fulfil every expectation of him, and more so.

So it was with a quiet determination that he approached Abbey Cwmhir, and the rest of his life.

The porter met them at the gate and there was a flurry of activity as lay brothers in their plain brown tunics appeared to see to their horses. The party dismounted and retrieved their possessions. Hal and his father were shown into a receiving room off the main gatehouse, where they were offered meagre refreshments and fresh cold water to wash their hands and faces. They were left alone then, neither daring to speak, awed somewhat by the quiet serenity of the place.

Another brother appeared and nodded for them to follow him, through into the cloister gardens and then along a path that led to a large, arched doorway. He led them through the door into a fine open room with high stone arches and windows. Hal noted the stone benches that lined three of the walls.

'The chapter house,' his father whispered knowingly.

The monk said nothing but indicated that they sit, and disappeared through another doorway that looked to have stairs beyond. After what seemed like an eternity to Hal, during which his stomach twisted nervously, the monk reappeared.

'Father Abbot will see you shortly. He is aware of your arrival. Please wait here.'

And then the man was gone and they were alone again.

Sir Robert turned to his son. 'You are ready?' he whispered. He sounded as nervous as Hal. Perhaps it was the effect of this place.

Hal closed his eyes briefly before meeting his father's. 'I have resolved to be ready,' he said, straightening his back and trying to sound more convinced than he actually felt.

A slight noise caused them to both turn their heads in the direction of the door as Abbot Rind appeared. He was a medium-sized man of middle years and indistinct features, except for an extraordinarily large bulbous nose, which Hal found himself staring at rudely. Realising he was doing so, he hastily averted his gaze.

'Sir Robert de Brampton, of Brampton Barre.' His father announced himself formally and stepped forward to bow towards the abbot.

The abbot appeared to sneer slightly before training his features into a fixed smile, imperiously stretching out a beringed hand for Sir Robert to kiss.

'And this is my son, Henry de Brampton. I wrote to you of his coming?'

'Of course.' The abbot stepped over to Hal and extended his hand for him also to kiss. Hal offered the required obeisance and stepped back. He was surprised to find the man smelt strongly of wine.

'You desire to enter our Order by way of the novitiate here?'

Hal nodded solemnly. 'I do, Father Abbot.'

'And that is of your own free will?' The abbot threw a penetrating glance at Sir Robert then, but Hal could answer honestly on his own account.

'It is.'

'You will serve at least one whole year as a novice here before being required to take your full vows and receive your tonsure. You must leave all your worldly possessions behind and be clothed with humility from the moment you enter our house.' He looked Hal up and down, taking in his fine clothes and sheathed sword. The barely concealed sneer was back.

Hal registered the look on the abbot's face and wondered if it was their obvious wealth that was so distasteful to him, or just that they were noblemen from the wrong side of the Welsh border.

'We have also brought a gift for the abbey. A sizeable donation to your work here,' Sir Robert interjected.

The abbot turned to him, the fixed smile returned, his eyes at least registering interest.

'We will receive that gratefully,' he nodded. 'Although it is not required, of course,' he added quickly. 'Now you must say your farewells. Prior Gwrgenau takes charge of the novices. He will come and find you here.' He turned his attention back to Hal. 'You can leave your weapon with your father. You will have no further need for that.'

With an imperious nod and a swish of his long habit, the abbot turned and left them.

Hal undid his sword belt and handed it to his father, who grabbed him by the arm.

'Henry... Hal... I am proud of you, son,' he whispered urgently.

Hal felt moisture come to his eyes and blinked rapidly.

'And I will make you ever prouder,' he whispered in return. 'That is my solemn vow.'

His father grabbed him in a quick embrace before turning to leave.

'God bless you, my son,' he said quietly as he turned back at the doorway, and then disappeared from Hal's sight.

Hal felt suddenly very alone and bereft. The stone walls loomed around him, prison-like. It was cold and quiet and claustrophobic. He felt an almost overwhelming urge to run after his father, to change his mind, to leave and go back to the warm familiarity of Brampton. But he knew it was not possible, and that it would break his father's heart.

A guffaw of laughter made him spin around in surprise, as from the direction of the cloister two figures appeared in the plain white garb of the Cistercians. They were not tonsured so were obviously novices, and were laughing and play-wrestling with each other. They came to an abrupt stop in front of Hal. One was thin and tall, with dark hair and eyes, and he soon adopted a more dignified air when he spotted the newcomer. The other was smaller and rounder with fair hair and ruddy cheeks and he was grinning broadly. They were young, the tall one maybe the same age as Hal himself, the other younger, or at least appearing so.

Behind the two a more serene figure appeared. He was dressed in full Cistercian garb and had so little white hair in his tonsure that he appeared bald. He glided rather than walked towards them, but his bright blue eyes were warm and smiling.

'Welcome, Henry de Brampton, to Abbey Cwmhir.' He dipped his head in Hal's direction. 'I am Prior Gwrgenau, and these two reprobates are Julian,' the tall one nodded, 'and Rhodri,' who beamed at Hal. 'They have been novices here long enough to know what is, and what isn't, acceptable behaviour within the cloister precincts in the middle of the day, but they are slow learners, it seems.' It was said with a serious tone but the prior belied his true feelings by the lift of the corners of his lips. 'They will show you where to go and help you settle. I will meet all three of you in the church for Sext within the hour. You have time enough. Do not be late.' This last was directed at Rhodri, who smiled somewhat sheepishly.

The prior turned his attention back to Hal.

'You will find you get used to being within our walls, and I trust that you will find your home here with us before too long. You have much to learn about us and our ways but that will come soon enough. If I can give you one piece of advice now, it is to take one day at a time and live that day to the best of your ability. Don't be concerned about tomorrow, or about the future that may seem to stretch long in front of you at this moment in time.

'One last thing, Henry. As a mark of the start your new life here you will be expected to take a new name. It is usual for the abbot to choose that for novices, but here it is left for me to choose. I usually pray and ask God to inspire me with a suitable name, but He has been unusually silent when it comes to you. I wonder if perhaps you have a name in mind?'

'Hywel? It was my Welsh grandfather's name, on my mother's side.'

Gwrgenau paused, looking thoughtfully at him.

'Yes, I think that will suit well,' he said eventually. 'Hywel it is. You will take your novitiate vows in front of the community in the chapter meeting tomorrow, and from then you will be known to us as Brother Hywel.'

'Hywel!' The voice was low, but insistent. Who was this Hywel? And who was trying to rouse him? He tried to block out the sound, tried to return to sleep.

'Hywel, Hywel, wake up, before you wake the whole community with your moaning!'

Hywel? He suddenly registered his new name and was aware that someone was shaking him, quite forcefully.

'What?' he growled crossly, opening his eyes and pulling off the hand that was laid on his shoulder.

'Shhh! You fool. It's Rhodri, and you were making such a noise in your sleep that it woke me.'

'And me,' came a muffled voice from the other side of the room. Julian was on his side facing away from them, but obviously awake and reluctantly so.

'Sorry.' Hywel sat himself up in the bed and looked around. The small dormitory the three of them shared was in pitch darkness. 'What time is it?'

'Before we need to be up, that's all I know,' Rhodri replied, sitting down heavily on the side of Hywel's bed. 'What were you dreaming about? Sounded terrifying.'

Hywel closed his eyes and was back in the dream. Hild was with him, down on the riverbank, the sun shining on them as it had the second time he had seen her there. And she was carrying that same basket, and smiling that special smile at him. Then she had taken the basket and walked to the reed beds and lowered the basket into the water. Hal had walked over, curious to look into the basket, and what he saw made him draw back in horror and scream. It was a baby – but cold and lifeless.

That was the moment that Rhodri had called him awake. He realised that his hands were clammy and his tunic damp with sweat. He pulled himself back into the present, dropping the shutters on his heart again.

'It was nothing.' He tried to make his voice sound normal but it came out in a kind of strangled whisper. 'Just an upset stomach. Too many beans have made me bilious.' His stomach rumbled loudly.

'Too little to eat, more like. I'm struggling with the meagre diet here too. Come on.' Rhodri stood up and grabbed Hywel by the hand. 'I know where to find something that will settle your stomach and make us all feel better. You coming, Julian?' He walked over and shoved the other novice, who groaned and rolled over onto his back.

'Might as well, as I'm wide awake now!' he grumbled.

With Rhodri leading them, the three made their way quietly down the stairs and through the refectory to the kitchen beyond. There was sufficient moonlight through the high windows to light their way. Once inside the kitchen, Rhodri found a candle and lit it, and headed straight for a tall cupboard in one corner of the room.

'Here, hold this.' He handed the candle to Hywel. 'Julian, can you reach the shelf on the top of the cupboard or do you need to give me a leg up?'

'Please,' Julian said, 'I'm not chancing my back trying to lift your heavy bones.' He stepped over and easily reached up to the shelf. 'What am I looking for?' he asked, feeling around with his hand.

'The abbot's wine. It's kept in a flagon, up there,' Rhodri replied.

'What?' Julian pulled back his hand as if bitten by a viper and stepped away, horrified. 'No! We are not stealing the abbot's wine, Rhodri. Are you mad?'

'Not stealing, just sampling. That was all that was on my mind to do,' Rhodri replied, obviously feigning innocence.

The sound of the kitchen door closing and a key turning had all three suddenly frozen to the spot. Hywel blew the candle out quickly. They expected a voice, steps, but nothing came. After a few moments of silence, Rhodri crept over to the door to try it.

'It's shut and locked, from the outside,' he said.

'Try the other door.' Julian sounded panicked.

The door to the courtyard outside was also shut and locked, the keyhole empty. Then the peace was shattered by the sound of the bell calling the community from their beds.

'Vigils, oh no! We can't miss it, not all three of us,' Julian groaned. He ran flustered from one door to the other, rattling the handles noisily. They were still well and truly locked.

Rhodri had sat down on a bench by the table. 'Not a lot we can do about that now. We'll have to stay here until someone comes. Might as well make ourselves comfortable.'

'But that might be for a very long time,' Julian moaned. 'Lauds is not for hours yet.'

Hywel smiled to himself. He was beginning to think that life in the abbey was not going to be dull in the company of these two. He was actually quite enjoying this little adventure. He relit the candle and set it down by Rhodri. He wandered over to the corner cupboard and found he too could easily reach the upper shelf. He felt around until his hand met the cold clay of the wine flagon, and he carefully brought it down, placing it in front of Rhodri on the table.

'We might as well try it, now we are here,' he said. 'Julian? Will you join us?'

The tall novice came over and folded himself onto a bench but sat disconsolately, with his chin in his hands.

'Well, I'm going to try it. It's a very long time since I had some fine wine.' Rhodri unstopped the flagon and brought it to his lips, taking a small swig. He handed it to Hywel, who did the same. It was good, very good, and he enjoyed the way it warmed his throat as it went down.

'Julian?' He handed the flagon to Julian, who took it from him but stared at it rather than taking a drink.

'What are we doing? Rhodri, do you realise how much trouble we are in here, and you want to make it worse by stealing this?' He placed the unstopped flagon back on the table.

'Well, my feeling is that we are in trouble enough anyway for missing Vigils, so we might as well make the most of it. You'll regret not trying it at least. Go on, Julian,' Rhodri insisted.

The other novice groaned again, but grabbed the flagon and took a deep swallow. At the exact same time the kitchen door swung suddenly open and Brother Puw, the cellarer, entered, followed swiftly by Prior Gwrgenau.

Julian spluttered and hastily hid the flagon under his bench.

'Well, rather large rats I would say, brother.' Prior Gwrgenau spoke first, addressing his companion.

'Yes indeed, brother. As I told you, I heard what I thought was vermin in the kitchen on my way down to Vigils and thought I'd best lock them in so as to deal with them thoroughly after prayers.'

'Well, it seems they are still trapped here, brother cellarer. What do you suppose we should do with them?'

'That I will leave to you, brother prior,' Brother Puw laughed. 'I'm sure you have a good idea.'

'If you would follow me,' the prior addressed the three rather subdued novices, 'I have just the thing for you to do to while away the hours until Lauds. Did you not say you needed the soil in the vegetable beds to be turned over, Brother Puw? It won't hurt for them to do it in the rain, will it?'

'No, no. Not at all. A good soaking would be good for the soil, and it won't do those three any harm, either!'

'Oh, and Julian,' the prior added, 'you can leave the abbot's wine here on the table, if you wouldn't mind.'

Julian acquiesced, glaring at Rhodri's back as the three filed out of the kitchen and into the early morning rain.

Adjusting to life at Cwmhir did not come easily for Hywel. The Rule was strict, the food sparse and basic, and the silence deafening at times. But he was absolutely determined to engage fully with every aspect of Cistercian life. He had much to prove and a future position to secure, after all. This was his life now and there was no turning back. He studied, was religious in his attendance at the Offices, and compliant with every task he was asked to perform. He enjoyed the work hours most, especially when he could be outside with the livestock. The abbot had a pair of fine horses and the abbey also housed a few ponies for the brothers' use, as well as three large farm horses. Hywel was at his happiest if he could help out in the stables, and he impressed the lay brothers there with his knowledge and instinctive understanding of the horses.

As to the Offices, the liturgies became more and more familiar and the responses became more natural as time went on. Hywel learned early on that singing was not his gift. Plainsong was far different from the bawdy songs of the alehouses that he had loudly sung along to. The sound that came from his mouth the first time he tried to sing along with the plainchants was so loud and discordant that it disturbed a turtle dove nesting in the roof rafters, and made several of the brothers turn around in horror. Rhodri's giggles were the last straw. From that moment, Hywel decided he would mime along during sung worship.

The hardest times of all for him were the times of quiet contemplation and meditation. In the long hours of silence it was hard not to think of his guilt, of Hild and of Cenred. He would take to pacing up and down the cloister, until he was glared at once too often for disturbing the brothers at their quiet devotions. He would try counting the stones in the cloister wall, or the flower heads in the gardens, anything to stop his mind thinking of things he didn't want to think about.

Hywel was jealous of how the other brothers seemed to be able to connect with God in private prayer. It wasn't that he didn't believe in God. There were even times when he was sure that he felt God's presence, especially in the church during the Offices. It was just that he didn't know how to connect with God on a personal level, or what to say that God would want to hear. He was too ashamed, too guilt-laden, to impose himself on a holy God, so opted rather to pretend his devotion. It was never questioned, so he supposed it was working well enough.

The presence of Rhodri and Julian at Cwmhir certainly made the transition from Brampton easier. They were fun to be with, although both were obviously serious about their vocations. They had both chosen the Church rather than had it chosen for them, and they both seemed to have a real connection with God, unless they too were acting well. Julian was definitely the more studious of the two and loved his book learning, but he wasn't against a little bit of honest fun from time to time. Rhodri was just a constant source of laughter, but surprisingly also had an extraordinary aptitude for figures, which found him often working at the almoner's side, or helping the cellarer with his accounting. When Rhodri wasn't causing others to laugh, he was the willing butt of their jokes. He took it all good-humouredly. After the episode with the abbot's wine, the three friends were a little more circumspect with the escapades they got up to, but it didn't stop them having fun at each other's expense.

On one particular occasion, Hywel and Julian came together to hatch a plan, both keen to repay Rhodri for the wine incident. The abbey had a cat that liked to hide out in the stables where there was a steady supply of vermin for him to catch. Hywel had befriended the semi-feral cat and taught it to come to him with a whistle, rewarding him with a morsel of cheese each time. The cat also liked to climb the apple trees in the orchard.

One day, when the cat was sitting minding its own business up a tree, Julian came running to find Rhodri.

'The poor cat is stuck up a tree, Rhodri, you must get up there and help him down,' he pleaded piteously.

Ever good-natured, Rhodri ran to the cat's aid. When he had climbed a fair way, a well-timed whistle from a hidden Hywel caused the cat to jump down. It easily navigated the branches on its way and left a bemused Rhodri stuck halfway up the tree. And he was well and truly stuck, the strap of his sandal caught on a small twig. Hywel and Julian looked on in horror as Rhodri bent awkwardly, trying to release his sandal and in doing so lost his hold and began to fall headlong from the tree. Only his foot was still well-held, wedged tight between a branch and the tree trunk, and the poor novice found himself hanging upside down, suspended by one leg and embarrassingly bearing all. The Cistercian Rule forbade the wearing of undergarments.

Julian and Hywel rushed to his aid, but their hysterical laughter made it almost impossible for them to do anything useful to help him. A lay brother with a ladder eventually arrived to rescue the poor lad, but not before a considerable audience of brothers and lay brothers had assembled, some with looks of horror or disgust on their faces, but the majority losing their composure and smiling, or bursting into barely restrained laughter at the sight. It was a tale that would be retold in whispers in that community for many years to come.

A year later, all three novices stood before Abbot Rind to take their vows and receive their tonsures. They had encouraged each other continuously and become firm friends during their novitiate. Now they stood seemingly ready to commit themselves to God, to each other and to the community they had been called to be a part of.

Create in me a clean heart, O God,

And renew a steadfast spirit within me.

Do not cast me away from Your presence,

And do not take Your Holy Spirit from me.

Psalm 51:10-11, NKJV

7
Unravelling

Spring 1205

Barely a month after Hywel had received his tonsure, he found himself summoned to the abbot's rooms. He made his way anxiously through the chapter house and up the stairs beyond, to the great wooden door that led to Abbot Rind's comfortably furnished apartment. The abbot seemed personally less observant of the Cistercian ideal of simplicity when it came to his own comfort. From a previous visit, Hywel remembered the curtained wooden bed that dominated one side of the room, and the fine wall-hangings. The room also contained an elegantly carved round table and armed chairs, and shelves bearing books and stoppered flagons. The abbot seemed to have a constant supply of good-quality wine available for his exclusive use. *Those are the advantages that come with position, I suppose*, Hywel mused to himself. More fuel to the fire of his own ambition. He guessed meat found its way onto Abbot Rind's table also. His mouth salivated at the thought.

The door opened as he reached the top of the stairs and the abbot himself gestured for him to enter. Hywel could not think why he had been summoned. Prior Gwrgenau had always disciplined them when they had needed it as novices. He supposed now that he was a full brother, he was answerable directly to the abbot. If only he could think what he had done?

But then, as he stepped around the abbot and into the room, he realised that they were not alone. Standing beaming at him was a familiar figure clothed in the finest of travelling clothes and creating an imposing sight. Robert! Hywel resisted the overwhelming urge to run and grab his brother in a full embrace, recalling the expectation of a more dignified greeting. He sensed a slight movement to the side and turned to see that his brother had not arrived alone. A young woman stood by the table, also in fine clothes, her fair hair fashionably braided and coiled beneath a simple headdress. She was wearing a warm smile on her face.

'You have visitors, as is your right, Brother Hywel.' The abbot addressed him without emotion. 'I will permit you the time between now and Vespers to entertain your guests. They have had refreshments here with me.' He nodded to a table still showing the remains of a substantial meal. The leftovers alone were more than Hywel had seen served to him at any mealtime for months. Hywel felt a flash of annoyance that he had not been invited to eat with them, but he wasn't going to let ill-feeling spoil the sheer joy of this moment of reunion.

'You are welcome to show them the public areas of the abbey, the gardens and church, of course, but please do nothing to disturb your fellow brothers in their work or devotions. Perhaps a walk down by the brook might be more conducive to conversation? You can go now.'

The abbot dismissed them abruptly, as was his way. Hywel wondered just what sort of a host he had been to Robert and his wife. Perhaps missing out on eating at his table was not so great a loss. He led his guests silently through the abbey precincts and out through the gates before turning to welcome them properly.

'Phew!' His brother exclaimed as Hywel embraced him warmly. 'I'm glad to be out of there. That abbot of yours is a strange one. Sorry, brother, but we have had to endure an hour of his near-silent company. His face never showed any emotion, although I tried more than once to engage him. When he did deign to speak, it was to address Anne here. I think the only reason we were invited to eat with him was so he could enjoy female company for a while. I guess I can understand that.' He laughed.

Hywel smiled along. 'Come on, let's get a little way away from here for a while. Unless you want a tour of the abbey?'

'No, no, Hal! Lead away. Anne might like a look in the church before we leave, but I want to spend as much time as possible with you. Somewhere we can talk freely. I've got much to tell you, and much to ask.'

Hywel led them down towards where the trees lined the brook; there were secluded places there where they could sit for a while. The sun was warm for the time of year and the skies clear blue. He turned to Robert.

'I changed my name, brother. I am Hywel now, not Hal any more.'

'Ah, that makes more sense! I thought your abbot had a problem with his speech when he called you Hywel. "Hal", "Hywel", I suppose they do sound similar enough. Interesting choice, brother. Was it forced on you?'

'No. It was my choice. New start, new name. And it helps to associate with the Welsh here.' He smiled at Robert, hoping he understood why he had forsaken his old identifier.

'Yes. Yes. I think I understand,' his brother replied thoughtfully, looking back at his brother. 'We are here to "associate" with the Welsh also – well, with our own Welsh cousins, anyway.'

'What? Not to see me?'

'Of course.' He gave Hywel a playful shove.

They were nearing the Brook Clywedog now; although swollen with the spring rains it was running fast and full, more like a river than a brook. It made a pleasing sound as it tumbled past them over several small waterfalls. Hywel watched Robert hold his young wife's hand as they clambered over some tree roots and into a clearing at the water's edge, where a fallen tree trunk rested conveniently for her to sit on.

The Lady Anne was quite lovely to look at. Slight of build, with fair skin and eyes of sapphire blue. When she smiled, small dimples appeared in her cheeks and, although her face was still round and soft with youth, Hywel could see that she was going to grow into a fine beauty. His brother had done very well for himself. Robert and Anne made a well-matched pair.

He watched them together. Robert was attentive, as he would have expected, but it was more than that. He saw the looks that passed between them and the way she followed him with her gaze. She was obviously besotted with him and he seemed equally enamoured of her. Hywel was pleased. Robert deserved to be loved, and to love in return. He seemed more settled. Content.

'So, what brings you here, then?' Hywel asked Robert as they sat side by side on the grass, watching the dragonflies playing on the water. The late spring sun that had caused the insects to emerge was pleasantly warming.

'Well, Father sent me to check on you. He wanted to know whether you had stuck the year and made it to your tonsure. Which suits you, by the way,' Robert teased, rubbing Hywel's bald crown.

'Surely you didn't come all this way into Wales and drag your poor lady wife along with you just to see my tonsure?' Hywel smiled over at the Lady Anne, who smiled sweetly in return. She was sitting demurely with her hands clasped in her lap, calmly watching the interplay between the two brothers.

'No,' Robert laughed. 'Father had some letters for our uncle Meredydd, something to do with some land that was our late mother's dowry, that he wants to gift to Abbey Cwmhir for your sake. He was going to undertake the journey himself but I persuaded him to let us come. I wanted to show Anne some of Wales and give her the chance to meet our Welsh relatives. But mostly I wanted her to meet you,' he smiled rather sheepishly then, 'and for you to meet her, of course. I miss you brother,' he added quietly.

'And I you,' Hywel replied genuinely. 'How is our father? He is well?'

'Yes, well enough. He is not having to do so much these days, as he has handed much of the responsibility of running things at Brampton over to me. He is enjoying a slightly slower pace of life. He moved out of our home when Anne and I married, and he took Cenred's cottage, which he has had added to and refurnished and made very comfortable for himself. He insisted that we needed to have our own space. We have also added to the main house to make a separate bedchamber.' He glanced over at Anne, who blushed coyly.

Hywel felt the familiar twinge at the mention of Cenred's cottage, and found it difficult to imagine it looking any different from how he remembered it, how it had looked when Hild had lived in it. He tried to stop his mind going there by changing the subject.

'What do you think of Abbey Cwmhir, Lady Anne?'

'It is a beautiful spot, brother, I think, and very peaceful,' she replied sweetly. Hywel liked her already.

'How do *you* like the quiet?' Robert asked Hywel.

'I like the peace most of the time, but I do miss talking!' Hywel laughed. 'I'm still practising how to control my tongue. It has been difficult, but I am improving.'

'So you are happy here, brother?'

That was a hard question for Hywel to answer honestly. Robert needed to take positive tidings back to their father. Hywel could not risk disappointment or worry on his behalf. But happy? He had not been truly happy for a long, long time.

'I know I am where I am supposed to be,' was all he could manage, praying that was enough to satisfy his brother's curiosity.

'It isn't all prayers and meditation, is it?' Robert asked. 'Forgive me, brother, but I still find it hard to imagine you filling your days with those things.'

'Much of our day is just that, and I am becoming used to it, Robert. I enjoy the work hours most, especially when I can be outside with the horses.'

Robert snorted. 'Might have known you'd find some horses to befriend.'

'I have made some human friends too, and they have given me many reasons to laugh in the time I've been here.'

'That is good to hear. Really good.' Robert grabbed his arm warmly. 'I wondered for a time whether you would ever smile again,' he added.

The three of them sat enjoying each other's company for a while. It felt comfortable and familiar and Hywel wanted to make the most of it.

'There is one more question I need to ask you.' Robert had adopted a more serious tone.

Hywel looked up from his contemplation of his feet. He had removed his sandals and was absent-mindedly enjoying the feel of the cool water between his toes. His stomach twisted uncomfortably at his brother's tone, but Robert's face gave nothing away. What was he wanting to know? Was it about the past? Hywel braced himself.

'Is it true what I hear? Do Cistercians really deserve the title "bare-bottomed monks"?' Robert's face broke into a huge grin as he saw Hywel's face blush crimson.

'Robert!' It was his wife's voice that remonstrated with him.

'Sorry, my love,' he laughed as he levered himself up and went over to her, kissing her hand by way of apology.

'Sorry, Hywel, I just couldn't resist it.' Robert turned back to Hywel and offered his hand to him, grinning. 'Here, let me help you up.'

'Oh no, I fell for that once before. I don't trust your kind of help, brother. And I certainly don't want to risk you finding out first-hand the answer to your rude question by falling face down onto those wet stones.'

Hywel stood gracefully and bowed in the direction of Lady Anne.

'My apologies that you have had to wed yourself to this oaf, my lady.' He sent her a sympathetic look.

She giggled in reply. 'Oh, I'm getting used to him,' she said, as she lifted her hand to tenderly touch her husband's cheek, the look on her face of pure devotion. Hywel felt the knife in his own heart twist.

'We must head back,' he said, rather brusquely, 'especially if you wish to see the church before Vespers.'

Robert offered his hand to help his wife to her feet, and caught her arm as she swayed slightly.

'Are you well, my love?' Robert asked her, concerned.

'I am,' she breathed. 'But a few minutes sitting in the cool shade of the church would do me good.'

Hywel watched then as she placed her hand protectively over her belly and gazed up into her husband's face. With child? It hit him hard. Of course she would be, he thought. It was inevitable and to be expected. And they both knew and weren't telling him. It was their own little secret and they were obviously overjoyed. He had to swallow back a wave of emotion. He turned away and walked back up towards the abbey, leaving them to follow at their own pace.

Hywel's mind was in turmoil. He had been overjoyed to see Robert, happy for his happiness, so pleased to spend this short time with them both. But something within him railed at all that his brother had. That had been, and forever would be, denied to him.

It was a quiet, thoughtful parting after Anne had had her time in the church. Hywel did not know what else to say to his brother, his mind was so full, but he plastered a reassuring smile on his face as Robert grabbed him in a hug and held on a little longer than was comfortable. Hywel kissed his new sister's hand and then watched as the two mounted their fine horses and rode away together. He felt lost somewhat, and as he turned back and walked through the abbey gates, back into the confines of the cloister, back to what was now his normality, another unexpected emotion rose up from deep within. A long-buried anger. Not at Robert. No, he was genuinely happy for his brother. Robert had his long-awaited position of responsibility, his own home, his beautiful wife, married love and a child on the way. All those things he well deserved. It was just so unfair. What did *he* have? He had known love and had had it torn away from him. He had fathered a child and… The pain hit him afresh and he sunk to his knees on the stone floor of the cloister.

He stayed there in an attitude of prayer, his head in his hands, breathing deeply, trying to bring his emotions under control, looking to find some elusive peace for his soul. The bell for Vespers sounded and he made himself rise and go through the motions, following his brothers into the church.

His mind was still whirring so that he could not concentrate on the liturgies; he found himself instead distracted by the strange shapes made on the stone floor by the late afternoon sunlight pouring through the great window. He thought he could see the image of his father. He closed his eyes and remembered the look on his father's face on the day he had discovered his son's sin. The disappointment, the pain, the weariness. Then he remembered his father's face when he had left him here at Cwmhir a year ago, the look of pride and the hope in his eyes.

Through the mist of his swirling emotions, Hywel suddenly had clarity. He knew then what he must do. A new determination arose within him. He would show them all. He would rise to the top, go as far in the Church as was possible for him to go. Make his father proud of him, erase the past. Let Robert have his ordinary life: Hywel was going to make sure his life from now on was extraordinary.

As prayer ended, with a grim determination he headed for the small room off the cloister that acted as a library. Prior Gwrgenau was also heading that way, and Hywel opened and held the door for him. Together they silently entered and Hywel made for the shelves that carried the largest ecclesiastical manuscripts. He was going to study, harder than ever before. He was going to outshine them all, and get himself noticed. He was glad Prior Gwrgenau was there. He would witness his renewed earnestness and note it.

The days of fooling around as a novice were past. His days as a foolhardy youth governed by his passions were gone. Hywel needed to make a name for himself. He needed to absolve himself of his past failures. It was a sort of madness that possessed him.

Prior Gwrgenau watched with curiosity as Hywel pulled down the large manuscript and laid it out on the desk. He watched as he took a wooden aestel[3] and started to silently read the lines. Gwrgenau smiled to himself. The writing was tiny and the light dim. He wondered how much Hywel was actually able to see, much less understand. What had possessed the usually easy-going young man that he was suddenly so unnaturally studious?

'Brother, can I help you? Is there something in particular you are looking for?' Gwrgenau came up behind Hywel and spoke softly.

'Brother Prior. My thanks. I am content,' he replied tersely, and turned his attention back to the mass of script in front of him.

'It is perhaps not the best thing for you to be reading at this hour. The light is failing, and even by candlelight that is a difficult read,' Gwrgenau persisted, concern in his voice.

Hywel sat back and closed his eyes, breathing deeply, as Gwrgenau continued to speak kindly to him.

'What troubles you, brother? Seeing your family? It is bound to have unsettled you.'

Hywel sighed. 'I am troubled about how much time I have been away from my duties and my studies.'

---

[3] A pointer used by monks to read script, to protect the ink from finger marks.

Prior Gwrgenau knew well enough that was not the truth of it, but thought it wise to not counter him. The young man was obviously struggling with something internally.

'Prior?' Hywel suddenly addressed him.

'Yes, my son?'

'How did you get to your position? How long did it take you? Do you have ambitions to be abbot one day? What does it take to be in a position of status within the Order? What do I need to do to prove myself?'

Hywel hadn't waited for the prior to answer any of his questions. He rambled on, his words spilling out of him like a beaver's dam breached by a fast-flowing stream.

'I have ambition, you see. I will make abbot one day. I have to do well, and it is expected of me by my family. I feel I have an advantage already. My uncle is Abbot Jerome of Grand Selve and held in high regard by the Cistercian fathers of both Clairvaux and Citeaux. My family is of noble birth, is wealthy and has given generously to the abbey. They are also close to Roger de Mortimer, your patron here. I am well educated and have been well prepared to succeed at whatever I turn my hand to.'

Gwrgenau was rather aghast at the tone and content of Hywel's words, but he chose to school his features and let the man finish. It was as if something had caused a barrier to break within Hywel, releasing things that had been held back for a long time.

'Take my fellow novices,' Hywel was still speaking. 'Julian is clever, of course. He likes his books, and he is a good enough man, but the truth is that his mother was only a serving woman, and he a nobleman's by-blow. Rhodri is good with numbers and a friend to all, but he is merely a wool merchant's son, a commoner. Not abbot material, surely? Neither has as much advantage as I, try as they might. Assuredly, of the three of us I have the greatest chance of success and position, here at Cwmhir at least?'

As he finished speaking, a strained silence fell. Then a slight noise made them both turn to the door. In the doorway stood Julian and Rhodri. That they had been there long enough to hear Hywel's derogatory words was evident. Julian looked stunned. He quickly placed the book he was holding on the table and turned and fled the room. Rhodri was red with rage, his fists clenched white at his sides. He stepped forward towards Hywel, who had stood up in horror, his hands held out beseechingly. The prior quickly stepped forward and placed his hands gently on Rhodri's arms.

'Brother,' he said firmly, and Rhodri raised his eyes to meet Gwrgenau's. The young monk took a deep breath and unclenched his fists, nodding finally at the prior, who released him. Then Rhodri was gone also, and Hywel was left alone with Gwrgenau. He sat back down heavily and dropped his face into his hands.

'Brother, I think you know that your words have done great damage here. I know not what has possessed you since your brother's visit, or even before that, but I have no doubt that the thoughts you voiced here were not meant unkindly. They do, however, reflect what is going on inside you, and that causes me great concern.'

He watched as a huge sob wracked Hywel's hunched body. Compassion filled his heart towards the young man and Gwrgenau stepped quietly forward and placed a hand on Hywel's shaking shoulders. He waited until the storm of sobbing subsided before speaking again.

'You will have to find a way to repair what now lies broken here. The community requires us to live together in harmony. Our words have the power to bring life, or to bring death and destruction, and you have betrayed your friends by your words. But it is also evident that you carry a huge burden on your young shoulders, and I would hope that we can help find a way for you to deal with that.' He paused, waiting for his words to sink in. Hywel was sitting, spent, his head on his folded arms, his fingers gripping his elbows.

'Enough for now. I will excuse you from Offices for the rest of the day. Go to your bed and I will pray that sleep comes to soothe your troubled soul. God alone knows what must be done with you, and I must seek His will on your behalf.'

He watched as Hywel rose painfully from his seat and pulled his hood up to cover his head. He left the room a dejected figure. Gwrgenau closed his eyes and offered up a quick prayer for Hywel, for Julian and Rhodri, and for the peace of his whole community, as the bell calling them to Compline rang out across the abbey.

O God, hear my prayer.

Listen to my heart's cry.

For no matter where I am, even when I'm far from

home,

I will cry out to you for a father's help.

When I'm feeble and overwhelmed by life,

guide me into your glory, where I am safe and

sheltered.

Psalm 61:1-2, TPT

8

Pilgrims

For the second time in two days Hywel found himself summoned to the abbot's presence. Only this time he knew full well what he had done, and was desperately sorry for it. He had lain awake well into the dark hours, sleep of any kind eluding him. He had heard his fellow brothers moving around, his once friends, as they prepared themselves for bed, knelt to pray, rose in response to the bells, left to attend the Offices. He could say nothing. They said nothing. For once the Rule of silence was strictly adhered to between the three. Even without words it was obvious that the atmosphere between them had changed, the tension palpable. And Hywel knew he was the cause of it. He and his stupid words, not meant for their ears, certainly, and not meant to hurt. But cruel and unthinking nonetheless. Hywel was more than contrite. He was devastated. He felt the weight of this latest folly add to the weight of the huge guilt he already carried, and it was almost unbearable.

He entered the abbot's rooms silently, his head bowed and his eyes lowered. He braced himself for what was to come. He deserved whatever punishment they thought fitting. He would take it and make amends and do what he could to put right the wrongs he had caused.

The abbot sat in his favoured chair by one of the tall windows that lit the room pleasingly. By his side stood the figure of Prior Gwrgenau. Both wore serious faces, but Gwrgenau gave what appeared to be a reassuring nod and his eyes were kind. It was good for Hywel that the prior was here.

He had shown himself compassionate and understanding the night before. He had proved himself wise and good over the months Hywel had known him. Hywel trusted him. Abbot Rind he was less sure of, but showed him the required deference, bowing from the waist, and coming to stand silently before him, his head bowed.

'So you must leave us, Brother Hywel.'

The abbot's words hit like an arrow to the chest and Hywel's head shot up. *No. Not that. Anything but that.* How could he possibly face his father ever again if he were forced to leave the Order, his mother's dream for him crushed, over a few misspoken words?

'Father Abbot...' Hywel opened his mouth to plead his cause, but the abbot raised his hand to silence him. Hywel saw out of the corner of his eye that Prior Gwrgenau had moved towards him.

'Brother, hear us out,' the prior spoke reassuringly.

'Brother Prior has informed me that you had something of a crisis moment yesterday, after your family visited, and that it has caused you to question your vocation. A serious matter indeed for one who has only recently taken his vows.'

That wasn't right. He wasn't questioning his vocation. The last thing he wanted was to go back on his vows. He had to stay, to prove himself, to become all that he was destined to be.

'No...' Hywel began to speak again.

Prior Gwrgenau flashed him a warning look, so he shut his mouth and lowered his head again. Something was going on here and he wasn't sure what, but in that moment he decided to trust the prior and hold his peace.

'Brother Prior,' the abbot was speaking again, in his usual monotone, 'has nominated you to accompany a group of pilgrims on a pilgrimage to the Holy Island of the Saints, Ynys y Saint.[4] You will be gone for some time, but I trust that you will return surer of your desire to be a brother here, and clearer

---

[4] Ynys y Saint, which means Island of the Saints, is the early medieval name for Bardsey Island, now known in Welsh as *Ynys Enlli*.

about your life's purpose. I have agreed to this, not least because you are younger and fitter than most in our community, and you have a way with horses, I believe. This particular group of pilgrims will be travelling mostly on horseback.'

Hywel felt a huge sense of relief wash over him and he relaxed. He wasn't being sent away permanently. He missed much of what the abbot had actually said after the 'return' bit... something about horses? Confusion must have registered on his face.

'Prior Gwrgenau will explain more. You will need to be ready to leave in the morning. God go with you.'

He was being dismissed. Was that all? No punishment, no enforced penance? Hywel was perplexed but he obediently turned to leave, the prior following close after him. As they reached the chapter house below, he felt a hand on his arm.

'Brother, sit. We must talk now.' Gwrgenau led him over to the stone seats lining the far wall of the room. It was cool and peaceful.

'You did not sleep much?'

Hywel looked up at him through weary, bloodshot eyes, and smiled ruefully.

'I did not sleep much either. I was praying for you, brother.' Gwrgenau sat down next to him with an audible sigh. 'I know that you are carrying some heavy weight on your soul and I do not expect you to confess all to me here and now. That is between you and God.

'Something is making you believe that you have to prove yourself by your actions and your achievements. You carry a pride within you, and an innate confidence in yourself, which, when combined with ambition, manifested yesterday as condescension and self-importance, to the detriment of those who did not deserve it.

'I have watched you, Hywel; you have done all that is required of you here, and with good grace mostly, so that we assumed you were ready to take your vows. But I know that it is possible to put on a convincing outward show while inwardly being in turmoil. I see now that you are not free enough within yourself to be able to fully commit your life to God and to His service.'

He paused, apparently to ensure he had Hywel's full attention.

'The pilgrimage Father Abbot spoke of is led by someone I know very well, an old soldier, Madoc by name. He knows the route well and has led many such groups of pilgrims over the years. He asked me to go with him this time; he likes to have a spiritual guide to accompany them, and having a Cistercian with them certainly eases things with obtaining accommodation in the Cistercian houses along the route. I was tempted to agree to go, but then I thought of you. You need this more than I. And well, I prayed, and God seemed to highlight this as a solution. It will indeed get you away from here for a while, and also give you time and space to deal with whatever it is that is holding you back in your devotion to God.'

Hywel sat listening, thoughtfully. He wasn't sure. Wouldn't time outside the community be a diversion from his true purpose? Surely all he needed to do was make penance, apologise and seek his friends' forgiveness, and then continue with his intended plans? How would riding across miles of countryside with a group of pilgrims, from who knew what backgrounds, help him? And yet the thought of being outside the four walls of the abbey, experiencing new things, riding over hills and mountains, appealed.

'If I don't agree to go? What then?' he asked.

'Then I will be honour-bound to tell Father Abbot the whole truth about what happened yesterday. At present all he knows is that you were upset and spoke unkindly while out of control of your emotions. He doesn't know what you said, nor that you are after his position.' He smiled wryly. 'Hywel, believe me, you cannot continue here as you are. Either you take this opportunity to get away for a time and seriously seek God's direction for your life, find some peace for your soul, or I will be recommending that you leave here for good.'

They sat in silence as Hywel mulled over what the prior had said, what his refusal to go on this pilgrimage could mean for him and his future. He seemingly had little choice but to acquiesce.

'Brother, I know that you have knowledge of horse ailments. The reports have come back to me as to how you have helped treat a wounded horse, more than once.'

Hywel nodded, interested as to where the prior was going with this train of thought.

'When an animal, or a man for that matter, suffers a deep wound and it begins to fester, it does not do much good to clean the surface of that wound and to dress it. It is even possible for a wound to heal on the surface, I believe, and yet still fester deep beneath the skin. Unless that wound is cleaned out, excised of any foreign object and the impurities released, it will never truly heal. And we have both seen what an untreated festering wound can do. Limbs and lives can be lost.

'So it is with our souls, Hywel. We can bury our true thoughts and feelings, our guilt and our pain, our unconfessed sins, even. We can believe that they are hidden, that there is no gaping wound needing to heal, just a surface scar, maybe. But deep beneath the surface, those things fester and poison us from the inside out. You have done well to hide your inner feelings for months here, until they burst to the surface yesterday, and I'm sure you would be able to bury them again. But sooner or later something would bring them to the surface, and you could cause further damage to the harmony of our lives. Hywel, you must dig deep and deal with what has you bound up inside before you come back to us. If you can do that, with God's help, I believe you will also discover your true destiny – what it is that God actually has planned for you. I am sure of it.'

Hywel looked at the prior sitting calmly beside him. He knew there was wisdom in what he had said, but still was not sure how a pilgrimage would help. He also realised that Gwrgenau would not be moved on this. So, pilgrimage it was.

'I will go,' he whispered.

'With our blessing and our prayers,' Gwrgenau answered.

It was a cool and dreary morning, reflecting Hywel's mood. He hadn't slept much again, but had risen with the bells and attended Offices as he should. He had tried to pray. Tried to connect. But he found his mind wandering and his apprehension growing as the hours passed and the time for his departure neared. He hated uncertainties, and this definitely felt uncertain. What would be required of him? Who were his companions? How long would they be away? Would he be welcomed back to Cwmhir after it all, or would he have to return to Brampton with his tail between his legs?

He stood just inside the abbey gates with Prior Gwrgenau, who smiled reassuringly at him. There was no one else gathered to see him off. He felt the loss of Julian and Rhodri's friendship even more acutely. Before he had betrayed their trust in him, they would have come to wish him well on his journey, he was sure of it. He glanced around but the cloister and gardens were quiet.

A slight commotion outside the gate caught his attention.

'The pilgrim party is here, I think,' Gwrgenau said brightly, and walked towards the gates where the porter had appeared to unlock them. Hywel followed slowly, carrying a small satchel which contained his own meagre possessions: a change of clothes, a small knife, a cup and a bowl, and a letter signed by the abbot that he was to present at any Cistercian house where they might seek accommodation.

The pilgrim party awaited him. An odd mix of people, on an even odder selection of mounts – a couple of Welsh hill ponies, an old farm horse and a fine-boned black stallion that was standing throwing its head about and stepping sideways in frustration at being made to wait. Hywel smiled to himself that he had taken more notice of the horses than he had their riders.

His attention was then taken by the huge dappled grey that stood riderless and patient, looking straight at Hywel with a knowing expression on his face. Hywel stepped forward instinctively and put his hand out to stroke the huge soft muzzle. The horse snorted and tossed his head but allowed Hywel to pet him again.

'I see you have introduced yourself to my horse, brother.'

Hywel turned at the voice, which was more of a growl, not quite menacing but near enough.

This must be Madoc. He looked every inch the old soldier. He was not above average height; Hywel towered over him, but he was broad and imposing. His bare arms showed he was still muscular and well built, as he stood with his hands on his hips, watching Hywel impassively. He was full-bearded and had a full head of hair; both hair and beard were red, liberally streaked with white, and his face was weathered. He stood well-armed, with a broad sword belted securely at his waist, Hywel was unsurprised to see. Once a soldier, always a soldier, it seemed.

'Well, if you can drag your attention away from the horse, perhaps we can get on our way,' Madoc said gruffly, showing just how athletic he still was by easily remounting the tall grey.

Hywel turned to see that Gwrgenau was barely supressing a smile. His own smile in response was a nervous one. At least the *horse* was friendly, he reassured himself.

A lay brother appeared, leading one of the abbey's ponies. It would have been too much to ask to be loaned one of the abbot's fine steeds, Hywel supposed. Well, the pony would suffice. He knew it to be healthy enough.

As he went to take the reins of his mount, Hywel realised that two figures had followed the pony from the direction of the stables. It was Julian and Rhodri. They came to a standstill a little way away and Hywel had to hand the reins back to the lay brother in order to move to meet them.

'Brothers.' He wracked his brain for what he could say that could possibly undo what he had said. 'My tongue ran away with me. What you heard... I'm sorry. I ask that you forgive me. I will forever regret causing you pain. You did not deserve it, either of you,' he added, beseechingly.

The two stood together, listening to Hywel's little speech. Julian's face was passive, Rhodri more stone-faced.

'Julian?' Hywel appealed to his friend. He watched as Rhodri took a step closer to Julian and placed his hand protectively on the other man's shoulder. *Interesting*, Hywel thought; Rhodri's anger made more sense now. He was used to being teased and usually took it in good humour. No, his anger in this instance was for Julian's hurt. His soft heart was hurt for his friend's hurt. Hywel saw that now, and realised that Rhodri would have probably felt the same way about him once. Before this.

Julian looked directly back at Hywel for a few moments and then offered him a slight smile. He nodded once in Hywel's direction.

'Rhodri?'

The younger monk was obviously struggling more with how to respond. He was searching Hywel's face and must have seen what he was looking for. He released his hold on Julian and stepped forward, extending his hand and opening it palm upwards towards Hywel. In it he held a small wooden cross, hand hewn, and it was being offered as a gift, a peace offering. Hywel felt his eyes welling up.

'Thank you, brother,' he said as he took it.

'God go with you,' Rhodri whispered.

'And with you, my friend,' Hywel replied with a small smile.

'Now can we be off?' Madoc's grating voice broke in. Hywel grimaced and turned his attention back to mounting his pony, pulling up alongside the old soldier.

'Ready when you are,' he said, as confidently as he could muster, before turning back in his saddle to raise his hand in farewell to his friends, to Prior Gwrgenau and to Cwmhir.

Madoc pulled away from him almost as soon as they were out of sight of the abbey. He obviously preferred being at the head of the party and the company of the small lady riding the old, rather plump farm horse. Behind them rode two young men on the hill ponies, and Hywel pulled alongside a third young man riding the black stallion at the rear of their small party.

They rode in silence for some miles, Hywel lost in his own thoughts and enjoying being on horseback, the wind in his face, breathing in the broad open skies. They climbed out of the valley to the north of the abbey, following a well-worn path through the trees and over the hills.

He was increasingly aware of the black stallion beside him, more so than the man riding him. The horse was obviously not used to being held back and wanted to run. He was tossing his head and getting agitated.

'Fine horse,' he ventured to engage his companion.

'Troublesome horse,' the young man replied sharply.

Interesting response. 'Is he yours?'

'My father insisted on buying him for me. Said if I was determined to do this pilgrimage that I would do it on horseback, to minimise the time I was away from the business. He insisted on this horse and he insisted on all of our party travelling on horseback also. He ensured everyone had a mount – of sorts. I think he bought me this horse out of spite, to perhaps make me give up and return home. He knows I am no horseman.' He illustrated this by pulling the reins too harshly to the right and causing the temperamental horse to rear in frustration.

'Here, let me,' Hywel said as he reached over and took the reins from the young man's fists, holding them loosely and using his voice to calm the agitated horse.

'You know horses?' It was asked in the same toneless voice.

'I was brought up with horses, and taught about them well.' Hywel swallowed back the memories. 'I seem to have a connection with them and they with me.'

They had pulled up under a large oak, their companions not so far ahead that they would lose sight of them.

'Do you want to ride him?'

The young man was eyeing Hywel's more steady-looking pony. Would he like to ride this beast? Of course he would. He relished the opportunity.

'If that would make you more comfortable.'

They both dismounted and swapped reins before remounting. The stallion also carried several large saddlebags. Hywel was sure that they weren't helping the horse's unhappy frame of mind, but they could tackle that later.

'What is his name?' he asked as they started out again to rejoin the others.

'Brenin. Welsh for "king". He's strong-willed enough to bear the name.'

Hywel thought it suited him too. A fine horse, and he was up for the challenge of riding him.

'And what name do you go by?'

'Matthew,' the young man replied. 'Son of Simon the goldsmith. My father is a dealer in fine metals and makes bejewelled items from them. He is wealthy as a result.'

That was all the information Hywel was seemingly going to get, and it was said in a disinterested tone. Hywel examined Matthew from the corner of his eye. He was small and wiry, and his hair was shaved so close to his head he looked almost bald, and boy-like – probably younger than he actually was. He was dressed in simple clothes which did not tally with his so-called wealth, and were all in black. No colour. Like his voice and his demeaner. Colourless.

He obviously wasn't a keen conversationalist so Hywel rode on next to him in silence for a while longer. The stallion had settled under his confident handling, and Matthew also seemed much more settled on the smaller, more docile pony. The sound of laughter – great guffaws – came from one of the riders ahead of them, grabbing Hywel's attention. *At least someone is happy*, Hywel thought. He tried another tack to engage Matthew.

'Can you tell me who our companions are? Madoc I know by name, but the others?'

'The one laughing is Tomos, and the other is Rhys. They are shepherds, I believe, and brothers, apparently, although it isn't obvious by their appearance.'

From what he could make out at a distance, Hywel could see his point. They looked markedly dissimilar.

'The lady riding beside Madoc is a widow, from Rhaeadr Gwy. She goes by the name of Myfanwy.'

He felt silent again. So Hywel let it go. He would have plenty of time to get to know them all; he assumed he was going to be in close proximity to this group of people for quite a while.

'Madoc is being paid by my father to guide us and specifically to protect me. I am an only son. He expects me to survive to take over his business.' Matthew didn't seem thrilled by the idea.

'Can I ask why you are set on this pilgrimage, when your father is so obviously against it?'

Matthew looked over at him, his eyes hard, seemingly assessing Hywel and why he was asking.

'For the same reason anyone goes on pilgrimage,' he replied with a condescending air, 'to gain favour with God and purity of soul.'

With that, the young man spurred his pony forward, leaving Hywel riding alone.

Strange, Hywel thought to himself, *the way he reacted to my questioning of his purpose?* He let his thoughts wander again as he settled down into the saddle, swaying instinctively in time with the horse, holding the reins loosely in his hands.

Is that why everyone goes on pilgrimage? *It isn't why I am here*, he thought to himself. *I wonder if it really is the reason any of these people are here.* He was sure over the weeks ahead he would come to know why they were each on this journey, and perhaps, eventually, why he was.

Blessed is the man whose strength is in You,

Whose heart is set on pilgrimage.

Psalm 84:5, NKJV

9
Llandinam

Hywel was enjoying the feeling of being on horseback, enjoying the freedom of being outside stone walls, feeling his soul expanding as his lungs did, breathing in the fresh air. By the position of the sun in the sky, they seemed to be heading almost due north from Cwmhir, along marked tracks that led across gently undulating grasslands and through wooded groves. The hills of Powys sheltered them on both sides but did not rise so high above them so as to be menacing. It was a dry day and warm enough, although puffy white clouds threw intermittent shade as they floated gently across the sky.

Hywel hung back at the rear of the riding party and took the opportunity to inspect his companions more closely. Madoc took the lead on his huge grey, and behind him the diminutive widow rode on her broad-backed farm horse. She sat astride her mount and her short legs meant the stirrups sat high on the horse's sides. Hywel smiled at the comical sight. He could hear her singing softly to herself as she rode.

The two brothers rode side by side on their matching ponies, but nothing much matched about them physically. Rhys rode tall, his long legs hanging almost to the ground, obviously abandoning his stirrups completely. He was dark-haired and square-shouldered. The other, Tomos, was blond, his legs definitely shorter, and his body rounder. He was talking and laughing almost constantly, while his silent brother just nodded from time to time. Matthew rode alone, a sullen figure and seemingly unwilling to engage.

Hywel felt a sinking feeling inside when he realised that these five were to be his constant companions for however many weeks stretched ahead of them. What did he have in common with any of them? He longed suddenly for Julian's scholarly mind and Rhodri's quick wit.

The party stopped to rest and water the horses as the sun reached its zenith, making use of a clear, fast-flowing stream. Hywel pulled up and dismounted Brenin smoothly. The stallion seemed to have accepted his handling and was being compliant enough. He relieved him of some of the weight of Matthew's numerous saddlebags and added them to his own meagre belongings on the back of the pony he had brought from Cwmhir. He led both horses to the stream.

Returning to the group, he watched Myfanwy as she dismounted awkwardly, with help from Madoc, and then busied herself retrieving provisions from the sack tied to the farm horse's back. Hywel was surprised to see that not only was she short in stature but she stooped also, her neck bent painfully, so that she could not lift her head high enough to meet his eyes as she approached him.

'Sit, brother, please,' she said cheerily, 'here on this rock. Rest yourself now. We must see that you are well fed. I rose early today to prepare some sweet pies for our meal, and I have some cheese here also.' He sat as ordered, and she handed him a small round pie wrapped in cloth and a piece of hard yellow cheese. Both smelled wonderful to his already rumbling stomach. Hywel took them from her with a grateful smile, only then seeing how gnarled and misshapen her hands were. She bobbed a little curtsey as she served him, as if he were some great potentate, before shuffling away to serve the others, who had gathered to sit in an awkward circle.

'Perhaps you would say a prayer of thanks for our meal, brother,' Myfanwy asked suddenly. Hywel had already raised the enticing pie to his mouth and felt his cheeks flush. He glanced around to see every face looking back at him expectantly, except for Madoc, whose lips were twisted in a half-sneer. His knowing eyes caught Hywel's and made the young monk feel even more exposed.

'Ah, yes… of course.' He stumbled over his words, his embarrassment increasing by the moment.

Hywel wracked his brain for the right words to say. After all those months in the abbey, why could he not remember a single simple prayer of thanks? He swallowed hard, aware of the eyes on him, and bowed his head, raising one hand as if offering a benediction. It seemed the right thing to do.

'We offer you our thanks, O Lord, for this our daily bread, I mean pie… our daily pie… and cheese… And keep us from temptation… forever and ever. Amen.'

There was a moment of silence. Hywel lifted his head and lowered his hand. Myfanwy and the two brothers were looking at him with kind, if confused, faces. All three smiled indulgently at him and lowered their heads to eat.

Hywel heard a muffled snort and looked over to see Madoc's shoulders shaking with mirth. Matthew's look was one of pure disdain. He hastily turned his back on Hywel and ate his food quickly before rising to leave the group, moving several yards away and pulling his black hood over his head as he knelt, in an attitude of prayer.

'He probably knows better than I how to pray,' Hywel mumbled to himself, while making short work of his lunch. He was mortified. Of course, he was supposed to be here as a spiritual support to the group, but he felt inadequate to the task, and his inadequacy had just been well and truly demonstrated. Who did they think he was? Of course, he was Brother Hywel, monk of Abbey Cwmhir, to them at least. A spiritual leader. He laughed inwardly at the thought. Yet, if that was who he was supposed to be, then he must try his best to live up to that. He resolved he would learn, be more prepared for the next time he were called upon. Maybe, like Matthew, he ought to spend every spare moment praying.

Madoc sidled over to sit by him, handing him a flagon of ale to drink from.

'Nicely done, brother,' he quipped. 'I needed a good laugh!'

Hywel stared back at him, affronted by the man's tone. 'I don't appreciate being ridiculed,' he snapped.

'Oh, now, don't get all high and mighty with me. We will just put it down to you being unprepared for Myfanwy's adulation. But I must warn you, brother, this won't be the last time you are called upon for your *spiritual* leadership. And you won't want to disappoint these faithful ones, now, will you? Look to it that you don't.' The last had an edge of threat to it.

Hywel wanted to respond, but decided wisely to let it go.

Madoc rose and wandered over to offer his flagon to Tomos and Rhys. Myfanwy reappeared before him. Her hair, where it escaped around a simple cap, was still mostly blond, despite the deep wrinkles around her eyes. Hywel guessed she was of middling years.

'There now, brother, I trust that you enjoyed my humble offering?' she asked, her face all smiles. 'I am so grateful for your company with us on our journey, brother,' she enthused, not waiting for his reply. 'To have a real man of God with us makes it an even more blessed pilgrimage. We are honoured by your presence.' It was genuinely said and she moved away with another small bob of a curtsey.

Hywel took a deep breath, his stomach twisting slightly. What was the word Madoc had used in describing Myfanwy's attitude? 'Adulation' – yes, that was it. For some reason, he guessed, his habit, tonsure and title gave him a status he was undeserving of. Man of God? Him? He had no idea how he was going to live up to that title, and he had days and weeks ahead of having to do so. He felt terrified by the thought. He was going to have to do a really good job of trying to convince the pilgrims that he was what Myfanwy believed him to be.

He caught Madoc watching him. He felt uncomfortable under the older man's scrutiny, as if he, at least, could see right through him.

Hywel felt the need to ride out his discomfiture, and as they headed off again, he spurred a lighter-loaded Brenin forward and past the other riders. The countryside was unfamiliar to him, but the track was marked clearly enough. He let the horse stretch his legs into a trot and pulled further ahead from the group, relishing the space. It was too long since he'd ridden a fine horse, and the temptation to spur Brenin into a gallop was strong. He had missed the thrill of a good hard ride.

Hywel was suddenly aware of the sound of heavy horse hooves coming up fast behind him. The grey pulled noisily alongside him, puffing and snorting, making Brenin rear and skitter sideways. Hywel pulled on the reins and spoke to calm the horse before turning to Madoc indignantly.

Before he could utter a word, Madoc grabbed the reins from his hand and pulled Brenin towards him, so that the horses were almost touching. He leant into Hywel and growled, 'What in hell do you think you are doing?'

Hywel was so startled by the ferociousness of the question he pulled back, confused.

'Do you have any idea where you are, or where we are heading? Did you not stop to think how speeding your horse and taking the lead would look? Those poor souls!' He nodded back to where the rest of the horse party stood some distance away. 'They and their horses tried to keep up with you. Not only was that cruel on their poor horses but dangerous also. Look, there…'

He thrust his hand in the direction they were facing. Hywel could see nothing of concern. The track had narrowed, certainly, and was less distinct. It wound upwards towards a ridge.

Madoc pulled him forward a few more paces, and then he saw it. The track he had been blindly following led straight over the ridge and disappeared into nothing. If he had continued at the speed he had been riding he would have plummeted down a rocky scree slope on the other side. He knew how dangerous that would have been, to horse and rider alike. He rubbed a suddenly sweaty hand down his thigh, trying not to further upset the horse beneath him.

'I'm sorry, I did not think.'

'No, you did not. You are so sure of yourself and your supposed abilities, young man, that you are blind to the needs of others. You left the track we must follow some time ago and have been following a sheep trail – it almost led to disaster.' Madoc released Brenin's reins and pulled the grey around.

'Now we must return to the others and you will *never* again take it upon yourself to lead at any time, unless I say so. In fact, I think it might do you good to take up the rear, to learn what it means to be last and not first. Certainly while I am responsible for this group. They may look to you for spiritual leadership, but you have yet to prove yourself worthy of being considered a leader. You may be able to fool them, brother, but not me. Thankfully I am only responsible for their physical safety. God help them if you are their spiritual hope.'

Hywel was in tumult, part guilt-ridden at his mistake, but also smarting from Madoc's reproof. He had not meant to lead the others astray; he certainly meant no one harm. He just hadn't thought, and had indulged himself for a few moments. No one had been hurt. And it was not his fault that this whole venture was forcing him into a position of spiritual leadership that he was unqualified for. He was angry at himself for his stupidity. He was angry at Madoc for shaming him. And he was angry at the situation he found himself in, which he was so ill-equipped for. How had Prior Gwrgenau ever thought that this would be a good idea?

He steeled himself for more reproach as they rejoined the others, but found Myfanwy and the brothers laughing together, and seemingly unaware of the drama that had almost unfolded. He waited for them all to ride on, with Madoc in the lead, before pulling in behind. Matthew glanced back at him with a questioning look, but Hywel pulled his hood up over his head and lowered his face. He wished complete disappearance was possible. He did not want to be here, had nothing to say to anyone. Even to God. But perhaps he should try to pray?

The words would not come, so he wallowed alone in his misery, dutifully following Madoc's plodding lead.

As the afternoon wore on, they came to a river, flowing wider and slower than any of the brooks and streams they had crossed so far. They did not cross it, and instead turned their horses slightly westward towards the now setting sun, following the wide river until they reached a small hamlet. The fine stone church of Llandinam sat on a small promontory above the river, surrounded by a collection of dwellings of various sizes.

'We will stop here for the night,' Madoc said, pulling his horse to a standstill. 'Unfortunately we are unlikely to be offered hospitality or a roof over our heads. The *clas*[5] community here is unaffiliated to any order. It is headed by a self-appointed canon and I know enough of him to expect little. There is guest accommodation available in the village, but only if you are prepared to pay well. And as only one of us has any wealth to speak of, I do not think we would be welcome. But there are flat stretches here along the river, and a baker in the village who will sell us fresh bread to break our fast on the morrow. It should not be cold tonight, and there is no sign of rain.'

'We will do well enough under the stars,' Myfanwy smiled over at Madoc.

'You, of course, can seek more comfortable accommodation, as you have the means.' Madoc had turned to Matthew, who looked decidedly put out at the suggestion.

'There is no place on a pilgrimage for comfort or self-indulgence,' he bit back at Madoc. 'It is bad enough that we have to make this journey on horseback and not on foot. How do we achieve mortification of the flesh if we are unwilling to feel even a little in the way of discomfort?'

Madoc seemed unmoved by Matthew's retort and proceeded to dismount and lead his horse to an area of grass

---

[5] A *clas* in early medieval Wales was an autonomous, non-affiliated monastic community with its own clergy based around a church, rather than an abbey.

on the riverbank. As the others joined him he gave quick instruction and, working together, they had soon unloaded the horses, collected twigs and small branches, and had a small fire burning. More pies and cheese appeared from Myfanwy's provisions and Hywel, more prepared this time, kept the prayer of thanks brief and to the point. They found spots to make themselves as comfortable as they could, as the sun lowered in the sky. Hywel was weary enough to sleep, despite the lack of a bed. He wrapped his cloak around him and settled down to rest. He tried to recite some of the words of the evening liturgy in his head, as he thought he ought to, but sleep quickly took him.

He woke early, the grass damp beneath his legs. The sun was on the rise, but a lingering light mist made the air feel cool. He glanced around their camp. Myfanwy, Tomos and Rhys were still huddled up in their makeshift beds, but the spaces where Madoc and Matthew had been lying were empty. The horses were standing contently grazing where they had been left the night before. Hywel stood stiffly, stretched his back and walked down to the riverbank. Upriver he spied Madoc, looking like he was lowering a fishing line into the water. Fresh fish to break fast? He salivated at the thought.

He turned then towards the village and made the decision to start the day right. He would go into the church to pray.

The double nave stone church was simply built on ancient foundations, but as Hywel approached he could see the foundation rows of a square stone tower being built in Norman style. There was no shortage of wealth here, then? He found the wooden door with its arched stone surround, and entered the church quietly. Through clear glass windows, the rising sun lit up enough of the interior for Hywel to take it all in.

A quick glance around confirmed Hywel's earlier estimation. This was not a poor parish. The table at the high altar end of the first nave was covered with a gold-threaded, richly embroidered altar cloth. On the altar stood a fine gold crucifix and two tall silver candle holders. He took in painted illustrations on more than one wall, a statuette of Mary, silver implements and censers, and a wooden reading stand with exquisite carvings, holding a leather-bound book.

He also saw that he wasn't alone in the church. Matthew had obviously had the same thought as he. The black-robed figure was lying prostrate in cruciform before the high altar. Hywel sighed to himself. How long had the other man been there, he wondered, and why did he have to surpass him in his show of piety, every time?

Hywel moved quietly into the second nave and found a spot where the sunlight coming through the window was warming the stones. He knelt there to pray, but he missed his Cistercian brothers, the soul-stirring plainsong, the familiar words of the psalmody recited together, the set prayers. Without those, he did not know how to approach God. He listened instead to the sounds of the morning outside of the window, a blackbird singing, distant calls of greeting between villagers, the rattling of a cart as it passed, and the tuneless whistle of its handler.

He grew frustrated with himself, and was even on the verge of going over to ask Matthew to pray with him, when another sound caught his attention. A door creaked and a figure appeared to one side of the altar. The man was dressed as a priest, but in such fine raiment as Hywel had rarely seen. He had glimpsed the Archbishop of Canterbury from a distance in Westminster, and this man's clothing was comparable in its rich fabrics and stitchwork. He was a large man with a round, pasty-white face and heavy jowls. He was not smiling. He cleared his throat loudly, looking down at Matthew's prostrate form. The young man raised himself gingerly from the stone floor at the same time as Hywel rose and stepped forward to stand by him, both facing the Canon of Llandinam.

'You are welcome to pray here, of course,' he said. He was staring at them, his mouth set in a hard line, belying the content of his words of greeting. They were clearly not welcome. 'The Cistercian habit marks you as a monk, brother,' he nodded reluctantly at Hywel. 'But your attire, young man, I do not recognise as belonging to any order or church that I know of, and I am surprised to find you lying uninvited on my nave floor.' He sneered in Matthew's direction. 'Some heavy sin lays on your back, perhaps? I would usually offer you confession in exchange for a small donation to our poor church. But...' he sighed, '... unfortunately, I must ask you both to take your leave. I have services to perform for a local knight and his family and need to prepare myself and the church.'

He turned abruptly and walked to the heavy main door, held it wide open for them to leave, and closed it firmly behind them.

'Well, he wanted rid of us!' Hywel quipped as they walked away together, trying to make light of the awkwardness.

'Pompous, arrogant, son of the devil! He will face God's wrath for his vanity and ostentation. This is a sordid and ungodly place and I am sorry to have entered the church at all!' Matthew turned to Hywel, his face puce. 'And you, *brother*,' he spat out the word. 'How could you as a Cistercian, in good faith bear the gaudiness and wealth on show in there?'

He didn't wait for Hywel's response but strode off back in the direction of the camp. Hywel followed him at a slower pace, somewhat bemused at the heat of Matthew's response. He wondered to himself, was it true piety that had caused his anger? Or, as he suspected, rather that the man's pride had been hurt and his demonstrative devotions interrupted.

They arrived back at the camp to find Madoc returning with two good-sized trout hanging from the line in his hands. He greeted them both with a nod, but Matthew ducked his head and walked past him to the water's edge, bending to splash his face and wash his hands repeatedly, as if to ritually cleanse himself from some stain. Madoc raised his eyebrows questioningly at Hywel, who just shrugged in response.

'See to the fire, if you will, Brother Hywel, while I get these fish cleaned. Tomos and Rhys have gone into the village to buy bread and milk.'

Hywel collected some more sticks to add fuel to the fire and blew life into the embers still faintly glowing from the night before. The fire smoked and then suddenly sparked to life. Tomos and Rhys reappeared, laughing, and laden with provisions. Myfanwy helped Madoc spear the freshly gutted fish on sticks and they sat together, turning them slowly over the flames. The smell as the fish oils dripped into the fire was mouth-watering.

'Are you partaking of the fish, brother? Is it permitted?' Madoc asked with a small grin.

'Special circumstances,' Hywel replied with a grin of his own, his stomach grumbling loudly.

His offered prayer of thanks this time was genuinely felt, and speedily spoken as he took the piece of hot fish proffered to him, and ate it hungrily. The fresh-from-the-oven bread and warm creamy milk acquired from the village added to his enjoyment of the simple meal, and he felt a sense of unexpected contentment as he glanced around at his fellow feasters.

Tomos was chatting away, as he did, interspersed with guffaws of laughter, his brother smiling and nodding indulgently, but saying little. Myfanwy was fussing around, pouring milk and serving bread, but with a constant smile. Matthew had eventually joined them and Madoc was sitting by him talking in low tones. It seemed to be having a calming effect on the young man.

Hywel realised then, in contrast to the cold reception they had received from Llandinam's unpleasant canon, that there was no want of joy, kindness or good feeling here in the company sitting around that little fire. He felt sudden warmth seep into his soul.

How truly wonderful and delightful it is

to see brothers and sisters living together in sweet

unity!

It's as precious as the sacred scented oil

flowing from the head of the high priest Aaron,

dripping down upon his beard and running all the

way down

to the hem of his priestly robes.

This harmony can be compared to the dew

dripping from Mount Hermon,

which flows down upon the hills of Zion.

Indeed, that is where Yahweh has decreed his

blessings

will be found, the promise of life forevermore!

Psalm 133, TPT

10
Llanllugan Abbey

Madoc seemed in no hurry to break camp and set off. The mist had lifted from the river and the sun was warm on Hywel's back as he stretched his legs and leant back on his hands, watching his companions. His stomach felt satisfyingly full and it was very pleasant indeed resting down there by the riverbank. He closed his eyes but his mind was not as at peace as he had hoped. Better to occupy himself than let his mind wander down paths he didn't want to retrace. He heaved himself up and walked over to the horses. Madoc was already there, checking his horse's hooves.

'All is well?' Hywel asked.

'Yes, thank you, brother. He caught a stone under his shoe yesterday, but it has left no lasting damage. No need of your *renowned* horse expertise here.'

'Is that why you have delayed our departure this morning?' Hywel ignored Madoc's slight, whether intended or not.

'No. We covered a good distance yesterday, and our next overnight stop is not so far a ride. You are fit and young, and used to being on a horse. Not all of our party are so blessed. They will be feeling the effects of being on horseback all day yesterday, followed by a night on the hard ground. One in particular.'

Hywel followed Madoc's gaze as his eyes lighted on Myfanwy. The little woman was walking stiffly towards the fire. She bent painfully to retrieve a discarded cup.

'Myfanwy. She suffers? Is it her joints?' Hywel had seen it before. The painful bone condition that led to crippling incapacity over time.

'You would do better to ask her and not me about that, brother,' Madoc replied and walked away, leading his horse behind him.

Hywel plucked some long blades of fresh grass and approached Brenin, offering it to him with an open hand and speaking softly to him. The horse turned his large brown eyes on Hywel and seemed to take a moment to assess him, before bowing his head to take the proffered grass. Hywel gently took hold of his rein, intending to follow Madoc back towards the camp, where it seemed their guide had decided it was finally time to pack up and leave. He then had another thought. He led Brenin over to where Myfanwy's farm horse was grazing contentedly, his tail swishing at the swarm of gnats that had gathered because of the river's proximity. He grabbed the reins of the other horse, who needed some persuading to leave his grass patch, and led both horses back.

'Can I help you load your horse?' he asked Myfanwy, who had turned to greet him with a smile.

'Oh, thank you, brother. I would be grateful. These old bones of mine are a bit stiff this morning and they won't do what I want them to do.' She was looking down at her disfigured fingers, trying to flex them and wincing visibly as she did so.

Hywel bent to pick up her belongings and began securing them to the horse's back.

'Your joints pain you?' he asked quietly.

She didn't answer straight away. Just fussed around repositioning some of her possessions.

'Some days more than others, they do pain me, yes. But I do well enough. I once stood straight and proud, you know.' She laughed briefly, but the pain was evident on her face.

'I'm sure you were quite a beauty.'

'*Were*, brother? Well, thank you! I didn't think I was that ugly now!' she replied teasingly.

Hywel had the good grace to dip his head in embarrassment.

'Now, don't concern yourself. I never was a great beauty, but my condition has certainly disfigured me, and you were kind to compliment me. My past self, anyway.' She laughed again.

'Forgive me for asking, but if you are in so much pain, why did you come on what might be an arduous journey lasting for many weeks?'

She turned to him then, and awkwardly twisted her neck so that she could look up into his eyes.

'Brother, this is my journey of hope. I must make it, because it is where I will find my healing. I have waited a long time to be able to make this journey. The opportunity was denied me for far too long, but now I am free to make my own choices. And I have chosen this.'

She broke off then and turned her attention back to her horse standing patiently by.

Healing? She expects to be healed from her infirmity? It wasn't unheard of, Hywel supposed. It was the reason very many souls made these pilgrimages, after all. He marvelled at her simple faith and wondered where she had come by it. He did wish her well in her quest, but couldn't quite match her belief.

'I pray God will heal you,' he said, and was surprised how genuinely he meant it.

'I *know* He will, brother,' she replied softly.

The horse party set off at a steady pace, following the course of the river until they reached the small settlement of Caersws where a bridge took them over the wide river to its other side. For a few miles more they stayed with the river before turning more directly northwards again. Hywel kicked himself for not asking Madoc earlier where they were headed. He had reluctantly held back at the rear of the party as instructed. Myfanwy rode beside him, as if some new connection had been made between them. She didn't speak much, but Hywel was aware of the odd sharp intake of breath or painful shifting of position, as the ride was uneven in places. The weather was kind at least, although clouds appeared as the day wore on, and Hywel began to feel chilled. He could only imagine how the chill affected Myfanwy, and he felt for her. But she was uncomplaining, her ready smile never far from her face.

'Do you know our destination for tonight?' he asked her as their route followed a smaller tributary of the great river. It was certainly easier riding now, mostly flat and green, with the waterway winding along attractively beside them.

'Llanllugan Abbey, brother. I'm surprised you do not know it. It is Cistercian, I believe?'

Hywel had heard of Llanllugan but had had no idea that it was on their route. It wasn't an abbey that Cwmhir had close connection with, for one main reason – it was a female house. The only one in the northern part of Wales, he understood. It had closer connections to the great abbey at Strata Marcella, and was only fairly recently founded.

'Will we find welcome there?' Hywel was doubtful that a small community of nuns would appreciate the arrival of a pilgrim party consisting mostly of men, even with a Cistercian brother among them.

'Madoc seems to believe so. He knows the abbess personally,' she smiled over at him. 'No need to be afraid of a few nuns, brother!'

Hywel grinned back. 'If you say so, Myfanwy. I'll wait to make my own judgement on that one.'

Llanllugan was neither a big nor an impressive abbey. It seemed to consist of a small, simple wooden church and a rough stone-built house, surrounded by a collection of rustic-looking farm buildings. They approached as the sun was beginning to set. They had not pushed themselves or the horses, and it had been a leisurely ride, but Hywel still felt weary in the saddle and ready for rest. He wondered if it would be another night in the open air. It didn't look like there was much in the way of visitor accommodation within the abbey complex.

As they drew near and dismounted, a nun came out to greet them. Her habit was white, as Hywel's, and she wore a simple wooden crucifix on a cord around her neck. She walked with an easy grace. As she came closer, Hywel could see a pleasant face with kind eyes framed by wimple and veil. A small smile lifted the corners of her mouth. Hywel noted that her face was also unblemished by age; she did not look that much older than him.

'Sister Gracia, or should I call you Mother Abbess now?' Madoc stepped forward to greet her, his tone softer than Hywel had ever heard it.

'Madoc, our friend, you are most welcome here.' She held a hand out to grasp his, before acknowledging them all. 'And your companions, of course. Come, bring your mounts and we will get you all settled for the night.'

She turned with a demure swish of her skirts and led them towards a barn-like building. It was a well-enough constructed wooden building with a thick thatch and had high double wooden doors on one side. It was to these the young abbess led them. She pushed open one of the doors and then stood aside for them to enter. Madoc led his horse inside, pushing the other door open as he went, and nodding for the rest to follow. He seemed familiar with the place, leading his horse over to the far left where fresh straw was stacked high, and hay bags hung on well-placed nails on the walls, as if the horse visitors at least had been expected. A large half-barrel of water was well-equipped with dippers. Madoc tied the grey, and the horse happily helped himself to some hay.

Well, the horses will be comfortable, Hywel smiled to himself. He looked around the barn and saw that the space at the other end had also been prepared. A simple wooden table and two benches sat to one side, and more fresh straw was piled up on the other, with some folded blankets resting on top. Bedding for them, he presumed. So they would sleep under cover tonight.

'We will be most comfortable here, as always, sister,' Madoc smiled over at Gracia. 'But Myfanwy here… Could we impose on your hospitality and ask you to find her a softer bed and a less-draughty space to spend her night?'

Gracia gave him what looked suspiciously like an affronted look, before turning to the woman in question.

'Myfanwy, I would never expect you to have to sleep with the animals.' She glanced back at Madoc with a twinkle in her eye. 'We have a comfortable guest bed, and space at our sisters' table to accommodate you, my dear.'

Myfanwy blushed slightly but did not reject the offer. 'I would be most grateful, Mother Gracia. It would be a great honour to be able to share space with you and your godly sisters.'

'It is nearing the time for Vespers and you are all welcome to join us in the church. As are you for all the Offices during your stay.' She glanced at Hywel. 'If you choose to rest, however, I do hope that our bells do not disturb you. I will return after prayers with some warm food for your supper. Please, make yourselves comfortable.'

She moved over to help Myfanwy, who was struggling to lift a bag down from her horse's back. She silently took the bag from the older woman's hands and gestured for her to walk ahead of her out of the door, which she closed quietly behind them.

'Lovely,' Tomos said with a sigh, watching her leave. It was a bit forward to speak of a nun in such a way, but Hywel silently agreed. It wasn't that she was stunningly beautiful, rather that the young nun radiated a kindness, goodness and grace – yes, that was it. She lived up to her name.

'She is young to be an abbess?' Hywel had been trying to keep his curiosity to himself, but he was personally invested in the answer to that question. He was young too, but he had ambition.

Madoc had been busying himself unloading his horse, but turned to him with a half-smile. 'She might be considered young, but she was by far the most qualified to take the position when the late Mother Abbess died. It is a very small community here, just six sisters, and she leads them well. A more genuinely spiritual woman than Gracia you will rarely find, brother.

'Now, I suggest we get these horses seen to. They need a good rubbing down tonight. Unless you want to attend prayers, brother?' He looked pointedly at Hywel, as the first ring of the bell for Vespers sounded.

'No, I'll stay and help you here,' Hywel replied. 'God knows I can pray any time.'

He and Tomos and Rhys set to, helping Madoc to make the horses comfortable. It was only after they were done that Hywel realised that Matthew was not with them. He felt a momentary twist of guilt as he realised that yet again the other man had surpassed him in his religious duty. He alone of their party had joined the sisters for Vespers.

The four of them moved over to the table, lit some candles and sat down. Before long, Matthew returned with Gracia, entering the barn just as Hywel was laughing loudly at a very funny story Tomos had just shared. Matthew scowled at him disapprovingly, and lowered the steaming pot he was carrying onto the tabletop. It smelt very appetising. Gracia added some bread and a flagon of ale to the table.

'You will find bowls, spoons and beakers on the shelf behind you.' She indicated the store with a nod of her head. 'God bless this food to you all.'

'Thank you, sister.' Hywel spoke for them, adding hastily, 'We will all join you later for Compline, before retiring for the night.'

Gracia nodded and smiled, and then left them to it.

The hot stew of beans and vegetables was very satisfying and they made short work of finishing it between them.

'So we are all attending Compline, are we?' Madoc asked Hywel, one eyebrow raised, as he rubbed his belly contentedly.

'I feel about ready to make a comfortable bed in that straw and settle for the night.'

'My apologies, Madoc. But I do think we should attend to show our appreciation for the sisters' hospitality, and to God, of course, for His provision for us. And we are on pilgrimage, after all.'

Madoc snorted. 'You are right of course, brother! We follow your lead. Although it seems your fellow pilgrim has already set an example to us *all* by his attendance at Vespers.' He turned so that only Hywel heard what followed. 'Is it because of Matthew that you committed us to attending the prayer Office? Did his attendance at Vespers shame you? I would warn you against making this any kind of personal competition between the two of you. You are very different beasts. As different in nature as your young stallion and Myfanwy's farm horse. Trying to be what someone else purports to be would be as ridiculous as Brenin trying to pull a plough. It will not end well.'

Madoc didn't wait for Hywel to respond but stood up and moved over to rearrange the straw and blankets for his bed.

Hywel sat gazing into the cup he held in his hands. The ale had been as good as the food and there was a mouthful left, but he was lost in his thoughts. He needed to examine his heart. What had he meant by promising their attendance at Compline? He had no right to speak for them all. *Was* it just a reaction to the guilt he felt at missing Vespers? He never would have missed attending Offices back at Cwmhir. *Did* he see Matthew as a rival in piety? He admitted to himself that Matthew did challenge him, but wasn't sure Matthew's style of religious observance sat well with him. He didn't think God would hold it against him for missing an Office to give aid to his companions and their horses, anyway.

He was confused by it all. And if he allowed himself to dig further, he knew he carried much greater guilt than that of missing a prayer Office. If this company of pilgrims really knew what burdens he carried, how much he had hurt so many by foolish and selfish actions and words, they would definitely not look to him as any kind of spiritual lead.

He sighed and swallowed the last of the ale. He still did not understand why he had been sent on this pilgrimage; all it seemed to be doing so far was to expose him as a fraud and pretender, in his own mind, at least. Oh, and it seemed that old soldier Madoc might have the measure of him too.

The prayers and sweet singing voices of the nuns of Llanllugan had soothed his troubled mind somewhat by the time they settled down on their straw beds for the night. Hywel had sat with the others for Compline, even though a space had been offered to him in the nuns' choir stall. He was surprised to realise that he hadn't wanted to elevate himself above his companions in any way. Nor did he want the good nuns to realise that he could not sing a note in tune!

He had watched the faces of the other pilgrims during the short service. Myfanwy had sat transfixed by the candlelit wooden crucifix, her face glowing and a contented peace radiating from her. Rhys and Tomos had been engaged and wholehearted in their responses. Rhys had even hummed a low and beautifully tuneful harmony along with the nuns' song. Matthew had knelt throughout with his head bowed, and Madoc had sat with his eyes closed and his arms folded across his chest, his face unreadable. Hywel himself had responded to the familiar words of the liturgy and found comfort in them. He was glad to have attended, just for those few moments of peace, and the feeling that perhaps he was not as far from God as he imagined himself to be.

Sleep came easily enough, but Hywel was disturbed by the early morning bell for Vigils. Not disturbed enough to rise from his warm and comfortable bed, however. In the dim light of the barn he could make out the sleeping form of Matthew, and allowed himself a brief moment of self-satisfaction that the other man had not risen for Vigils either. Hywel pulled the blanket closer over his shoulder against the early morning chill and let his heavy eyelids lower again.

He was startled to full awareness by a muffled crash that seemed to come from outside the barn. He wondered if he should go and investigate, but sleep was again calling to him. Except now his bladder was uncomfortable. He gave in to the inevitable and rose as quietly as he could, pulling the blanket around his shoulders like a cloak, to make his way out into the chilly night air.

The half-moon was still visible in the sky, enough light for Hywel to see his way, enough light to see also that he was not alone. He could make out the familiar figure of Rhys, but the tall man was on his knees leaning over something laid out on the floor.

He approached and Rhys started.

'Brother, only you,' he whispered breathlessly, glancing back at Hywel, before turning his attention back to the form before him. Hywel realised then that it was Tomos that Rhys hovered over with concern. The other man was on the ground, but was not still. His limbs were twitching and his head rolling from side to side, until with a final massive convulsion of his body, he finally did lay still, twisted awkwardly, his head thrown back.

'Rhys? Can we do anything?' Hywel had joined Rhys on the ground beside his brother, watching Tomos as finally his whole body relaxed.

'No, best not to touch him. I'll just sit with him until he wakes. He will sense my presence and it will be comfort enough. The worst is past now.'

'Here, let me cover him at least.' Hywel took the blanket from his shoulders and laid it over Tomos' prostrate form.

They sat together in silence for a moment, the only sound Tomos' steady if slightly noisy breathing. Hywel could feel Rhys trembling beside him and reached out to place a comforting hand on his arm.

'This is not the first time, is it?'

'No,' Rhys sighed. 'Tomos has had these episodes ever since he was a lad of fourteen. He fell out of a tree and was knocked senseless. He did not wake for three days and we thought we had lost him. But then he did wake and seemed to recover well. Within a week he had the first attack. They did not come frequently nor last for long at first, but lately they have come more often and have lasted longer. I think it was the sudden sound of the bell clanging tonight that brought this one on. He had risen to relieve himself and I for some reason was prompted to follow him out. I think God knew he would need my protection again.'

Rhys sat down on the ground, twisting his knees from under him and rubbing the life back into his legs. 'We may be here for some time, brother. That is, if you choose to stay.'

'I'd be happy to keep you company.' Sleep was a far way off now. 'Will he be well when he awakes?'

'He may be a bit confused and appear dazed, and that can last for a few hours. I will need your help both to get him back to his bed and to keep his condition a secret, brother.'

'Why a secret? Does Madoc not know? He perhaps should know as he is responsible for our safety on this pilgrimage.'

'No.' It was emphatic. And for the first time Hywel picked up a fierceness in Rhys' voice and demeanour. 'I will not have him exposed to the judgement of others. He has suffered enough without being branded a fool, or even worse, demon-possessed.'

Hywel could understand his concern. He knew well enough how misplaced superstitions and warped beliefs could engender fear and cruelty in people.

'We have come on this pilgrimage to seek God's help; we need no interference from men, well-meaning or not,' Rhys continued. 'I have sworn to protect and shield my brother, and I will not break that promise until God releases me from it.'

'Are you seeking healing for him, then?' Hywel thought back to Myfanwy's simple faith.

'If it is God's will, brother... I pray that it is, for my brother's sake.'

'And for yours too, I would say.'

Tomos stirred and groaned.

'Now, then, Tomos, all is well, although I am sure you are uncomfortable lying there on the ground. Let's get you back to your bed.' Rhys spoke with his more usual softness, and gestured for Hywel to come around to Tomos' other side. Between them they helped the dazed man to sit up, and then half-dragged, half-lifted him to his feet.

When they were sure Tomos could put his weight on his feet, they took an arm each to hold him upright, making their way as noiselessly as possible back inside the barn, where they lowered him onto his straw bed. He turned onto his side, curled into a ball, and was snoring almost immediately.

Rhys turned his face to Hywel and made a point of putting his finger to his lips. Hywel knew it was to signal his silence about what he had seen and heard that night. He was not fully comfortable with keeping the brothers' secret, and had made no vow, but he nodded his head in response. *For now*, he thought, *I will honour Rhys' wishes, but if there comes a time when this secret must be exposed, then before God, I will do that.*

So in my sickness I say to you,

'Lord, be my kind healer.

Heal my body and soul; heal me, God!'

Psalm 41:4, TPT

11
Valle Crucis

Hywel carefully observed Tomos and Rhys over breakfast the following morning, across the rough wooden tabletop that separated him from them. To any other onlooker there were no signs to indicate what had passed during the night. Both brothers were tucking into the fresh bread and hard-boiled hen's eggs the kind nuns had provided for them. Both were quiet, Tomos perhaps uncharacteristically so, but conversation was sparse anyway, the general mood around the table reflecting the damp, misty weather outside.

Hywel had risen early with Matthew to attend Prime, and, surprisingly, Madoc had accompanied them. Myfanwy had also made an appearance, looking rested, as they gathered together in the early morning chill. Tomos and Rhys had both been sleeping soundly as they left to head to the church, but were up by the time the small group returned bearing the victuals to break their fast.

As if sensing Hywel's perusal, Rhys paused mid-bite and looked up to cast a wary glance over at him. Hywel gave him a small smile in return and nodded his head slightly. He was content enough for now to agree to keep his silence, but would look to keep a close eye on the brothers as they continued their journey together. He doubted that Tomos' condition would stay a secret for long.

Once breakfast was done and the table cleared, the business of loading the horses and getting on with their journey took everyone's full attention. The mist was still lingering and it was a sorry-looking party that readied themselves to leave Llanllugan. The simple hospitality of the nuns had warmed and blessed them and the damp weather did not fill them with much enthusiasm to leave.

Mother Gracia had come to fare them well, carrying provisions for them to take away.

Hywel stepped forward to take the bulging bag from her hands.

'Our thanks, sister, for everything… I mean, Mother…' he hurriedly corrected himself.

'Is it hard for you to call me that?' Gracia smiled knowingly at him.

'Forgive me,' Hywel felt his face redden. 'It's just that you are so young.' He wasn't making the awkwardness any better.

'You can see me more easily as a sister than a mother. That is understandable, considering we are close in age.' She paused. 'Believe me, brother, I did not expect or look for this position.' She was looking directly at him, and he felt like she was reading his very thoughts. 'Hywel,' she spoke his name softly. 'You may have to learn what it truly means to be a son before you can earn the right to be called "Father".'

Did she know of his ambition? He shifted uncomfortably under her gaze. How did she know? Had Madoc been talking to her? Had Gwrgenau talked to him?

'I'm not sure I understand.'

'No.' She smiled again. 'But I think you will, in time.'

Madoc had appeared, leading a skittish Brenin. 'Time we were off, brother. Gracia,' he nodded to the nun.

'One more thing.' Gracia placed a soft hand on Hywel's arm. 'That horse of yours needs to learn how to submit to someone who knows better than him. He will be happier and more content for learning to trust another, and in realising that he does not have to be in control. Perhaps the same is true for you? God has asked me to pray for you, brother. He has His plans for you, but don't be surprised if they don't match your plans for yourself.'

With that, she was gone, leaving Hywel holding the horse's reins.

The damp soon pervaded everything: Hywel could feel it as his habit grew heavier and his back began to ache. He could only imagine how it was affecting poor Myfanwy's bones. As the day wore on the mist became a drizzle, and then a steady rain, and the misery of it pervaded deeper still. They all rode in silence, heads bowed and bodies slumped. It was a relief to see the stone walls of Strata Marcella finally appear. It had thankfully been but a short day's ride and they were all more than ready to dismount, dreaming of dry beds and warm food.

'You will need your letter of introduction here.' Madoc pulled alongside Hywel as they approached the abbey. 'We are not guaranteed a warm welcome, although your habit might work in our favour.'

Hywel looked down at his bedraggled state, his habit far from white. He was not sure he would even be recognisable as a Cistercian.

Madoc had been right. The welcome, if it could be called such, was muted, especially when it became apparent that their party contained a single female. Any accommodation available inside the impressive abbey walls was limited only to the male members of the party. The abbey's grange farm, which consisted of a collection of ramshackle wooden buildings, was the alternative offered to them. It was not a hard decision for any of them to insist that they all stayed with Myfanwy, so it was another night in a barn, only this time much less accommodating. Food had been provided for them, but it came cold. The damp air inside the flimsy building made making a fire big enough to warm themselves or their food an impossibility.

Hywel mused, as he gazed into his bowl of cold, congealed vegetables, how easy it was to take the simple comforts for granted. Warmth, hot food, dry bedding. He found himself longing for home… not Brampton, surprisingly, but Cwmhir. And as he lay down in his damp clothes on the hard dirt floor, his arms his only pillow, he dreamt of his dry, cosy cell, and rope-sprung bed, and the comforting snores of his friends.

It was a restless night and sleep was elusive. His companions seemed to have slept poorly also, as before the sun was up they were all risen and making haste to leave. The dawning day was mercifully dry, and there were signs as the sun rose that it was going to be brighter too; the skies not cloudless, but neither overcast.

As they rode away, Hywel looked back at Strata Marcella. There was no question that the abbey was a majestic site, where it sat on a wide plateau along the banks of the River Hafren.[6] The tall abbey church, only recently completed, and the range of fine stone buildings surrounding it were also impressive. But fine buildings meant nothing without common kindnesses. The abbey was definitely big enough to accommodate guests, and probably had fine apartments designed for the purpose. But their mixed party had not been considered worthy to receive a guest's welcome, despite Hywel's letter of introduction.

Strata Marcella was the largest and reputedly already the most successful abbey in Wales, and perhaps a community that Hywel would once have aspired to be a part of. To rise to position in such a place would have been an honour indeed. Yet, would it? However fine and well run the abbey was, to not be able to extend the simplest of welcome to weary pilgrims… that did not sit well with Hywel. Princes might have endowed it and even lie buried in its precincts, but that did not make Strata Marcella any more prominent a place than the humble community of Llanllugan, where they had received such a warm welcome, and more than had their needs met in the simplest of ways. It was a lesson well learned.

As the sun rose higher and the clouds parted, the warmth began to penetrate their damp clothes and dry them. The

---

[6] The Severn.

subdued party that had left the farm that morning seemed to become more enlivened as the day went on. Matthew was still his morose self, and rode alone more often than not, but the others intermingled. Tomos and Myfanwy giggled together, Rhys sang a sweet melody under his breath, and Hywel found himself riding alongside Madoc. They were climbing steadily, the well-worn route probably a drovers' path. It was a much more pleasant ride than the day before, and Hywel was beginning to enjoy it now that the steam had stopped rising from his clothes. He was also curious about the man riding beside him.

'So, you have done this pilgrimage many times?'

'Yes.'

'Always as a guide to others, or for your own reasons?'

There was no reply. But Madoc had turned and was looking at him with a measured stare.

Hywel shifted in his saddle, uncomfortable under Madoc's scrutiny.

'I need no confessor, especially not you.'

Hywel smarted. He was only trying to be friendly.

'You don't like me much, do you?'

Madoc let out a small laugh.

'I don't have to like you; I just have to put up with you.'

They rode in silence for a few moments before Madoc turned his penetrating gaze on Hywel again.

'The truth is, brother, that I don't think you like yourself much. So much so that you pretend to be what you are not, and that pretence may well get you into trouble. So I am not sure yet that I fully trust you. But then, we all carry secrets, and we all learn to act a part when we have to. You are no different from any of us, monk or man. You have much to learn, as do we all, about who we really are.'

With that he pulled forward, leaving Hywel to mull over his words. He saw that Madoc had got the measure of him. It was not comforting, and yet there was a sense of relief. There was one person in this party that Hywel did not have to try to impress. Madoc had been right about one thing... he was learning more about himself all the time.

The route they were taking was the path that linked Strata Marcella with its newly founded daughter-house at Valle Crucis, but the distance was too far to force both horses and riders to make it comfortably in one day, so another night in the open air was inevitable. Thankfully the party came upon a small settlement at the crest of a hill, and were able to buy milk and cheese and flour from an amenable farmer's wife. They found a sheltered spot among some trees, close to a free-flowing stream, and soon had a good fire going. Quickly made flatbreads soon added to the veritable feast, and it was with warmed bones and satisfied stomachs that they lay down to sleep on the sun-dried, soft grass.

The morning was again warm and dry, and the day's ride from there to Valle Crucis easy enough. It was mid-afternoon as they descended the densely wooded valley to find the abbey, nestled among the hills. Despite its stunning location, in contrast to Strata Marcella, the abbey was little more than a building site. Stone foundations in the shape of a church had been laid, and the masons had begun their work of building the walls, but these had barely risen above head height. Wooden buildings made up the shape of a clearly defined cloister. There was visible activity all around – trees being felled and cut, carpenters sawing and hammering, monks in scapulars turning over soil in what looked like kitchen gardens, and masons noisily chipping away at huge stone blocks.

Despite the busyness, their little party was seen as they approached and a tall, broad monk, with his habit sleeves turned back to reveal strong, muscular arms, came towards them with a welcoming smile. His face was tanned by the sun, and his fair hair bleached almost white.

'Welcome, travellers, to our humble home,' he laughed as he gestured with his outstretched arm towards the half-constructed buildings behind him. 'I am Brother Titus, acting prior here, and you are most welcome. You look weary, all.

Come, come, let us find you some refreshment and a place to rest your bones.' He had gone straight to Myfanwy, taking the reins with one large hand to steady her horse and, with the other, holding her elbow to steady her as she dismounted.

A young monk and a swarthy-looking lay brother came to take the horses from them and, having unloaded their possessions, the party followed Titus as he led the way towards the wooden buildings that ran along the whole western length of the cloister square.

'Now, you will find all you need here.' He indicated a large room furnished simply with a fire, a wooden table and benches, and, much to Hywel's relief, beds. 'And you, my lady, you can have the abbot's own room. He is away from us at present, leaving me in charge. And you look like you could do with a soft bed and a warm fire tonight.'

Hywel could see why the brother monk was showing such concern, as Myfanwy was struggling to stand, even with the monk's steadying hand under her elbow. He had also heard the softly uttered cry of pain as her feet had found the ground when she had dismounted. Her face was pale and lined with tiredness, but she managed a small smile at the brother's kind words.

After the pair had left them, the same young monk who had seen to their horses appeared again with a large jug, and indicated the beakers already waiting for them on the table. The cool ale was very good, as was the opportunity to stand and stretch their legs. The urge to try out a bed was almost overwhelming, and as soon as he could, Hywel did so, stretching out his long, aching legs with a deep sigh. His stomach was rumbling, but he could wait for food. He would just close his eyes for a brief moment.

The bell for Vespers startled him awake. He joined the small company in the half-built church, marvelling at how they kept to the Offices and the set liturgies in the midst of so much upheaval and activity. As if to read his mind, Brother Titus came alongside him as they left.

'We keep Prime and Vespers together in the church, but are more lenient with the other Offices, brother. There is much work to be done here, and we pray as we work. But these moments of silence and rest are good for us all.'

Despite the noise and activity, Valle Crucis really did feel like a peace-filled place.

Titus had left Hywel's side and was now in deep conversation with Madoc.

As the pilgrims sat down to a warm, satisfying meal that evening, Madoc revealed what they had spoken about.

'Brother Titus has invited us to stay for as long as we need to. It is obvious that Myfanwy is suffering from the ride, the effects of the weather and a lack of comfortable places to rest. I am sorry for that. She has been ministered to by the infirmarer here and is now resting peacefully. Tomorrow is the Sabbath, and there will be no building work done, so Brother Titus has suggested we stay at least until the day following to make the most of the peace. He assures me we are welcome, and the community here are evidently hospitable. If we stay more than one day I have assured the kind brother that we will lend a hand anywhere we can. I think it must be Myfanwy's condition that determines the length of our stay above all else.'

There was no disagreement. Even Matthew did not complain, as he tucked into the steaming savoury stew that had been served to them. A rest from the road, even for the most religious of pilgrims, seemingly had its appeal.

The Sabbath dawned both bright and dry and, as promised, all work tools were left where they had been laid the day before. The rest day offered the opportunity for the community to adhere to the full number of Offices, the dry weather allowing them to meet together in the still-roofless church. Hywel found it both strangely comforting and reassuring to attend with them. Matthew was also present for the early morning Offices, whereas the other pilgrims had chosen to rest in their beds.

Word was brought that Myfanwy had developed a slight fever and was being nursed carefully and encouraged to rest completely. Hywel was glad. He found himself thanking God for the kind brothers of Valle Crucis as he joined them in prayer. They had gone out of their way to care for them. Good food, clean, dry beds, and a safe place for the pilgrims to rest and build up their strength.

Below the abbey buildings was a broad, green, grassy slope leading down to a wide pool of still water. It was to this place that Hywel made his way after their midday meal. The pool had all the makings of a fish pond, although no fish had appeared at their table. Hywel wandered around to examine it further; it was likely that it had been formed from damming and diverting water from the river that ran along the valley floor below the abbey. It was surrounded by trees in full green leaf, and the spring sunlight playing on the water was beautiful. Pond skaters skipped across the surface, leaving barely a ripple.

So preoccupied was he by the charm of the spot that Hywel walked headlong into a crouched figure, who gave out a muffled 'oof' and sprawled helplessly, splashing into the shallow water at the edge of the pool.

The figure, from his grubby-looking, now soaked habit, appeared to be a monk.

'Brother, forgive me. I must apologise for my clumsiness. I did not see you there.'

'Perhaps I was trying not to be seen.' The voice was heavily accented, but the tone genial.

Hywel reached out his hand to help the brother up. The hand that met his was calloused and wrinkled but gripped his own with surprising strength. The face was also wrinkled and topped by a thinning grey tonsure, but the startling blue eyes were kind, and the smile genuine.

'I am Jean-Pierre.' He vigorously shook the hand he still held, spraying them both with pond water. 'And you are?'

'Hywel. Brother Hywel, of Cwmhir.'

'Ah yes, our pilgrim visitor. But I have seen you before, no?'

Hywel thought quickly, but could not recall meeting this intriguing man before, even here at the abbey. His accent was familiar – rural French, perhaps – but not the face.

'Ha! But it is your eyes. I know your eyes, my friend. It is those I have seen before. Although perhaps not in your face, I think now.'

Hywel smiled, bemused. The older man was examining him closely, and it was as if he could see his mind working through those clear blue eyes.

'Ah yes. Jerome! My old friend. You have his eyes! Now, is that not a strange thing to see, French eyes in a Welsh face?'

'Not so strange,' Hywel laughed. 'I am Jerome's kin. His nephew.'

'Ah, so! Then I welcome you, Jerome's kin, as my own.'

He reached out and pulled Hywel into a firm embrace, which was stranger still as Hywel was so much bigger than the slight man, and many years younger. Yet the arms that surrounded him were strong and he felt energised by their hold on him.

'Brother, perhaps you should release our visitor, so that he can take a breath.' Titus had appeared and Hywel extricated himself from Jean-Pierre's arms. All three men were grinning.

'So you have met our French import, then? Brother Jean-Pierre is a great asset to our community.'

'Jean-Pierre is also on a mission, to discover why this pond is not filling as fast as I would like, and why it is not yet deep enough for the fishes.' With that, Jean-Pierre dashed away at remarkable speed for an older man, towards the river, leaving the two monks shaking their heads.

'He is a character; I like him,' said Hywel.

'He is, as I said, a great asset to our community, and we have come to appreciate even his idiosyncrasies. His mind is incredible, Hywel. It never stops. The ideas and the creativity that flow from that man are inspiring. He is fascinated with the natural world, and seems to have an innate understanding, God-given, I would say, as to how things work. The human body included. He knows plants, and he knows remedies, and he makes up concoctions that no one has heard of or tried before, but they are effective nonetheless, and so he acts as infirmarer here. He is also fascinated by water and how it flows, as you can see here.

'He was sent to us because of his knowledge of building techniques and design, in both stone and wood. Much of what you see being constructed is a result of his ability to see things before they are built. His drawings have informed the designs of most of what you see, from this pond to the church being built behind us. The majority of the brothers here came from Strata Marcella, but he came directly from France.'

'From Abbaye Grand Selve, I think? He knew of my uncle, the abbot there.'

'Ah! That might explain his unconventional welcome of you. He is not usually so effusive in his greeting of strangers!'

They both laughed.

'So you followed your uncle into the Order?'

The two had begun to walk together around the water's edge.

'He was an influence, no doubt. But not the whole reason.' Hywel did not want to think back. To his father's ambition for him, and how he had disappointed him. To the events that had preceded his entry into the Church. Such thoughts sparked the old feelings of guilt and shame, and on this peaceful, sun-warmed afternoon he did not want to go down those dark paths.

Titus paused and then lowered himself down onto the soft, cool grass. He sighed. 'It is good to rest, no? I love my work, especially where it involves wood, and I share the same work ethic as all of my worthy brothers. But I do appreciate the day of rest our good Lord provided us with.'

Hywel sat down beside the older monk and picked a long blade of reed grass, which he began idly twisting in his fingers. 'We have appreciated the rest from our pilgrimage, brother, and are most grateful for your hospitality.'

'We have not seen many pilgrims yet, but I'm sure as we become more established we will see more. My hope is that they always receive a warm welcome here. Anyone embarking on pilgrimage is worthy of that, in my estimation. I admire you all, and hope to travel the path you are travelling myself someday soon.'

Hywel felt uncomfortable. He hadn't chosen this path. Not like the others. He did not feel 'worthy' of anything in particular. He still felt himself a fraud in so many ways.

'People have many reasons for going on pilgrimage,' he said quietly.

'Yes, indeed. But mostly good reasons, I would say.'

Hywel thought of his own little party. He thought he knew their reasons. Myfanwy, with her faith for a healing miracle; Rhys, for his brother's sake; Matthew, out of his piety; Madoc – well, to guide them, but maybe too for his own hidden reasons.

But what about him? It had felt like he had been forced to come on this particular pilgrimage. So… a pretence? Was it still that?

'What is it that you are seeking by undertaking this journey, brother?'

Hywel swallowed hard. How was he supposed to answer that, when he did not know himself?

'Matthew told me that the purpose of pilgrimage was "to gain favour with God and purity of soul".'

'I'm sure that is how some see it,' Titus replied thoughtfully. 'I would hope it would be more than that for me. A desire to experience more of God, perhaps, to grow deeper in my knowledge of Him, and of myself, as I walked the pilgrim path.'

Hywel thought on that. Madoc had spoken the truth when he had said that he didn't really know who he was and perhaps was playing a part. His foolishness, his lust, his pride, had caused so much pain and hurt. He had once thought he knew who he was, and what his life's purpose was. Now he was less sure than ever. And even as a monk, he had failed. He was no man of God. God required better men than he to be His lifelong servants. He was not sure he wanted to get closer to a God who might expose him for what he really was. But something in the way Titus had spoken appealed to him.

'How? How does any one of us, sinful humans as we are, get to know and experience God more? And why does that mean we learn more about ourselves? What if in the process we find things out about ourselves that we would rather not know?'

Titus looked at him with kindness, but also with an unsettling intensity.

'How we experience God is unique to each one of us. He knows us intimately, Hywel, and knows how to reveal Himself to each one of us in ways that we can understand. I do believe that He wants you to know Him better and also to understand who you are in Him. I hope you will discover that He is a God who genuinely cares for you, and wants you to be the best that you can be. Perhaps the burden you carry, the sadness in your eyes, will be easier for you to release to Him then.' He gripped Hywel's hand lightly before heaving himself to his feet. 'And ask Him. I have always found that the best way to get the answers I am looking for. Ask God who He wants you to be, and how to be that person.'

He smiled then. 'Now I believe we will be summoned to prayer very soon, and I must find Jean-Pierre, before he loses himself in the undergrowth completely!'

Lord, you know everything there is to know about

me.

You perceive every movement of my heart and soul,

and you understand my every thought before it even

enters my mind.

You are so intimately aware of me, Lord.

You read my heart like an open book

and you know all the words I'm about to speak

before I even start a sentence!

You know every step I will take before my journey

even begins.

You've gone into my future to prepare the way,

and in kindness you follow behind me

to spare me from the harm of my past.

You have laid your hand on me!

Psalm 139:1-5, TPT

12

The Gift

The community of Valle Crucis sprang to life early the following morning. Prime was celebrated at sunrise and a hearty breakfast was supplied of steaming bowls of a thick, creamy oat porridge drizzled with honey, followed by freshly baked bread.

'Can we stay here?' Tomos mumbled, his round cheeks stuffed full and his eyes gleaming.

It was a pleasing thought to Hywel also, except that he knew that to stay too long would be a drain on this fledgling abbey's resources. They would have another day here at least. Madoc had been taken to see Myfanwy and returned to report her much improved, but needing another day of rest.

As they finished their meal, they could already hear that work had begun outside. Tomos, Rhys and Matthew left with Madoc to see where they could help. Hywel made his way to the stables and the horses. He found the stables already empty, except for Brenin, tied loosely at one end, and the same swarthy lay brother they had met on their arrival.

'Brother Hywel,' he introduced himself cheerily.

'I am Bryn.'

'Can I help you at all?'

The man was brandishing a huge broom and had obviously been left with the task of mucking out the stables. Hywel didn't mind getting his hands dirty. He was surprised that the feisty stallion was still inside and not out with the other horses, presumably at pasture somewhere nearby. He found another broom propped against the wall and, hitching up the skirt of his habit, he began to clear out the area closest to where Brenin was tied.

The lay brother stopped and stared.

'I don't mind mucking out, I assure you,' Hywel said.

'It's not that. That horse has let no one near it for the whole time it has been here. I barely avoided a kick even bringing him his oats this morning. I didn't dare try to lead him out.'

'Oh?' Hywel looked over at the horse, who was not taking any notice of him, rather chewing nonchalantly on the oats. 'So he has not left the stable since he arrived?'

'Not for lack of trying, but he didn't seem to want to go anywhere. And to be honest, I have had more to do than usual with so many extra horses to care for.'

'Yes, I can appreciate the extra workload, and am sorry for that. Perhaps I could get him to go out with the others?'

'You can try.' Bryn didn't look convinced. He turned his attention back to his broom and the stinking pile of mucky straw it was forming.

Hywel approached Brenin calmly and noiselessly. The horse knew he was there as one ear twitched, and a single front hoof pawed the ground. The chewing had paused.

Without a fuss, Hywel swiftly untied the rope tethering the horse and began to walk purposefully towards the open door. The horse stood stock still until the rope tightened and then he objected, tossing his fine head. Hywel held on fast, and kept moving. This was going to be a battle of wills, and he was going to win. A short tug of war later and the horse gave up, snorting as he followed Hywel out into the sunlight. The lay brother followed, a look of pure amazement on his face.

'He must be your horse.'

'Well, for the journey he has become mine, but I did not train him.'

'Then you have a gift, brother.'

Brenin was now standing calmly at Hywel's shoulder.

'Thank you,' Hywel replied. 'Now, if you can show me where to take him?'

Bryn led the way down a track and to a field partially obscured by a line of trees. The other horses were dotted around, enjoying the lush grass and the sun on their backs. Hywel spotted the pilgrims' mounts, and noted a few others, mostly work horses. Madoc's large grey stood watching as they approached. Hywel led Brenin into the field through a sturdy wooden gate, and when he was sure it was closed securely behind them, he released the horse. Brenin reared and snorted, shaking his head, as if to reassert himself as being a horse not to be trifled with. Hywel removed himself and stood the other side of the carefully closed gate, watching, Bryn at his side. Brenin made a dash for the fence and then ran along it, and turned and galloped back, obviously agitated.

'He's a horse that needs handling and riding more, but he doesn't make that easy,' Hywel said.

'You are a braver man than me to ride him.'

Suddenly Brenin stopped dead in his tracks, as the grey stepped over and into his path, lifting his own great head with a loud neigh and shaking it violently. Brenin seemed to cower ever so slightly before moving alongside the older horse and dropping his own head so that it almost leant on the grey's flank.

'Well, would you look at that?' said Bryn. 'Perhaps like all of us he just needs a little guidance and reassurance from someone older and wiser at times.'

Hywel thought more on his words as he walked back to the stables to help Bryn finish the muck-clearing. The two worked silently together to get the job done, so Hywel had time to muse. He thought of Prior Gwrgenau at Cwmhir, of Titus making time for him the day before, of Madoc, of his own father, and of Cenred too. He could equate himself with Brenin in some ways. Young, headstrong, proud, yet also unsure of himself, prone to making mistakes, and maybe even frightened at times. And then he realised how those older, wiser men had in their own ways positioned themselves to help him, as the grey horse had for Brenin. Or was it possible that God had placed them there in his life when he most needed their insights, reassurance and wisdom? He recognised that as the truth.

Perhaps Titus had been right when He said that God would reveal things to him in ways he would understand. God talked to him through the behaviour of a horse? He smiled to himself. And why not?! He felt his heart turn in degrees nearer to God, genuinely thankful.

He was still musing as he made his way back towards the church as the bell for Sext sounded. He was met by a grinning Titus.

'You might want to shake the straw off your habit at least; the sweet horse muck aroma will have to linger for now. Pity whoever sits close to you for prayers.'

Titus was himself dusting sawdust from his own clothing, and rolling his sleeves down to cover his sweat-sheened forearms.

Hywel brushed himself down as best he could but a wash would have to wait. Titus obviously did not mind the aforementioned smell as he duly sat down next to Hywel for the Office. He also accompanied him after prayers to a wooden table where pails of fresh water had been drawn for the monks to wash themselves before their upcoming meal.

'I have something for you. Will you meet me after you have eaten? I suggest by the pond so that we do not overly disturb the others.'

It was whispered as they stood close together, splashing water over their hands and faces. Hywel nodded his reply, curious.

He made his way to meet Titus as arranged, while the other members of the community made good use of their postprandial rest time.

'Thank you for your help with the horses today, brother. Bryn believes that you are particularly gifted in horse handling.'

'It does seems I have an understanding with them, I suppose. I was taught well,' he added quietly.

They were sat together on the grass bank as they had been the day before, the pond sparkling before them. There was more of a breeze and the blue sky above them was dotted with white clouds, making the air feel cooler.

'What you said about God revealing Himself to us in ways we understand, I think I experienced that today with the horses.'

'Go on.'

'Brenin, the young headstrong stallion, was naturally calmed by an older, more settled, horse. I think God might have put it into my mind to compare how those horses interacted with my own relationships, to the people who have helped me, in the past and now. I've never experienced that sort of enlightenment before, and I've observed the behaviour of horses many times.'

'That is good,' Titus replied, enthusiastically. 'I believe that God speaks all the time to us, brother, but often our hearts are closed to hearing Him. Perhaps you have consciously opened your heart towards God more as you have journeyed on this pilgrimage, and so you have heard Him speak. Not in an audible voice, perhaps, but through the things you understand and relate to.'

'So, I might hear God more from now on?'

'I pray so, son. That's why you are on this journey, after all. We are all on a journey closer to His heart. For you, it is treading the path of pilgrimage; for others, like me, it is serving Him in the everyday and doing the best with the life He has given us.'

'How do you hear God speak, brother?'

'Like you, sometimes in the things I am doing, just naturally; a thought comes to me that I believe is from Him. Other times He speaks to me through the wise words of others; sometimes through songs and liturgies, most often when reading and meditating on His word.'

Hywel thought that as a monk he really should understand all Titus had said and have experienced it himself. He would spend the allotted time reading the Scriptures, of course, and he had tried to practise *Lectio divina*,[7] but more often than not his eyes would alight on a word that would cause his gut to twist, and take his mind back to unwelcome memories: sin, guilt, woe, condemnation. He couldn't say he enjoyed those times of quiet reading and meditating. Was that God speaking, when he felt sinful and condemned, he wondered? Yet what he had been led to think about in his experience with the horses had encouraged him and made him thankful. Titus might have the answer.

'Does what you hear God say to you make you feel worse or better about yourself?'

'That depends on the state of my heart when I come before Him, I suppose. Although I would say that He speaks encouragement to my soul much more than He speaks conviction. I find the words from the lips of others much more likely to judge and condemn me. Or indeed the thoughts I have about myself.' He was looking intently at Hywel, his eyes knowing. 'I have something here for you, Hywel. I am hoping it will help you greatly.'

Hywel had noticed the package in Titus' hands, wrapped in soft, oiled skins. It appeared to be the size of a small rectangular box. As it was passed to him, he realised it was not a box, and, pulling the skins aside, he could see the dark leather cover of a finely bound book.

'Jean-Pierre asked me to hand this over to you. He says little, but thinks deeply, and felt I could explain better than he why this book is for you.'

Hywel turned it over gently and curiosity got the better of him as he opened the front cover and glimpsed the parchment

---

[7] *Lectio divina* means in Latin 'divine reading' and is a traditional, meditative, contemplative approach to reading Scripture.

inside. The text was tiny, beautifully scribed, but it was the gloriously coloured illuminations that made him catch his breath. The more pages he turned, the more he realised what a treasure of workmanship he held in his hands. This should be locked away somewhere, or kept for only the most deserving to handle. He wanted to hand it back, feeling his lack of worth, but it transfixed him.

'It's beautiful. Such workmanship. I cannot accept this.' Hywel was surprised at the lump in his throat.

'It is not yours to accept, or to give back. It is on loan, for you to keep and use for as long as you need it, and then for you to pass on to whoever God tells you to give it to. That is how Jean-Pierre had it in his possession. It came with him from Grand Selve – a gift from your uncle, I believe. But gifted with the same proviso: that he would keep it only until he knew it was time to gift it on. It would seem that you are the one he believes should be its new keeper.'

Hywel carefully started to rewrap the book. It felt an onerous task to keep and protect such a treasure, but it pleased him to think it came originally from Jerome. Perhaps it was right that he inherited it, if just for a while.

'There is one other proviso.' Titus had reached his hand over to pause Hywel's rewrapping. 'You must not keep it always wrapped. It was designed to be read. And you must read it. See here.' He opened the front cover, and Hywel could see one word clearly: *Psalmus*. This beautiful book was a Psalter. 'The writers of the Psalms knew how to speak to God, how to pour out their complaints, their griefs, their guilt. Find your voice in their words, Hywel; pray them out loud if you have to, and then stop and listen, and see if God does not speak back to you through the words written here. I believe He will, if your heart and mind are open to hear from Him.'

The following morning the air was definitely cooler and the mist had returned. Myfanwy appeared and sat with them to break their fast. Her visage was definitely less pale, and she ate heartily.

Soon it was time for the pilgrims to leave Valle Crucis. Hywel felt a pang as they led their horses out to be loaded for the journey ahead. He had felt at peace in this place, despite the noise and disruption of the building work. He vowed he would return, to see the abbey in all its imagined splendour, when it was finished and done. He wanted to admire what Jean-Pierre had designed, and knew it would be magnificent. He also wanted to see Titus again.

More and more he was realising that God was putting people in his path to help him on his journey. Some of those people weren't those he would naturally have chosen to be his companions. He glanced around at his fellow pilgrims, that little group of very ordinary people, from different walks of life and with different experiences of the world. He found himself smiling. It really wasn't bad company to be in.

He glanced back at the book he held in his hands, which had spent the night under his pillow and had not left his side since it was gifted to him. He hadn't opened it yet, but once more the temptation to look at those beautiful pages drew him to pull back the cover and trace his fingers over the words. He was still slightly overwhelmed with the responsibility of having it in his care. He resolved he would read it, whenever he could find the time and space to do so. But he would prefer to do so when he was alone. He didn't feel like sharing his new-found treasure just yet.

Brenin whinnied beside him and Hywel turned back to the task in hand. He rewrapped the book in its oilskins and pulled his spare habit out from his satchel to add a further protective layer. He wanted this beautiful book as protected as possible from the vagaries of the weather. As he did so, something fell to the ground with a soft thud. He looked down and saw the small wooden cross Rhodri had pressed into his hand as he had left Cwmhir. He had packed it away and, to his chagrin, forgotten it. Hywel bent down to pick it up, feeling the smoothness of the wood in his hand. It had the feel of having been held, he guessed in private prayer. If Rhodri had made this, he had also used it. Perhaps Rhodri had used it to pray after Hywel's words had hurt him so much. The thought made Hywel's stomach twist.

He examined the cross, turning it over in his hand. Just a simple wooden cross, obviously naively carved out of one piece, the edges not perfectly straight, the slipped chisel marks obvious.

'That is a fine little cross and just the right size to hold in one hand. Ideal for a pilgrim.'

It was Myfanwy's soft voice.

'A gift.'

'Oh, so doubly precious to you, then?'

'I… yes, it is.'

The need to unburden himself was suddenly overwhelming, but Hywel checked himself. This dear lady didn't need to be loaded down with his pain. She had enough of her own to carry.

'I have this.' Myfanwy reached into the neck of her garment and withdrew a thin cord that held a tiny pewter cross. 'I love to have the reminder of what Christ did for us so close to my heart,' she smiled.

Hywel looked down at the face turned awkwardly up to him. A face that should bear the signs of pain, sickness, despair. Instead it radiated a quiet joy, and in that moment Hywel longed with a surprising intensity to have what she had.

She was speaking still.

'Mercy and grace. Our priest explained it to me. Mercy was not getting what I deserved, and grace was getting what I didn't deserve. That's what the cross means. Jesus took the punishment that I deserved for all that I have done wrong – that's the mercy bit. And then, because of that, God gifted me with full and free forgiveness – that's the grace bit. I think I've got that right. I don't read, you see, but I named my pigs as a reminder.'

'Pigs?' Hywel was struggling to comprehend any of what she was saying. It all sounded just a bit too simplistic. The cross of Christ was a holy mystery, surely? Something to meditate on and grow to understand over time, perhaps never in this lifetime. And yet she seemed to have a clear understanding that was real to her. And what did her pigs have to do with it?

Myfanwy laughed. 'Sorry, brother. My pigs – around the time I spoke with the priest, my sow produced a litter. I kept two and called them "Mercy" and "Grace" as an everyday reminder of what I had learned. I had things I was ashamed of, you see, and the priest showed me that the cross meant that I could be forgiven for them. I just had to put my guilt burden down and ask for God's forgiveness in return. My pigs were a daily reminder that I was saved by God's mercy and grace. As I'm sure that small cross is to you.'

Hywel closed his eyes momentarily so that she would not see his turmoil, gripping the cross in his hand so hard that it hurt. He turned away from her, back to loading his saddlebag, and lied.

'Yes, of course.'

Lord, I'm fading away. I'm discouraged and lying in
the dust;

revive me by your word, just like you promised you
would.

I've poured out my life before you,

and you've always been there for me.

So now I ask: teach me more of your holy decrees.

Open up my understanding to the ways of your
wisdom,

and I will meditate deeply on your splendor and your
wonders.

My life's strength melts away with grief and
sadness;

come strengthen me and encourage me with your
words.

Psalm 119:25-28, TPT

Part Three
Pilgrim

13
Brothers

It had been a straightforward journey north from Valle Crucis to the town of Mold. Here, Prince Llewellyn's garrison held the town and castle, and here they found welcome on account of Madoc. From the first approach the old soldier was hailed by the sentry, and as the party were escorted through the heavy wooden gates into the bailey courtyard, there were cries of greeting, some less than complimentary, but all good-natured. It seemed Madoc was an old friend and comrade of the small group of men left stationed here, many looking as old and war-worn as he.

Hywel felt a familiarity as he dismounted, the size and construction of Mold Castle being similar to Brampton Barre; except here there was no stone keep, just a well-fortified wood-built defence atop the high, grassy motte. There was the usual hustle and bustle involved with finding accommodation for them and their horses, but the large hall they found themselves led into was warm and inviting. A huge table filled the centre of the room and a fire burned to one side of it, the thin trail of smoke finding its way out through a round hole in the roof. Although the spring days could get comfortably warm, the evenings were still feeling chilly, and a light rain had beset them for the last few miles of their journey. The fire was welcome, as was the food that began to appear on the table, and the jugs of warmed ale.

Later, as the pilgrims found themselves seated among their amenable hosts and having been well fed, Hywel's attention was drawn to Madoc. He was sat some distance from him, surrounded by soldiers, some already well in their cups. But he was smiling, his face more open that Hywel had ever seen it. Someone said something in Welsh, and Madoc went beet-red for a moment. His comrade slapped him so heartily on the back that Madoc spat out his mouthful of ale before guffawing loudly. As the evening progressed, Hywel noticed Madoc moving around the table, sharing time with his friends, laughing at their jokes, giving as good as he got. It was good to see him so relaxed, so at home, and enjoying himself, his guard down. Hywel felt perhaps finally he was getting a glimpse of the real man.

He also envied him. To have those easy-going relationships with friends that meant you could just be yourself. It had been like that with his brother and father, and with Cenred, at Brampton. But he had spoilt it. He had also had an easy-going relationship with Rhodri and Julian at Cwmhir, but he had spoilt that too. As he drained another cup of ale and his companions grew even more jovial around him, he in contrast felt more and more morose, until he could bear the sound of laughter no longer and wandered out into the night to find some peace.

He found himself in the stables, perhaps instinctively. Brenin snorted a greeting, and Madoc's grey snickered. The two stood side by side in the same stall; it seemed they had formed an understanding, and Hywel was glad. He settled himself down on a straw pile. The beds in the hall might be softer, but here was comfortable enough for him. The familiar smells and sounds of the horses soothed him and he fell into a deep sleep.

He was awakened by a violent shaking that made his ale-fuelled head spin.

'Brother!' It was whispered with urgency. 'Your help is needed.'

Hywel peered up into the bearded face of Madoc. The man was holding a lit wooden torch in his hand.

'What?' He was half-asleep still.

'Come now. We need your strength... and your discretion.' He pulled roughly on Hywel's arm to help him to his feet, and beckoned him to follow.

'How did you know I was in the stables?'

The two were making their way across the bailey to where a ditch ran around the base of the motte, a high fence behind it.

'I saw you leave.'

Madoc said no more. Hywel was surprised by how sober the old soldier seemed. His comrades had definitely been imbibing to the point of merriment. It seemed Madoc either held his drink well, or perhaps, more likely, he had not allowed himself to get insensible.

He had stopped and was crouching down at the ditch side, whispering again.

'I have him. I'll send him down to you. If you and Hywel get beneath his body and lift, I will pull from here. Between us we can get him out.'

'Who is it?' Hywel joined him and peered into the dark ditch. Below him, Madoc's torch lit up Rhys' white face. At his feet, in the mud-filled ditch, lay the inert body of Tomos.

A small shove from behind and Hywel found himself scrambling down into the ditch to join them. His feet sank into the foul-smelling mud.

'I'm sorry to have called on you, brother. He had another episode. I was not ready to catch him when he fell and he slipped down, and he is too heavy for me to lift out on my own.' The whisper was anguished and Hywel felt a surge of compassion.

'I am here now, and we will see to him. Don't concern yourself, Rhys. I am glad to be of help.'

'I did not want to raise the alarm. I don't want all those strangers to know of his secret affliction. So I told Madoc you knew.'

'Less talk, more action, I would suggest,' the urgent whisper came from above.

Tomos was insensible and a dead weight, and it took all the strength of the three of them to lever him up and out of his muddy pit. When he was laid out on the damp, flat grass, they stood around him, breathing heavily, their hands on their hips.

'What now?' Hywel whispered once he had breath enough to talk.

'He will not wake for whoever knows how long, and we cannot leave him here.' Rhys had crouched back down to wipe mud from his brother's face with his sleeve.

'Nor can we carry him back into the hall without waking up at least some of the company,' Madoc added. 'I suggest the stables. Brother Hywel seemingly found it comfortable enough in there to sleep soundly.'

Madoc took his feet and Rhys and Hywel his arms, and they made their ungainly way as quietly as they could, back across the bailey to the stables. It was a welcome relief for their aching backs to lower Tomos' sleeping form onto Hywel's still-warm straw bed.

Rhys settled himself beside his brother, his hand protectively on his arm. Seemingly spent with the anxiety and physical effort, he was soon snoring softly. Madoc and Hywel, in contrast, were wide awake. Both made themselves as comfortable as they could at the far side of the stables, sitting with their backs resting against the rough plank wall, reluctant to leave the brothers alone.

'You already knew about Tomos' affliction?'

Madoc shifted slightly beside him. 'I did.'

'Oh. Rhys thought it a secret. He… well, he asked me to swear not to tell you, not to tell anyone.'

'And you thought it best to swear so? When you knew how dangerous keeping such a secret could be to Tomos, to the whole party?'

'I did not swear. I would have told you if I had felt it necessary.'

Madoc half-laughed, half-growled. 'Do not concern yourself, brother. It mattered not if you had kept your secret. I knew long before we set out on our pilgrimage the reasons that Tomos and Rhys wanted to join us. I knew their mother.' He paused as if remembering a distant memory. 'Many years ago now, I knew her. She had a poor reputation in her village, but her sons being of different fathers was not her fault. She was a beautiful woman, but poor and alone, and taken advantage of, more than once. You understand?'

'I do.' *Only too well.*

'My wife was her childhood friend. After my wife's passing, I visited to take her a small token of remembrance from my wife's possessions. I met her boys then. It was not long after Tomos' accident and he had already had more than one falling episode. I could do little to help them, but when I heard that the boys, now grown, wanted to join a pilgrimage... Well, I made it possible. For their late mother's sake.'

Hywel was stunned for a moment. So much had been revealed in that short speech. Madoc had been married? His wife had died? And he had known the brothers for years. Had known all along of Tomos' affliction and Rhys' vow to protect him. He had found them a place in this party, possibly even funded it himself? Hywel's admiration grew for the man sat beside him.

'You are a good man, Madoc.'

'Just a man, brother, like any other. With many faults.'

But a kind heart beneath all that gruffness, Hywel thought to himself, as the man in question closed his eyes and laid his head back, talking done.

The sky was beginning to glow with early morning light when Hywel finally fell into a fitful sleep. When he awoke an hour or so later it was to the sounds of the new day. A cockerel was crowing loudly not too far away and it made Hywel wince. The space beside him was empty, but Rhys and Tomos still slumbered in the far corner. He needed a drink; the effects of the ale and lack of sleep had left his head throbbing and throat dry. He staggered out into the bright sunlight and almost collided with the bulk of Madoc, carrying a large jug of water. A serving woman a step behind him carried a tray laden with cups and a half-loaf of bread.

'Steady, brother!'

'Madoc, my apologies. I came looking for a drink. Seemingly you thought the same. We also need to rouse our friends,' he lifted his eyebrows and indicated towards the stables with his head, 'before they are discovered.' He glanced back to see a groom disappearing through the stable door.

'I think we are too late for that, brother. Still, I daresay it will not be the first time that guests have found themselves staggering drunkenly into the stable after a good night of carousing.' Madoc winked. 'I told them so in the kitchen, when I asked for victuals to help sober them up.'

It was a subdued group that left Mold later that morning. It had taken time to rouse Tomos, and Rhys was also struggling, his eyes red-rimmed with tiredness. Hywel had his own issues with a thick head from lack of sleep and too much ale. Matthew was his usual silent, morose presence, and Madoc was obviously sad to leave his friends. Myfanwy, though, looked pleased to be on her horse and on their way. She alone of the group seemed to have slept well, having been whisked away by the serving women and provided with a warm corner and soft blankets beside the hearth in the kitchens.

Hywel pulled his horse alongside her as they followed the road away from Mold heading northwards. She was singing softly under her breath, and Hywel recognised it as a song of praise taken from the Psalms. One that they had sung together before leaving Valle Crucis.

Bless the LORD, O my soul;
And all that is within me, bless His holy name!
... forget not all His benefits:

Who forgives all your iniquities,
Who heals all your diseases.[8]

He instinctively felt for the saddlebag nestled against his leg, and the reassuring form of the Psalter secured within. He needed to find that psalm when next they stopped. The words had been a balm to his troubled soul when he'd heard them sung in full. He knew he needed to trace the words written on the page for himself. 'Who redeems your life from destruction'[9] was a line that had spoken to him. He wanted to believe his life wasn't irredeemable.

Hywel did not want to interrupt her song, but she became aware of his presence and stopped her singing, turning her bent neck to smile over at him.

'It is a lovely day, brother. How blessed are we to have such good weather on this auspicious day!'

Hywel nodded. It was fine and dry, certainly, and the road well marked and the going easy for the horses. But he could not quite grasp why the day was so significant. And then he realised, it was not the day, but where the day's journey would lead them. Basingwerk Abbey was their destination, and beyond Basingwerk was St Winefride's Well. Myfanwy was singing about a healing God and believing for her miracle. And that was where she hoped to receive it. The holy pools were where many others had seemingly been touched by God. A destination for the faith-filled. Her face was shining in expectation. He knew he did not have her faith, but clamped his lips together rather than voice his doubts. More than anything he did not want her to be disappointed, to have her simple faith shattered, her hope turned to despair.

He glanced back at Tomos and Rhys, riding in silence behind him, and wondered if they had similar hope and

---

[8] Psalm 103:1-3, NKJV.
[9] Psalm 103:4, NKJV.

expectation. Would their journey to the holy well end in healing also?

One thing was for sure, they would not be one small party on their own for the rest of their pilgrimage. As they drew nearer to Basingwerk, already the road was filling. Being on horseback they found themselves overtaking more than one group of pilgrims travelling on foot. Some walked barefoot even, and Hywel as a monk wearing his habit had the good grace to feel he should perhaps at least have forsaken the comfort of a fine horse and walked beside them.

Before long they had no choice. So many pilgrims lined the way that continuing on horseback was not possible for any of them. Matthew was the first to dismount, and, unsurprisingly, he also removed his fine leather sandals. Hywel allowed himself a small smile as he watched him hobble and grimace, his soft feet unused to the rough stones.

Soon they were all walking. It was strange to be suddenly absorbed into a larger group. It was a good-natured crowd, and the shared stories and laughter lifted Hywel's mood. It seemingly affected Tomos and Rhys similarly as they too were soon laughing and talking amiably. Strangers were united by one purpose, and as the tall church of Basingwerk Abbey appeared in the distance, it was as if the excitement and joy of the pilgrim band grew yet stronger.

Basingwerk was ready for the pilgrims. A large abbey already, there were signs of even more extensive building work in progress. The fine abbey church was stone-built, as was an impressive chapter house and monks' dormitory. Stone foundations had also been laid for more monastic accommodation, and an outline for a large cloister. A range of fine wooden buildings made up the guest accommodation to the south of the church.

It was still early afternoon when they arrived, and as the pilgrims filed into the abbey grounds they were warmly greeted by members of the community. Hywel recognised lay brothers in their simple brown tunics, and several young novices in white habits with not yet tonsured heads. He was surprised to also see a good number of full brothers also busying about, welcoming their visitors, leading them towards the accommodation area, relieving them of the burdens they carried.

Their horses were quickly taken from them to be stabled, as they joined the crowd of pilgrims. To one side there were even stools lined up against a wall, and monks knelt before weary travellers with basins of water to wash tired and bloodied feet.

There were also welcoming tables set up with refreshments to serve the visitors, and Hywel made his way over to where a young monk with warm brown eyes was handing out bread. Beside him stood a larger, older monk, his habit sleeves pushed up to above his elbows, ladling steaming soup from a huge iron pot into wooden bowls.

'Brother, welcome,' the young monk smiled at him, handing him a warm bread roll.

'Brother Hywel, from Abbey Cwmhir. Thank you for your welcome, brother. And for this good food.'

'Hywel? A fellow Welshman? I am Bedwyr!'

'I can only admit to a Welsh mother, but that is good enough, surely?'

The young monk laughed his agreement.

'You are well met to meet the needs of pilgrims here. And it looks as if most of your community is engaged in some way?' Hywel turned to take a bowl of soup from the other monk, nodding his thanks. A queue of hungry people was forming behind him. Seeing the need, he felt a sudden compulsion. 'Can I be of help at all?'

'Thought you would never ask!' the older monk laughed. 'Here, take this.' He thrust his soup ladle in Hywel's direction. Hywel scooted around to the back of the table and put his own food down to take the proffered spoon.

'I will see the kitchen sends you more supplies, Brother Bedwyr,' the older monk said, as he turned to leave. 'You will manage well enough with our newly welcomed brother here?'

'Of course, Father Abbot.'

Hywel was ladling soup into a bowl for Tomos, but the ladle stopped, suspended midway when he registered Bedwyr's words.

'That monk is the abbot?' He couldn't hide his incredulity.

'Yes,' Bedwyr laughed. 'Abbot Geoffrey likes to get his hands dirty, so to speak. He loves to serve our pilgrim guests.'

'Oh.'

Conversation was postponed as they busily served the long queue of hungry customers. When there was a lull, Hywel turned to Bedwyr, full of questions.

'It is unusual for an abbot to work alongside the lesser members of an abbey community, is it not, especially in the menial tasks?'

'Maybe elsewhere. But not here at Basingwerk. We don't consider anyone a "lesser" member, as you put it, or any task "menial". Abbot Geoffrey least of all. He believes that it is his highest calling to serve God by serving man – if that means serving soup to hungry travellers, or kneeling down to wash their muddy feet.' He nodded over to where the abbot was now kneeling, carefully washing the feet of a weary-faced pilgrim.

Hywel was thinking of Abbot Rind back at Cwmhir. Of his relatively luxurious accommodation, his love for fine wine and collecting fine horses, his aloofness and superiority. It was what Hywel had expected of an abbot and he hadn't thought it wrong before. He had aspirations himself, after all, to rise up in position. To be revered as a leader in the church, and honoured by men was surely not a bad ambition? Watching Abbot Geoffrey on his knees with muddy water staining his habit felt wrong, somehow. What was the point of working hard to get into a position of respect and authority to then abase yourself in front of everyone?

'I can see the confusion on your face, brother,' Bedwyr interrupted his train of thought. 'I felt the same when I first came here. It didn't seem to fit the right order of things in my mind, or my experience either. But kneeling to serve doesn't lessen Father Abbot's authority, or the respect he engenders. In fact, it does the opposite. We watch him pour himself out and we want to follow his example. He leads us with a quiet and loving authority, disciplining us when necessary. But because we know the goodness of his heart, his innate humility, his love for his fellow man, we take the discipline and the encouragement with equal gratitude. He is being as Christ was, you see, the Servant King. He does not abuse his position of authority by lording it over us, rather he uses it to teach us a better way. The mark of a true godly leader.'

'And all the community accepts it?' Hywel was genuinely intrigued.

'Basingwerk is unique, I think, in that we have come to see the main purpose for our existence as being to serve others – those who come to visit St Winefride's Well, and those who make this their starting point for the journey to the Island of the Saints. That is both a spiritual and a physical service we seek to offer. So on days like today, when the pilgrims number many, we all take our place in serving their physical needs. Later, Father Abbot will lead us spiritually in the prayer Offices, and also pray individually with as many pilgrims as want it. We all offer ourselves to pray with them. It is our desire to do so.'

'You have given me much to think about, brother.'

And he had. Suddenly Hywel remembered Gracia's words about sons and fathers. He thought he was beginning to understand what it meant to be willing to be a son in order to be a true father. Surely what he had observed of the Father Abbot here was the epitome of that.

Hywel looked around. The open areas of the abbey grounds were clearing of their crowds now. Some pilgrims had refreshed themselves and then chosen to rejoin the road to St Winefride's Well. Others had found places to rest inside and outside the accommodation buildings. The queue at the food table had dwindled. Still the members of the community moved quietly around, serving the needs of their guests. Abbot Geoffrey was no longer visible, but soon the bell for Vespers would be sounding, and likely he was preparing to take his place at the altar in the church to lead the faithful in their prayers. Hywel wondered if he would at least change his soiled habit before doing so.

What would it be like to live and serve in a community like this? he thought. *How would it be to have a truly humble and servant-hearted man as abbot?* Prior Gwrgenau at Cwmhir was such a man, but Hywel did not know whether he ever had aspirations for the position of abbot. And what about himself? What sort of abbot would he want to be if he ever got to that position? Deep down inside he knew his unworthiness to lead anyone, either by authoritarian means or by example. Perhaps, after all, that was not the path for him.

He felt a strange admiration for Geoffrey and the Basingwerk way. That, perhaps, was the type of leadership he should be aspiring to. One where to lead meant to serve, whatever that looked like; even if it looked like grubby knees, rough-worn hands and a tired smile.

Madoc approached his table and accepted a proffered bowl of soup. He looked surprised to see Hywel behind the table serving, and he nodded in what looked distinctly like approval.

'I have made the decision that we stay here for the night and accept the kind brothers' warm welcome. Myfanwy was keen to press on to St Winefride's, and Matthew is none too pleased to be stopping to rest again, but the abbot here informed me that very many pilgrims have passed through here today, which would mean having to wait many hours to be admitted to the healing pools. It would be better for all of us to get a good night of rest and leave early in the morning.'

Hywel nodded his agreement and Madoc wandered away.

'Go, Brother Hywel, and find yourself a place to bed down for the night. We are finished here and will be called for prayer soon.' Bedwyr grasped his hand warmly. 'Thank you for your willingness to serve alongside me.'

'No, thank you, brother. Your welcome and *your* willingness to serve, I think, have shown me a better way.'

Good and upright is the LORD;

Therefore He teaches sinners in the way.

The humble He guides in justice,

And the humble He teaches His way.

Psalm 25:8-9, NKJV

14
Healing

The road from Basingwerk to St Winefride's was broad and tree-lined. It rose steadily out of the valley where the abbey sat, to where the shrine and healing pools were situated. Despite their early start, Madoc's little group of pilgrims were not alone on the road, and as they reached the crest of the hill and the ground levelled out they were joined by yet more travellers, seemingly coming from all directions. Spring was the optimum time for a visit to a holy site, especially when the weather had been fine. The sun was high in the sky again and the air warm as they dismounted.

It was a like stepping into a town square on a busy market day. There was a stall serving sweet buns, another serving ale, another with fresh dairy goods. There was a booth offering holy relics at exorbitant prices. There were groups of travellers sitting together in companionable groups, sharing stories and refreshments. A minstrel played a flute and a number of small children danced around his feet, laughing. It seemed a bit incongruous for a sacred site. But the pilgrim trade was good business, it seemed. And the wait to take a turn to dip in the healing pools was made all the more pleasant with such distractions.

A queue had already formed leading up to a wide gateway, sentry-guarded by two large but pleasant-faced lay brothers. A small, stone-built church stood beyond, and as each pilgrim entered through the gate, they were directed within to pray before being escorted to bathe in the pools. Myfanwy, Tomos,

Rhys and Matthew all joined the queue. Hywel felt no desire to dip in the holy water himself and so chose to wait with Madoc, holding the horses.

His attention was taken by a man standing on a small dais, a professional storyteller whose strong, Welsh-lilted voice carried well. Hywel stepped closer to hear his dramatic retelling of the legend of St Winefride. The storyteller had his listeners enthralled as he described how Caradoc, the unholy chieftain of Hawarden, had lusted after the pure and virginal Gwenfrewi (Winefride), niece of the saintly Beuno; how the wicked man had tried to force himself on her and then, being refused, had swung his sword and beheaded her in a blinding rage.

All this occurred right on the doorstep of the very church where St Beuno and Gwenfrewi's parents were inside celebrating the Mass. Coming out of the church, Beuno confronted and cursed Caradoc, beseeching God to show him as little mercy as he had the girl, at which the fiend dissolved into the ground where he stood, never to be seen again. Then, without flinching, the saint picked up his niece's head and placed it back on her body, placed his mantle over her, and returned to the church with her parents to complete the celebration of the Mass.

Miraculously, as they prayed, the maiden was restored to life. On the spot where her severed head had fallen, water sprang from the earth, a spring which soon was claimed to have healing powers. That same spring still fed the holy pools that continued to attract those in search of God's healing grace.[10]

The storyteller acted the whole scene out wonderfully, and elicited his desired reactions from the crowd, who gasped and sighed and groaned and cheered in all the right places. To Hywel's ears, it seemed a fanciful tale, however well it was told. But he could not deny that there was something special about

---

[10] The tale of St Winefride's miracle is one of legend. More information can be found at www.stwinefrideswell.org.uk (accessed 24th January 2022) or www.stwinefridesholywell.co.uk/st-winefride (accessed 24th January 2022).

the site where they were gathered. Maybe it was the heartfelt devotion of the many who had come to this site rather than the waters themselves that made it feel like a holy place; the prayers that had been prayed, the tears that had been cried, the desperation that had propelled the faithful to come. He had heard the stories of the miracles claimed, and standing among that crowd of pilgrims, he could well understand the hope that drove many to this place. He had no physical ailment that he needed to be freed from, but he had other things that bound him. Whether here, or maybe at one of the other holy sites on their pilgrimage, he hoped that somewhere he would find his own miracle, his own touch from God. He found himself praying genuinely for Myfanwy, and for Tomos, to find theirs here.

The pilgrims emerging from their visit to the pool were directed both to kneel at the statue of St Winefride and to pay their homage at St Beuno's stone. Only then could they receive the badge of the pilgrim, to prove they had visited the site. Myfanwy and Tomos came towards them, clutching their badges and beaming broadly. Rhys followed a few steps behind them, his face more peaceful than joy-filled. Even Matthew seemed to have been somewhat affected by the holy waters. He was not quite smiling but neither was his face fixed in its perpetual scowl.

Myfanwy was talking excitedly and they gathered around to hear her.

'How merciful God is to me! How blessed I am! I have received my healing. He has made me well. I know it. I feel it. Look.' She held out her hands.

To Hywel's eyes those hands were still gnarled and misshapen. And her neck was still painfully bent. But her joy was unmistakeable. He would not rob her of it in that moment, to point out the obvious. She was not made whole, however hard she tried to persuade herself. No one else dared say so either, or if anyone had wanted to speak, Tomos was too quick for them.

'I too am healed. I know it. I cannot prove it, and for some of you it may come as a surprise that I was even afflicted. But I was, and now it has gone. I will spend the rest of my days serving God in humble thanks for His mercy towards me.' He turned and embraced his brother, and then, not yet satisfied, embraced Myfanwy and Madoc and Hywel and even a surprised Matthew. 'And you are all my dear friends and witnesses to God's goodness in my life!'

By now a crowd had gathered and Tomos was swept up into it, telling everyone who would hear how God had healed him in the holy waters.

Hywel felt the large presence of Madoc come alongside him.

'I will not have anyone speak words that might steal their joy and their faith. Not in my hearing.'

Hywel nodded his agreement.

'Miracles have to be proven, surely, to be believed.' Matthew had joined them, his face inscrutable. 'Can we call it a miracle if there is no obvious sign of it?' He was looking over at Myfanwy as she hobbled alongside Tomos, receiving the well wishes of strangers.

'That is the strange thing about faith, Matthew; things don't always have to be seen to be believed.' Madoc spoke with what sounded suspiciously like conviction.

'So you can believe you are healed even though there is absolutely no evidence of it? And that is called faith? I'm not sure that sits well with me.'

'I struggle with that too, Matthew. But I guess we must wait and see, and pray that Myfanwy's faith, both in her miracle and in her God, is not misplaced,' Hywel added.

'And Tomos? I was not even aware he was afflicted.' Matthew looked at him questioningly.

Hywel was not going to break that confidence, even now. 'It will become clear for him also, I would say. For now, I will pray for him and his brother, and suggest you do too.'

The weary days of travelling that followed gave Hywel much opportunity to observe whether there was indeed any change in Myfanwy's condition. Her neck remained bent and her hands misshapen, but she did not cry out with pain, or look wearied or tired by her condition. That same glow he had seen on her face at the holy well remained. She rose without complaint every morning, mounted her horse and rode for hours, and served them when they made camp, always with a smile on her face, often with a song on her lips.

Tomos also seemed well. There had been no disturbed nights since they had left Mold. Hywel had questioned Rhys once, and he had confirmed that he had seen no sign of Tomos' malady since his visit to the well. Perhaps God had gifted him with his healing miracle after all. Hywel found himself starting to believe the impossible was possible.

There was a new purpose about their pilgrimage. All had their own reasons, it seemed, to get to their final destination – whether it were to give thanks for a miracle, to complete their devotion to God or, in Hywel's case, to find answers for the things that still plagued him.

He was reading from his precious Psalter when he could – the odd occasion when they stopped for an extended break in the middle of the day, or when their nightly accommodation came with a roof, dry bed and lighted candle. The Psalms were becoming more personal to him, and he found himself drawn more and more to the written words, hearing his own voice in so many of them. From time to time he also began to think he was hearing God's voice speaking to him through the written words. So many of the words were familiar; he had heard them in liturgies and read aloud in church. He had read some of them before in his own quiet times of meditation, but somehow now things were different. Maybe it was, as Titus had said, that he had become more open to hearing from God personally. Maybe his heart had softened, and his longing for God, to encounter Him, had grown also.

The pilgrim route took them to simple churches, like the one at Llanasa, where St Asaph's remains lay buried. It took them past ancient sites of worship, like the field where the strange tall stone, finely engraved with knotwork and a cross, stood to honour St Cwyfan. The terrain they crossed included vast swathes of high, windswept moorlands, and then deeply forested river valleys. From time to time they reached ground high enough to see the glint of the wide sea on the horizon.

They were rarely alone; those paths trod by many a pilgrim welcomed yet more. In some places they slept outside in larger pilgrim camps, sharing their stories and provisions. In other places they were provided with rooms or booths to shelter in. Always they were encouraged on in their journey by fellow travellers and by many of the locals they met or passed on the road.

Hywel was sure that the majority of those who travelled the pilgrim road did so with purposed devotion. Whether it was to gain favour with God, to seek absolution or to obtain a miracle, it was a pursuit of the Holy. Like the small party Madoc led, there were people from every walk of life: there were those whose clothes marked them as labourers or serfs, those of the merchant classes, a few clerics, holy brothers and sisters in their habits, and even the odd knight in hauberk,[11] or noblewoman on a fine horse. But on this journey they were one, united in their pursuit of something greater than themselves.

What was he doing on this pilgrimage? No, it hadn't been his choice to come, but now he had got this far, now he had seen what this journey meant to so many of his fellow travellers, he found his own heart purposed to complete it. It felt now like it was a necessary part of his own life journey, his own soul healing, perhaps. His life up to this point had not gone as he had planned, and as for the future, he was more unsure of that than he had ever been. At least this journey had a purpose, and a physical end point. But it wasn't just getting to the Holy Island

---

[11] Tunic with coif, made of chain mail.

– Hywel knew that he needed to end this journey knowing the answers to the questions Gwrgenau had sent him away with, if he ever hoped to return to Cwmhir.

He longed for peace for his soul, and freedom from the burden of guilt that still plagued him. He wanted to know what his life purpose was; had God really called him, and for what? He could not turn back now. He could not return to Cwmhir unchanged, he knew it.

He thought back over the things he had already seen and learned on this journey. That true hearts made true friends, however different they were in status or wealth. That piety could be worn as a pretence, and as a cover for deeper realities. That to serve one another was a higher calling than to lead with a detached authority. That God spoke, that He could use the everyday things to reveal truth, and that His Word could come alive when read with an open heart. That God had put people in his life at the right time and for the right purpose. That miracles could happen and prayers be answered. He was a softer, perhaps more humble, person than the young monk who had exposed his selfish ambition at Cwmhir, but he still carried the guilt of his past. He still was to blame for hurting so many, and for ending innocent lives. The memories came back to him in a rush and he felt the weight of it again.

What are you seeking?

It was a voice in his head. His own thoughts, surely. What was he seeking? Absolution? Freedom from guilt? Purpose? A new start? A calling? Many things.

What are they seeking?

He looked around at his fellow pilgrims. Myfanwy and Tomos were laughing as they rode together. Rhys rode alongside him, singing a tuneful song just loud enough for the melody to carry on the wind. Matthew and Madoc rode in deep conversation at the head of the party. He noticed the small pilgrim group sitting on the road edge, dressed simply and sharing their meagre food provisions between them. He thought of the party he had passed earlier that had contained more than one cripple, and the wagon that had carried their possessions while they insisted on walking the path on painful feet. What were they each seeking?

The words of a psalm came back to Hywel's mind, as he rode his own path,

> *O God, You are my God;*
> *Early will I seek You;*
> *My soul thirsts for You;*
> *My flesh longs for You*
> *In a dry and thirsty land*
> *Where there is no water.*[12]

Are you seeking Me?

Hywel almost pulled on Brenin's reins to halt and turn around to see who had spoken; it was not his voice. But he knew the truth, because the words challenged him to the core. He did not know what the other pilgrims truly sought, but he knew God was challenging him directly. Was he on this journey to seek the things that maybe God could give him, or was his heart set on pilgrimage to discover God Himself? What was it that Titus had said would be his own reason for pilgrimage? It would have been a desire to experience more of God and to grow deeper in his knowledge of Him, and in doing so, of himself.

'I am trying to find You, God.' He whispered the words to the air, feeling inadequate in admitting even that.

Then you will find Me.

The River Aled sparkled below them, leading them down a wooded trail to the small settlement of Gwytherin. Here St Winefride had reportedly come following her miraculous recovery, and here she had become abbess of the sister convent to her uncle's monastery. Here she had lived out her days and served God, forever bearing the white scar that was said to be

---

[12] Psalm 63:1, NKJV.

the proof of His miracle-working power in her life. A small stone church bore her name, and a small *clas* community still made their home there. The site was well set up to welcome pilgrims, and they found kindly given hospitality for their weary bodies. It had taken four days of riding to get here from the holy well, and they were glad for the comfortable lodgings provided.

As the sun was setting and Hywel's bed began to call, he felt Madoc's hand on his arm.

'A word with you before you retire, brother.'

It was not said with his usual gruffness.

'I must leave you here. I have somewhere I must go.' If anything, Madoc's voice sounded strained. Hywel could not see his face clearly in the dim light, but he felt the hand on his arm tighten. 'I once said that I did not want you leading our little party, but now I must ask you to do just that.'

Hywel was surprised, glad he had earned this man's trust somehow. He was also concerned.

'How long for? I cannot lead them all the way to the Island of the Saints. I do not know the way, and I cannot protect them as you can. I am not you, Madoc.'

The hand on his arm relaxed and he heard a small chuckle.

'Do not fear, Hywel. I will not leave you for more than a few hours, and then I will relieve you of your charge. It does me good to hear that you are unsure of yourself. The man you were when we first met would not have admitted so. It makes me ever surer that the others will be safe in your care.

'The road you must take from here northwards is well marked and well travelled. You must head for Llangernyw, not many miles from here. You will know it for the ancient yew tree that grows there beside the church. It is thought to have sacred powers of its own, not that I give that much credence, but many pilgrims insist on stopping there to pray for protection for the rest of the journey. I will meet you there. Wait for me.'

And then he was gone.

True to his word, Madoc was nowhere to be found when the pilgrims woke and packed to leave the following morning. No one argued with Hywel's explanation as to why Madoc had left him to lead them. Nor did they seem to resent his leadership as he led them away from Gwytherin, back up the valley towards Llangernyw. Even Matthew was silently compliant.

Sure enough, the yew tree was easy to spot. It stood alone in the churchyard, a brooding presence with its wide-ridged trunk and dense, dark-leaved branches bowing almost to the ground in places. Pilgrims milled around it; one knelt among its thick roots in an attitude of prayer, another stood with his head resting on the trunk.

There was no sign of Madoc, so Hywel suggested they dismount and find a dry spot. It was a lovely day and the wide expanse of grass around the church allowed space for them to sit and for the horses to graze happily. No one seemed to want to speak. Madoc's prolonged absence was felt by all, Hywel especially.

As time passed he became even more concerned. They could not stay here indefinitely. He was sure they would need to press on soon. There was no accommodation for them here, and although they had spent nights in the open air before, they also hadn't covered enough miles that day. He began to wonder if he should suggest they move on, and latch on to another group of pilgrims. Surely the road would be obvious, although the intimidating mountains of the Carneddau loomed to the north-west and they would meet them sooner or later. He knew Llewellyn's stronghold of Abergwyngregyn lay in the foothills somewhere. Was that where the old soldier would have headed for next?

Just as he was coming to the conclusion that he needed to do something, the familiar form of a large grey horse appeared. The man on the horse looked tired, but also strangely at peace.

'Well met, my friends,' he said, not bothering to dismount. 'I am sorry to have made you wait.' He glanced over at Hywel and nodded, his lips twisting into a half-smile. 'I suggest we make haste to leave here, if you are all well rested.' He waited as the party found their mounts. 'Brother, will you ride with me?'

As they made their way along the very road Hywel had thought to take, Madoc turned to him.

'Thank you for doing as I asked, and no more, brother. My trust in you was well placed.'

'Thank you,' Hywel replied rather guiltily, thinking about how close he had come to breaking that trust. 'Can I ask where you went, Madoc?'

'I will tell you some day, brother. Not because I need a confessor, but as a friend.' He smiled a rare smile. 'Let's just say some of us have personal pilgrimages we have to make, pilgrimages that we can only travel alone.'

Hywel smiled back. He understood that more than ever now.

As the deer pants for the water brooks,

So pants my soul for You, O God.

My soul thirsts for God, for the living God …

Why are you cast down, O my soul?

And why are you disquieted within me?

Hope in God, for I shall yet praise Him.

Psalm 42:1-2,5, NKJV

15

Abergwyngregyn

Hywel was glad of Madoc's strong leadership as they began the climb up the steep, densely wooded hillside, the track not so well defined to the untrained eye. But the old soldier seemed to know where he was headed. As Hywel had suspected, Madoc was taking them to Abergwyngregyn, the *Llys*[13] of Llewellyn, Prince of Gwynedd. It wasn't a place that usually opened its gates to pilgrims, but it was a place where Madoc believed they would be welcomed, for his sake. And where good food and warm beds would be made available to them, along with shelter and feed for their weary horses.

The previous day their route had been fairly easy going to begin with, but as the afternoon had progressed, Madoc had made the decision to find a place to rest for the night rather than press on into the hills. He took responsibility for having delayed them at Llangernyw, but was unwilling to lead them on a route that could be treacherous in low light. They had found a small settlement at Eglwysbach, with its own tiny wooden church, and camped nearby for the night, before crossing the River Conway by ferry at Tal-y-Cafn.

The overnight rest had been timely, because now both they and their horses were feeling the challenge of the climb out of the great river valley. As the trees thinned the path levelled, and here and there were traces of a much older, wider road, a legacy of the Romans who had once traversed those very hills between

---

[13] Court, or seat of power of Welsh princes.

their forts at Caerhun and Segontium. They skirted the contour of the mountain, the high, dark peaks looming above them. The party said little, concentrating on the terrain, their eyes fixed on the reassuring back of Madoc as he led them. Hywel happily brought up the rear, like an ever-vigilant sheepdog, making sure those ahead kept in step and did not falter.

Finally, they began their descent down craggy paths lined by tall trees, until arrested by the crashing sound of fast-flowing water. One more turn and to their left the high Aber waterfall appeared, its white water splashing down a steep cliff face into a wide pool below. It was both beautiful and terrifying to behold. The water spray chilled the air around them, so they did not linger. The light was already beginning to fade and they still had a way to go.

Hywel was never so glad to see a wall of wooden palisades lining a deep ditch, a sight which understandably would have deterred other more unwelcome visitors. Abergwyngregyn consisted of a spacious, well-fortified bailey with a small, round motte beyond, just visible in the dimming light. As the weary travellers made their way through the wooden gatehouse, they were hailed – or rather, Madoc was – warmly. Wooden buildings lined the edges of the bailey enclosure, among them well-appointed stables where their horses would be well catered for. Facing them was a long, wide, stone-built hall, whitewashed, and with a steep, rush-thatched roof. At each end, cross wings stuck out; one end was likely kitchens and stores, but the other had finely decorated leaded glass windows, and a separate entrance that denoted private accommodation.

They were ushered into the great hall, where a large central fire burned warmly. Rush torches lined the walls, so that the inside of the hall was bathed in a warm glow. The internal walls were also painted white, and Hywel could make out a simple red decoration highlighting the archways that divided the room.

To one end of the hall was a wide dais, in front of a wall lined by colourful tapestries. It supported a finely carved wooden chair, but it sat unused. The master of the house was not in residence. In fact, it seemed only a small guard, a few retainers and serving women remained, but still the pilgrims found themselves offered finer food than they had seen in days, brought hot to the large wooden table that ran the length of the hall. Wide, window-lined recesses to each side of the hall would provide ample space for them to make comfortable beds for themselves on the soft, rush-covered floor. Hywel felt himself relax in the inviting surroundings.

'Madoc, you old rogue, it is good to see you, my friend.'

A tall, grizzled man, with a round belly that hung over his belt, greeted them, his eyes warm in welcome.

'This fine figure of a man,' Madoc patted the man's midriff, 'is the prince's steward, Owen the Grey.' Madoc made the introductions. 'These, my pilgrim companions, and I are grateful for your kind welcome here, Owen. We thought to at least be offered the shelter of the stables and some simple fare, but to be shown into the hall and offered food at the prince's table? That is more than we simple travellers could have hoped for.'

'Madoc, even if the prince were here, you know full well he would gladly have extended his welcome for you to join his table, for the sake of your faithful service to him, and to his mother before him in Powys. But your arrival is timely, for we are celebrating, and you must join us. Our prince is, as we speak, being wed to his new bride, the Lady Joan, natural daughter of King John. Much of his retinue has gone with him to Chester for the ceremonies. He will return with his bride within the month, but in the meantime we will make the most of his good humour that has left his stores well provisioned. He would want us to enjoy his generosity. Once the *saesneg*[14] lady is ensconced here there might be less cause to celebrate.'

He added something in his native Welsh and grinned mischievously at Madoc. 'She will be made welcome, as Llewellyn requires, of course,' he added. 'But there are many

---

[14] Welsh term for the English.

here who do not like that he has chosen to ally himself with the English king through marriage, however it might benefit him, or us as Welshmen. We will watch and see.'

'Do you think it will stop John's interest in these Welsh lands?'

'Who is to say? Despite the alliance, he is not a king to be fully trusted. Llewellyn knows that well enough. You will see in the morning that more building work is planned here – a stone tower with fortifications, on a rise above the river. A stronghold retreat like the one at Dolwyddelan, if ever the prince should need use of it.'

The pilgrims were enjoying the fine spread that had been set before them, when another visitor was ushered into the hall. He wore travelling clothes of a fine quality but looked to have been wearing them for some days. As he stepped into the light of a torch, Hywel heard a small gasp escape the lips of the man sat next to him. He turned, and saw that Matthew's already pale face had turned ashen. The visitor too had noticed him and strode over, laying a leather scrip on the table beside Matthew's half-empty trencher.

'Jacob.' Matthew acknowledged him with a slight nod of the head, his lips set in a hard line.

'My apologies for disturbing your meal.' The young visitor acknowledged the rest of the diners, before turning his attention back to Matthew. 'It took me days to find you, master. I found many pilgrim groups but none that included a young man on a fine black stallion. Until I found one that had seen a group on horseback leave the ferry at the river and head this way into the hills. I tracked you, forgive me, but it was important I find you. I thank the Almighty One that He led me here and to you. I bear coin and a message from your mother.' He nodded to the scrip, and then sat down heavily on the bench, his head sagging almost to his knees in exhaustion.

'Come.' Hywel rose from the table and lent the visitor his arm to help him stand. 'Let us find you a bed to rest yourself, and then you can talk more.' A serving maid appeared with a cup of something steaming and the young man took it and drunk it thirstily before allowing the monk to lead him over to his own recently prepared bed on the soft rushes.

Matthew was sat staring blindly at a piece of parchment held in shaky hands when Hywel returned to reclaim his seat beside him.

'Not bad news, I pray?'

Matthew did not answer, but folded the parchment neatly and returned it to the scrip. He reached over to the jug of ale that had been left on the table and poured himself a cup, put it to his lips and drained it, before pouring himself another.

'Drink with me, brother.' He filled a cup for Hywel and thrust it at him.

Hywel was not sure of the wisdom of that. He glanced over to where Madoc sat with Owen and saw that he was observing their exchange. The older man nodded.

Hywel took the cup of ale and drank half of it. Matthew immediately refilled it, having already drained his second cup and replenished it. The jug was all but empty now. Matthew gazed into it for a moment and then replaced it on the table with a sigh. For a young man who had advocated moderation and self-control in all things, this was not typical behaviour. Hywel instinctively let the silence sit between them, sensing his companion's internal struggle.

'We all carry secrets, do we not, brother? The mismatched brothers yonder and that mysterious affliction that is supposedly healed. The smiling widow whose emotional burden bends her back more than the physical ailment. Even our esteemed leader with his secret assignations that delayed our journey. And you, brother, it is obvious to all that you are not all that you claim to be. I have seen the guilt and fear in your eyes, more than once. There, so we are all deceivers, and all deceived.' He drained his cup and banged it on the table.

Hywel did not know how to answer. There was truth in the words, however bitterly uttered.

'Forgive me, brother. I am in no place to judge.' Matthew dropped his face into his hands, and when after a few moments he raised it again to look at Hywel, his eyes were moist and his look defeated.

'This here is a summons.' He indicated the scrip. 'I am called home, and the coin is to pay for the best horses and quickest route back for Jacob and myself.'

'You must take Brenin, then, of course.'

'No!' It was adamant. 'One horse is much the same as another to me. If I go, that horse stays. He belongs with you, that is obvious. My father will have to just accept the loss.' He paused. 'Except my father will never know.' He dropped his head onto his arms and Hywel laid his hand on the man's shoulder.

'I am sorry for your loss, my friend.'

Matthew glanced up at him with sad eyes. 'I believe you really are. You have a kind heart, Hywel. I have done nothing to earn your friendship – the opposite, in truth – and yet here you are at my side.'

'I am good at listening too, if it helps.'

Matthew sat up and dragged his sleeve across his face.

'I have lived a lie for many months, brother. Now I must unburden myself, and you, I think, will judge me less harshly than others might. As I said, you too have your secrets.'

The noise from the other end of the table had diminished as one by one people were making their way to their beds. Madoc still sat with Owen and one or two others, talking quietly. This corner of the table, this whispered conversation, was the most privacy they could expect.

'Everyone will likely know my secrets soon enough,' Matthew continued. 'My father is not dead... not yet. He has suffered an apoplectic fit and is not expected to live. He has lost the power of speech but seemingly still controls us all. My mother has asked that I return. I am expected to take over the business, you see. I have tried to run from it, but it seems I cannot escape. Unless I offend all who love me and continue to selfishly pursue my own path.

'And here is the shocking bit. I am not even a true Christian, Hywel, much as I have tried to be. As I cannot escape the life path set by my father, so I cannot escape my heritage. Sitting before you here is not Matthew, the son of Simon the goldsmith, but Levi. Levi ben Shimon.'

It was a shock, and Hywel knew it had registered on his face momentarily. Matthew a Jew? And on a Christian pilgrimage?

'Yes, I can see it in your face. Surprise, but no revulsion. That I am glad of at least. A filthy Jew? Isn't that what many so-called *good* Christian people in this country would label me? It was because of such persecution that we were forced to leave Oxford, the city of my birth, and move westwards into Wales. When the pronouncements of the Pope and then the dictates of the king threatened our livelihood, and our Gentile neighbours grew increasingly hostile, my father took the decision to leave and set up his business in Rhaeadr Gwy, where no one knew us, or knew who we truly were. He was more interested in profit than piety, and it proved worthwhile as his business has flourished and made him a wealthy man. He easily shook off the shackles of Jewry, changing our names and hiding our origins. He was determined to perpetuate the lie, going so far as to engage the services of a priest to instruct his only son in the ways of the Christian faith. That was his mistake.'

Matthew paused and reached for his now empty cup. Hywel rose and went to find a replacement jug, this time filled with water. He poured a cup for Matthew, who wrinkled his nose but drank deeply.

'How so?'

'That priest was a good man. A pious and godly man, but also kind and gentle and patient. He taught me the ways of Christ in more than just his words. You understand, perhaps?'

'I do.' Hywel's thoughts spun painfully back to Cenred. No learned priest, but a Christlike man nonetheless. He thought too of Gwrgenau, of Julian and Rhodri, and of Titus. Each in his own way had demonstrated Christ to him.

'The more time I spent with that priest, the more I wanted to learn about the God he believed in and the Christ he followed. I began to resent my father more and more, to despise his avarice and his easy duplicity. I wanted less and less to do with the business I had been trained to inherit. I wanted to be like that priest. I became determined to defy my father and enter the Church.

'I confronted him with my decision one day. I expected anger, an explosion of rage. Instead I got sneering indifference. He just looked at me coldly as if he did not know, or even care, who I was. And then he turned away from me and back to his work. "You can go, but if you do, you will never have my support. I will cut you off from your home and your family," were his words.

'I could not go. I had my mother and my sisters to think of. They would be left defenceless if anything should happen to my father. They did not deserve that. So I submitted and reapplied myself to learning the business, all the while still yearning for something else. My father had put an end to the lessons from the priest, but I would find ways of meeting with him in secret. I even sneaked my way into Mass on more than one occasion.'

'So how did you come to be on this pilgrimage? Did your father relent?'

Matthew sniffed in derision. 'Hardly. I think he thought that if I did this, I would get it out of my system. That I would be put off by the hardships and privations of the journey and come home more appreciative of the comforts of home and the finer things our wealth affords us. I also think my mother had a hand in it, seeing how unhappy I was. We compromised. My father made me promise that I would forever abandon all ideas of entering the Church if he allowed me to do this one pilgrimage. He provided horses to make the journey quicker and to ensure that I would be away from the business for as short a time as possible.'

'He wasn't concerned about you further embracing the Christian faith, and denying your Jewish roots?'

'I suppose it all added to the show – the deception of us being a good Christian family would be enhanced by his only son going on pilgrimage. I don't think he really cared what faith I privately pursued as long as I gave up the notion of entering the Church. He was more concerned with doing a deal to keep me tied to the business.'

'And have you further embraced the faith?'

Matthew paused, a rueful smile on his face. 'I have tried. I have tried so hard to live a pious and holy life. I have prayed, and denied myself, and sat in judgement of others. You have seen my foolish attempts to place myself in superiority over you all, and you have probably judged me in turn. But deep down, I know I am a fraud. It's not that I don't believe, but now I think I have to accept that I have been pretending, as much as my father has, to be something that I am not.'

Hywel understood that only too well. 'So, will you go home? And will you abandon your Christian faith?'

'I don't know the answer to either of those questions… Will you pray for me, brother?'

The face that turned to him then was softer than Hywel had ever seen it. Behind the hard exterior hid a man as lost as he, a man just yearning to be understood and to understand. To truly find his place in the world. To live at peace with himself.

'I will pray, Matthew,' and he meant it. 'But can I offer you one thought of my own?'

'And that is?'

'Regret is a heavy burden to carry. If you have a chance to heal your relationship with your father by returning home, then I would urge you to do so. You cannot know what you will find when you do return, but if you do not go, you will forever flog yourself with "What if I had gone?" I am in no place to tell you what you must do; I have made more than enough wrong decisions myself. But I am grateful that God has allowed me to restore some of what was broken by my foolishness, and believe that I will have the opportunity to restore yet more. I also do not believe that you are abandoning your pursuit of God by ending this pilgrimage early. If you truly seek Him, I'm sure you will find Him another way.'

'Wise words, brother.' The figure of Madoc loomed behind them, one of his hands coming to rest on each of their backs as he bent towards them with a whisper. 'And now I think we should all sleep, and leave all else for the morrow.'

Hywel was unsure how peacefully Matthew rested, but for himself, sleep did not come easily. The conversation with Matthew had been startling in its revelations. But he appreciated the man far more now that he had heard his tale. He felt honoured that Matthew had trusted him enough to be honest in the telling. He also wondered how much of the story Madoc already knew.

Matthew's revelations had also stirred buried emotions in him. Lying in darkness, with only the sound of his sleeping companions and the odd plaintive screeching of a barn owl outside, his mind wandered. He revisited the past in dreamlike quality, rehearsing how he would tell his story if ever compelled to. How honest would he be, what would he tell, and what omit? There was so much he was ashamed of, and Matthew's deceits seemed petty in comparison. Had he, too, run away? Maybe, but at least with his family's blessing. He had made his peace with his father, and in part with Cenred before he died, although he knew there was still guilt there, still unfinished business. He knew that he must return to make his peace with Julian and Rhodri. And he hoped that completing this pilgrimage would enable him to finally make peace with God, and with himself. He needed to move on with his life.

Hywel fumbled around for his Psalter, finding it safe in the satchel he had tucked in beside him. He longed to read it, to let the words bring him enough peace to at least sleep. But the darkness in the hall was impenetrable now. He sighed in disappointment. He really needed something to distract his wandering thoughts.

What was it that he had said to Matthew? That you did not need to complete a pilgrimage in order to find God? Where had that bit of wisdom come from? He had surprised even himself.

Where can I go from your Spirit?

He had read that. He couldn't remember when, but now he could almost see the words written on the page in his imagination. He closed his eyes and there they were.

Where can I go from Your Spirit?
Or where can I flee from Your presence?
If I ascend into heaven, You are there;
If I make my bed in hell, behold, You are there.
If I take the wings of the morning,
And dwell in the uttermost parts of the sea,
Even there Your hand shall lead me,
And Your right hand shall hold me.
If I say, 'Surely the darkness shall fall on me,'
Even the night shall be light about me;
Indeed, the darkness shall not hide from You,
But the night shines as the day;
The darkness and the light are both alike to You.[15]

The words comforted him, and his mind stilled. The darkness suddenly didn't seem as dark. Hywel turned over onto his side and sleep came quickly.

---

[15] Psalm 139:7-12, NKJV.

Your presence is everywhere, bringing light

into my night.

Psalm 139:11, TPT

16
Worship

The early morning mist still hung low off the mountainside when the small group of pilgrims gathered to see Matthew take his leave. His pale face was drawn and Hywel guessed he hadn't slept, but seemingly he had made the decision that he would return home, and once that decision had been made he was resolved to be on his way. Surprisingly, Hywel found himself being drawn into an awkward embrace and, yet more surprisingly, found himself suddenly sad at the thought of the young man's departure from their little band of travellers.

True to his word, Matthew had insisted on leaving Brenin with Hywel, and had used his coin to hire two more-than-adequate horses for himself and his companion from the prince's stable. Owen had also offered an armed escort of two of Llewellyn's remaining guard to see them over the mountains, and Madoc had persuaded Matthew to accept. Those men knew the trails well, and also knew how to handle the bandits they might encounter. The fastest route back to Rhaeadr Gwy for Matthew and Jacob was not going to be all on well-marked roads, with hospitable places to refresh themselves. It made sense to be as well prepared as possible.

The remaining five pilgrims stood huddled together against the morning chill, to send the riders on their way with their kind thoughts and prayers.

They did not linger themselves, once Matthew and his party were out of sight, and made haste to load their horses and take their own leave from Abergwyngregyn. The road they were to take was a continuation of the route the Romans had used. It took them along the coast, the wide grey sea to their right, their destination Bangor and then beyond to the Lleyn Peninsula.

It was a subdued group, strangely missing Matthew's presence, but there was also a sense of renewed purpose to reach their destination – on Hywel's part, at least, not just for himself, but in a kind of tribute to Matthew, whose own resolve to complete the pilgrimage had been so abruptly ended; Hywel would finish it for him. As before, they were joined on the road by other pilgrims, if not quite as many as they had encountered at Basingwerk and St Winefride's.

The pilgrims headed for Bangor, and the cathedral church that bore the name of its first bishop, St Deiniol. The church was a fine building, built of stone in cruciform, with high windows and an impressively long nave, situated on a low, flat area of land, a half-mile or so inland from the sea.

They arrived just before noon and joined the pilgrims making their way into the church to celebrate Mass. The bishop himself was present, and as part of the celebration, each pilgrim was invited to advance and kneel at the bishop's feet to receive a blessing for the journey ahead. It felt good to kneel in that sacred place, surrounded by so many other devoted souls, and as the bishop laid his hand on his head, Hywel found himself praying for Matthew and the journey he was now committed to. Different, but a pilgrimage of sorts nonetheless.

The sun was high in the sky as they left Bangor, following the road up a small mountain which gave magnificent views of the great island Ynys Mon to the north, the high mountains of Eryri to the south, and to the west, their destination – the Lleyn and at its end, as yet invisibly elusive, the Holy Island of the Saints. It was a pleasant ride, past the church and *clas* community at Pentir, where they stopped merely to accept refreshments. Madoc was pushing them on, as he wanted to reach the church of St Peblig and the nearby remains of the Roman settlement at Segontium before nightfall. The sun stayed with them long into the evening and they arrived with light enough to make camp for the night among the ruins of the silent, square buildings where once had been a busy Roman fort.

Hywel wandered around in the half-light of dusk, stretching his muscles after the ride and taking in the atmosphere of the place. He could imagine the fort, how it might have been, teeming with life, soldiers stationed miles from their homes in an inhospitable land, with warlike natives to challenge them, and a river and trade routes to protect. He had a similar sense of being cut off from the familiarity of things he had once taken for granted, standing on the edge of a life that held so many uncertainties. But on this pilgrimage he had found himself comforted by the company of the unlikeliest of companions, encouraged by the unity born out of travelling so many miles together, and the sharing of experiences. Those soldiers of long ago must have relied on comradeship also, to get them through the challenges of their unpredictable lives.

Later, the five pilgrims sat around a small fire, sharing the provisions they had carried from Abergwyngregyn. None of them seemed ready to sleep. Not Rhys or Tomos, looking more refreshed than they had all journey, a result of several nights of unbroken sleep. Nor Myfanwy, who was still showing no signs of pain, yet still visibly crippled. She was sat beside Madoc, who was staring mindlessly at his feet. She nudged him playfully with her elbow.

'Time for a story, old man, I think.'

Whether it was a smile or a grimace that passed over Madoc's face in response, Hywel couldn't tell in the firelight.

'I'm no storyteller, madam.'

'You may not pass as a travelling bard, but you can string together a decent tale. I am sure of it!'

'Do you want battle stories?' he growled good-naturedly. 'I have many of them, real-life ones, if you aren't inclined to sleep peacefully tonight.'

'Not me,' Myfanwy shuddered. 'One of the tales passed down from our forefathers might suit, to entertain our young

206

friends, perhaps? We are here where St Peblig founded his church. Perhaps we should hear the tale of his father, Macsen Wledig,[16] and the dream, and the woman, that led him to this corner of Wales?'

Madoc shifted position, leant back against the low wall behind him, and closed his eyes as if to recall a distant memory. And then he began, and although he might not have had the dramatic skill of the storyteller at St Winefride's, his telling of the tale was compelling all the same.

Deep in the memories of our forefathers a tale has been told, and retold, and remembered in the retelling. Of a proud, wise, noble and handsome prince and emperor who ruled the western edges of the great empire of Rome. Macsen Wledig was his name, and it was one day as he rode in a hunt, with men of rank and nobility, that feeling the effects of the midday sun, he was forced to rest and laid himself down, falling into a deep sleep. While his faithful attendants shielded him above and around with their shields and spears, the great man dreamt a great dream. In it he travelled many miles, traversing the highest of mountains and the widest of rivers, across a vast sea, to a fair island, where among the most beautiful of landscapes stood a magnificent castle. All those within that castle were clothed in the finest of raiment, two knaves played chess on a board made from silver and gold, and a great warrior king, crowned with gold, sat on an ivory throne. Also in that castle he saw the loveliest maiden he had ever seen. With hair of deepest red, and the sweetest complexion, she was dressed in fine silks, with adornments of gold, silver and precious stones.

The great Macsen awoke, but was forever altered by what he had seen in his dream, so in love with that fair maiden and the land she inhabited, that he lost all other loves – for life, food, sport and even for rulership. His servants were so perplexed by the change in him that they begged him to seek for wisdom from the wisest men of the land. This he did, and at their bidding, messengers were sent out to the far

---

[16] Macsen Wledig or *The Dream of Macsen Wledig* (Magnus Maximus). One of the tales of the Welsh *Mabinogion*, folklore passed down by oral tradition.

reaches of the world, to find this land that the emperor had dreamt of, and to find his lady love.

And so the story goes — believe it if you will — that it was here, after finding the island of Britannia, and then the fair mountains, hills, rivers and forests of our land, that finally Macsen's messengers came upon a castle stood on the banks of the river that flows from the mountains to the sea, here at Caer Arfon. And in that castle they found everything that their master had described: the youths at their game of chess, the king sat on his throne and the beautiful maiden. They had found Elen, only daughter of Octavius, ruler of this land.

And so the faithful messengers told them of Macsen's dream and declared his love for the fair maiden, but the young lady was not moved. 'Unless he comes himself from the great city of Rome, to declare his love for me in person, I will not have him,' was her response. So the messengers left and travelled the many miles back to their master, and he with haste prepared to return with them. But it was a perilous journey and beset with battles fierce, each of which he fought with all his might, to win both the land and the lady's hand.

Coming to Caer Arfon, he found his love, and on promise of a share of the lands he had conquered, she consented to be his. From their union came Peblig, and through Peblig, and his sainted mother Elen, Christianity came to this land.

And so the story ends, here at the church St Peblig founded, close to the hill with the chapel that bears his mother's name.

'Good story,' Tomos said, yawning widely. 'Although I would have preferred a bit more blood and gore. And I'm not sure such love exists between a man and a woman, except perhaps in dreams. I've certainly never experienced anything like it. What about you, dear brother?' He turned to Rhys, sitting silently beside him. 'I've seen the way the shepherdess Gwenllian looks at you, following you around with her eyes. One smile in her direction and she'd be all yours.'

Hywel could swear Rhys turned bright red, although it might have been the reflection from the embers. He said nothing in reply but his brother was grinning broadly at him.

Tomos turned his attention to the rest of the group. Myfanwy just smiled back at him, and Madoc laughed out loud.

'Well, that's that, then. If none of us four has tasted such violent love then we have no way of knowing if it is even possible. Unless, of course, you have.' He turned to Hywel. 'But no, you are a man of the Church, so you would know nothing of such passion, brother.'

Hywel felt his own face flush bright red, and his breathing quickened. Truth was, he understand all too well what had driven Macsen to pursue his love. He had loved Hild like that. It had consumed him, taken away all sense, spoiled every other pleasure in his life. It was his desire to have her, his blind pursuit of her, that had ruined everything. His love story had no happy ending, and had left him a man burdened with guilt and hidden shame.

'I was not always a monk.'

He was aware of four sets of eyes trained on him. What had made him speak? Was he going to bare his soul now, in front of them all? The thought brought bile to his throat. He laughed a forced laugh, which sounded odd, even to his own ears.

'Well, that may well be a story for another time.' Madoc came to his rescue, standing awkwardly and reaching down to give Hywel a hand to stand up. 'Would you come and help me check on the horses, Hywel? Rhys, Tomos, ensure that fire is out. I suggest you all get yourselves settled for the night.'

Madoc said nothing as he walked alongside Hywel over to where the horses were happily grazing. They needed no human attention, and Hywel knew that. He was glad for the excuse to move away from those firelit faces showing a little too much interest in his discomfort.

'Thank you, Madoc.'

'For what?' He laughed softly. 'I could see you squirming, lad, that is all. You do not have to say more.'

'I loved a woman once. Loved her more than life. Loved her to her destruction and almost to mine.'

Madoc stopped by his grey and ran his hands down the horse's great neck. Brenin saw and, to Hywel's delight, snickered and wandered over to stand by him, dipping his neck as if to ask for his own caress.

'Did she return your love?'

'Yes, I believe so.'

'Then whatever the outcome, you have been blessed to have experienced what many long to, and never do. If just for a time.'

'She died, our child with her.'

Madoc stopped his stroking of the horse momentarily.

'Then I understand a little more of the burden you carry, brother.' He stepped around the horse's head so that Hywel could see him face on – although the light was failing, so Hywel could not read his eyes clearly. Madoc reached out and put his hand on his shoulder, squeezing it, his voice low and gentle. 'I cannot take that burden from you, Hywel. Nor do I think it wise that you unburden yourself to our fellow travellers. They hold you in high regard, and with good reason. You have proved yourself a kind travelling companion. I believe you are a good man, and perhaps will even be a good monk in time. I understand your burden, Hywel, because I too have carried such, for far too much of my life.'

'Do you carry it still?' Hywel did not feel it appropriate to question Madoc for the details. It was enough that he seemed to understand.

'No. I laid it down. It took me longer than it should have to do so, and even now, from time to time, I am tempted to pick it up again. But it gives me hope for you, brother.'

'How did you free yourself from it?'

'You will find out soon enough. I cannot tell you when or how, but it will be a transaction that no man can arrange. It must be between you and your God.'

With that, the older man turned away and wandered back to the camp. Hywel leaned into Brenin, who stood and let him, just for a moment, before reverting to his more normal skittish state and trotting away. Hywel smiled to himself. He was

210

making progress with the horse at least, little by little gaining his trust. He wondered if it was the same with him and God. As this pilgrimage went on, the things that were said, the people he interacted with, the words he was reading... Little by little, he was learning to trust God more, lean into Him more, accept that He might really care about him. Gracia had said that Brenin would be happier once he learned to submit to kind leadership. What was it she had said? 'He will be happier and more content for learning to trust another, and in realising that he does not have to be in control. Perhaps the same is true for you?' If he understood her meaning, she would have been praying for this. For him to trust God enough to give Him the care and control of his life and its direction. He was getting there.

He slept deeply that night, but his dreams were full of a red-headed beauty, dressed in the finest of garments, jewels in her hair and her eyes of emerald green. The smile on her face was Hild's.

They rose the following morning, their clothes damp from the heavy dew that had settled overnight. If any of them had thought more on Hywel's embarrassment the night before, nothing was said. Myfanwy was cheery, and Tomos and Rhys pushed and shoved each other playfully as they packed up camp. Madoc just gave him a nod, his eyes saying more by way of reassurance than any words could have. It somehow did not matter to Hywel that Madoc now knew his secret, and he was grateful. Grateful too that he hadn't spilled the whole story to them all, unwilling to see reproach in all those trusting eyes.

Their journey now took them westwards, again following an ancient track well trod by pilgrims through the ages. They weren't alone, either, as they passed one group and then another, all travelling towards the same destination. They were headed for the pilgrim church named for St Beuno, where they would rest for a few hours and stay the night. The *clas* community that had grown up around that church at Clynnog Fawr was accustomed to welcoming pilgrims. There was also

St Beuno's own healing well close by. It was a must-stop on their pilgrim route.

To give the horses a rest, they opted to walk some of the way. Now that they were closer to the endpoint of their pilgrimage it was as if they wanted to savour this part of the journey even more. The very air itself felt cleaner and fresher, as if heaven itself were drawing closer. The shining sea with its white-crested waves was a constant presence on their right, and the peaks of the hills of the Lleyn stood like beacons encouraging them on their way.

Clynnog Fawr was a busy and welcoming place. There was well-constructed wooden accommodation for them, and enclosed pasture for their horses. Food was on offer: steaming stews in iron pots hanging over large fires. There was even a lamb roasting on a spit, the smell making Hywel salivate. Pilgrims, laymen, tradespeople and clerics all mingled, sharing stories and food. Madoc was warmly welcomed by more than one of them, his face obviously a familiar sight.

They found themselves a corner in one of the rush-thatched huts and stowed their belongings there before wandering back out to explore. Madoc drew their attention to a large, flat-faced, stone pillar that stood higher than the height of a man in the churchyard. It was whitewashed and towards the top engraved with a large half-circle cut into four equal segments with radiating lines. Where the lines converged, a small iron rod protruded.

'Do you know what it is?' Tomos asked, his face a picture of confusion. 'Is it some sort of strange monument to the saints? Or a device for divination, perhaps?' He shivered perceptibly.

Madoc laughed, and Hywel smiled. He had seen this type of thing before, in the courtyards of wealthy houses. They had been smaller, perhaps, and the ones he had seen had been laid horizontal and had more lines cut into them.

'It is a device for telling the time of day, is it not?' he said.

'It is, brother. Only this one is ancient and was likely designed purely for the community here. They divide their day into work and prayer, much like you do in the abbey. As the sun hits the rod, it casts a shadow, and those shadows move around the half circle. When the shadow falls exactly over a line it indicates the time at which the community must stop work and come together for prayer. The boy there is likely waiting to run to tell the priest it is time.' He indicated a grubby-looking child lounging against a grave marker, picking his nose, who stood guiltily to attention at Madoc's words.

Tomos stepped closer to the sundial and reached up to trace his finger along the third radial line.

'Look, the shadow is almost in line. If you are right, we will soon hear the bell call from the church tower there, and the community will come together to pray.' Tomos stood transfixed, watching the shadow edge closer to the line, occasionally glancing up, shielding his eyes against the glare, as if willing the sun to move the shadow faster.

He was not the only one dazzled by the strange sight, a small crowd having gathered. When at last the shadow reached its mark, there was a small communal gasp. Within moments, the clang of a bell rang out.

People soon appeared from all directions and made their way into the stone church. Some wore scapulars much like Hywel would wear to work in. But there were no uniform habits here, most of the worshippers, of both sexes, wearing simple woollen garments of varying hues of brown and grey.

The visiting pilgrims were made welcome inside the cool church, with its tall glass windows above the altar that allowed the high afternoon sunshine to stream in. Hywel took his place and knelt in prayer as the call to worship was uttered by a priest wearing a plain white *alb*,[17] with a rope belt knotted at the waist and a simple black *chasuble*[18] over his shoulders, secured at the

---

[17] Long white linen tunic worn by clergy.
[18] Cloak, usually hooded.

neck with a small, silver clasp. The contrast with the *clas* priest that Hywel had met at Llandinam was striking.

Here, all was simplicity, and as the service progressed, so the simplicity of worship also became evident. There were no written words of liturgy, no formality, no separate area for monks and lay people, male or female, as Hywel was used to. All came together with one purpose: to praise their Creator together. The priest began to recite, and the words were from a psalm. The people in the congregation added their voices. They knew these words by heart, and they were spoken with conviction. One by one voices began to sing along with the responses, until there sounded the most beautiful of symphonies, voices coming together in sweet harmonies, rising and falling together. Their worship filled the space, until it felt as if heaven itself had leant a choir of angels to the realm of humans.

Hywel looked about him in wonder. All around him faces were lifted in adoration, bathed in peace and joy. Some knelt and spread their hands in devotion. One or two lay prostrate on the floor. It was a deeply moving experience and Hywel wished for it not to end. Could it be that God Himself had presenced Himself there, as a response to their praise, as He had in Solomon's great Temple?[19] Hywel found himself on his knees, overcome by the heavy sense of the Holy in that simple place, among those simple people. He could not even pray, but where he knelt he was aware of tears coursing down his cheeks and falling to the cool stone floor beneath him.

---

[19] See 2 Chronicles 5:13-14.

Enter into His gates with thanksgiving,

And into His courts with praise.

Be thankful to Him, and bless His name.

Psalm 100:4, NKJV

Give unto the LORD, O you mighty ones,

Give unto the LORD glory and strength.

Give unto the LORD the glory due to His name;

Worship the LORD in the beauty of holiness.

Psalm 29:1-2, NKJV

17
Rebirth

The time spent at Clynnog Fawr had felt like a rest of longer than the one-night stay it had actually been. Not just physical rest, but also a refreshment of souls. The worship, the sense of community, the beauty of the physical surroundings made it a hard place to leave. But they still had a fair way to go to end this pilgrimage, and the next stage included a steep climb up a winding mountain path. From time to time they caught a view of the sea below them, waves crashing against the rocks. It was wild and beautiful, and Hywel was enjoying every moment of the ride, Brenin sure-footed beneath him.

He tried to recall how he had felt in the church the day before. They had attended other services, both evening and morning, before they took their leave, but none that had moved him as much as that first had. He had knelt, his head bowed until well after the singing had ended and the congregation had begun to leave. He could not say what the tears had meant; he had felt peace but he had also become aware of a deep sense of unworthiness, that he was dirty somehow, and yet still accepted, still welcomed into that encounter with the Holy. He could not put any of it into words, nor even thoughts that made any sense to him. He supposed perhaps it went deeper than that. He could not deny that he had experienced something of God, but would it change him? He knew that if he went looking for it, the guilt was still there. He resisted the urge to feel his back to see if he were still carrying an actual physical burden. It still felt like it at times.

The others seemed also to have been deeply affected by Clynnog Fawr and there was an atmosphere of quiet contentment among them as they plodded their way up the slopes of the small peak of Yr Eifl. Their destination was Pistyll, a few miles further down the coast, and no one was in the mood to ride the route hard. There was so much to take in. Nant Gwethryn offered them a midway stopping place and they found welcome refreshments there, before traversing more inclines and more descents to arrive at Pistyll in the late afternoon.

It was not as large as Clynnog Fawr, and there was no *clas* community, only a simple, rectangular stone church perched on a platform overlooking the sea, and a series of farm buildings. But there was quite a collection of pilgrims already there, making camps on the grassed areas around the farm. Madoc pulled up and dismounted.

'The farmer here agrees to provide for the pilgrims who pass by this way, in exchange for not having to pay the church tithes for his land. A fair agreement, but also I think he takes pleasure in it. Especially when the pilgrims are generous in return. We will find fresh water in a pool fed by a stream, and food available to purchase from the farmhouse, and soft grass to sleep on and feed the horses.'

'It is wonderful!'

Myfanwy was her ever-cheerful soul, but she was right. The setting was so lovely, and yes, they would have all that they needed for the night. And the weather had been kind to them again, the sun warm, with just the slightest of cool breezes coming in from the sea.

They were used to making camp quickly and efficiently now, and chose a sheltered corner close to some small oaks in full green. Water was collected and the horses seen to. Hywel was just thinking of perhaps going for a walk to shake off the stiffness in his thighs, or even lying down in the sun for a quick snooze, when a harassed-looking man came running over in their direction. Wearing the recognisable garb of a farmer, his tunic and hands and knees were covered in mud.

'Pilgrims, welcome,' he breathed heavily. 'I pray you will find yourselves well provided for here.' He gestured around in a welcoming way, but there was a frantic look on his face. 'Excuse me for asking, but you have arrived on horseback, so could it be that any of you are well-learned in horse handling?' He looked from Rhys to Tomos, and then to Madoc. Madoc in turn looked at Hywel.

'I know my way around a horse, but the young brother here is particularly skilled with horse handling.'

The farmer could not hide his scepticism, and looked Hywel up and down warily.

'Well, if you think you can help, can you follow me?' He had already turned around and was hurrying back towards the farm.

In a fenced paddock, a fine piebald mare was stamping and rearing, and running from side to side, in obvious distress.

'She is uncontrollable! I bought her in haste.' The farmer was stood panting, his hands on his knees. 'I was only trying to lead her out to pasture and she kicked and reared and put her hoof through the stable wall. See, she has cut herself.'

Hywel could see the trickle of blood running down her left foreleg, and what looked like a large wooden splinter protruding from a wound just above her knee.

'I have tried to calm her, and so has my lad.' The farmer indicated a pale, thin youth sitting on the fence at a safe distance from the horse. 'Last time I got hold of her reins she just dragged me over and into the mud puddle. I am at an end of what to do. Can you help?'

Hywel had already stepped into the paddock, closing the gate securely behind him. He advanced slowly, making a wide arc of the horse, speaking softly. The horse saw him and tossed her head and reared but he began to move towards her and did not halt in his advance until he was close enough to make eye contact with her. All the time he was speaking in the same low, soothing tone and keeping his movements slow.

Whatever he was saying, it seemed to be working; the mare stopped tossing her head and appeared to be assessing him. Hywel, for his part, could see she was in pain, her eyes wide with terror. He needed her to trust him if he was going to be able to help her at all.

Choosing his moment, he stepped slowly towards her and reached up to take firm hold of the reins still attached to her bridle. He came close to her head; then, standing to one side of her neck away from the risk of a swift kick, he lifted his hand and touched her gently between her eyes. She was visibly sweating and trembling. Still talking to her, he continued to stroke her face softly, moving ever closer to her side, until he could feel the warm bulk of her against his chest.

Madoc had been watching, along with the wide-eyed farmer. In fact, a small crowd of onlookers now stood transfixed as Hywel and the horse connected, no one daring to make a sound. Eventually, Hywel looked back over to Madoc and nodded for him to enter, as he gently walked the horse over to the fence and tied her loosely there. He wanted to get closer to that leg wound and moved slowly but confidently, running his hands down the horse's neck and leg.

He sensed Madoc's quiet approach and, not taking his attention from the horse, he spoke softly to him.

'I will need some water to clean her wound and some honey and clean linens to dress it. We will have to take our chances that she does not kick out again, but I will need your help to hold her.'

Madoc hastened away and came back quickly, laying the requested items at Hywel's feet.

'Will you hold her head? She seems to like Welsh poetry, if you know any.' He smiled sheepishly up at his friend as he knelt to work on the horse's leg. Thankfully, the splinter came out smoothly and Hywel was able to swiftly stem the blood flow and clean the wound, winding the honey-soaked linen strips around the limb. The mare stood quietly, watching him sideways the whole time, Madoc singing softly under his breath as he held her still.

Once he was happy the dressing was secure and the horse stood calm, Hywel offered the mare the pail with the remaining water, and she drank deeply. He called over to the farmer's lad.

'If you bring some fresh hay over, I will stand by her as you feed her. She will more likely take to you then. Do not show fear, walk gently and calmly towards her, no sudden movements.'

He stood by as promised as the lad did as he said, and watched with satisfaction as the horse bent her head to take hay from the boy's outstretched hand.

'Use your native tongue with her, and speak softly. She was just afraid, that's all. She will settle with time and patience. You have a fine horse here.'

'*Diolch*,'[20] the boy whispered, obviously rather in awe of the monk.

'Thank you, brother, thank you.' The farmer grabbed his arm as he left the paddock. 'That was remarkable. Please, let us thank you by feeding you and your friends around our hearth tonight. I would love to know more about how you did that.' He glanced back over to where the piebald still stood quietly, the lad at her head, stroking her face softly.

Hywel placed the pail of water that was still in his hands on a sawn tree trunk and rolled up his sleeves to wash his hands.

'You have a gift, brother.'

Hywel turned in the direction of the new voice. It must have been a pilgrim from another party. The man addressing him was dressed finely, and the accent gave him away as French. His hair was close-shaved and his face beardless in the Norman style. There was something familiar about his face but Hywel could not quite place him. He nodded his thanks and quickly returned to rinsing his hands.

---

[20] 'Thank you' in Welsh.

'I once knew someone who could calm horses just like that. You remind me of him, strangely.'

The man had continued speaking even with Hywel's back turned to him. Hywel would have turned and graciously acknowledged his words out of politeness if the next word uttered hadn't caused him to pause and steady himself by holding on to the sides of the wooden pail.

'Cenred. That was his name. I watched him more than once tame a wilful horse, or tend a wounded one.'

He was my friend. Hywel wanted to yell the words but they stuck like barbs in his tightening throat. What were the chances of meeting someone here who had met Cenred? Perhaps that was why the man was familiar to him? Had he dined at his father's table, perhaps? Roger Mortimer had often brought visitors over to Brampton, especially if they had a horse with a problem. Cenred had always good-naturedly put on a show of his handling or healing skills. The man was still speaking. Hywel didn't dare turn, scared that at close quarters his own face might be recognised.

'Mortimer, my wife's cousin, introduced us to Cenred at Brampton. I was sorry to hear he had passed away a year or so past. I thought it a great loss. But it is good to see others with skills like his. It was almost as if you learned from him.' Hywel's hands tightened painfully on the rim of the pail. 'But then that is unlikely, you being a Cistercian.

'Sad story all told. Rumour was that he died of heartbreak after losing his wife and child. If the child was indeed his and not another man's, as some have said. I've heard tell a son of the house might have had something to do with it. Shameful all round. Still, I leave you to your ablutions, brother. Fine show you gave us. Fine indeed.'

Hywel paused, listening for the sound of retreating footsteps. He waited until all was quiet and let his breath out slowly, finally releasing his hold on the pail. It was only then that he felt the pain. Looking down at his hands, they had blood on them, and it wasn't the horse's blood. He had held so tightly to the rough edges of the wood that he had dented and broken the skin. Spotted trails marked both palms, like some kind of strange stigmata.

Blood on my hands. The thought came to mind, and it was right. Whatever he might tell himself, however far he had travelled, whatever time had passed, he still had their blood on his hands. He was still guilty. The stranger had been right. It was shameful. He was shame-filled. There was no escape from the truth. No escape from the guilt.

Suddenly the urge came to get away. He glanced around but no one was concerning themselves with him now. He didn't care to join the others to eat, to be normal, to pretend that he hadn't just been confronted once more by his past. He dipped his hands back into the water and wiped them on his habit.

Above him on the rise, the small church stood like a sentinel calling. He headed there, hoping beyond hope to find it empty.

The church was tiny, with small windows running along one side, with a view of the sea beyond. The stone walls and packed earth floor made it feel welcomingly cool as Hywel stepped inside. He was thankfully alone. He felt his heartrate slow and took deep breaths of the lightly rush-scented air, as he moved purposefully towards the altar end of the church.

The altar was nothing more than a small, roughly hewn wooden table, and above it hung a wooden crucifix, the figure of Christ surprisingly highlighted in gold paint. Hywel stepped nearer, drawn to take a closer look. Above and below the figure of the dying Christ were two scroll-shaped banners inscribed in Latin, one word on each: *'Misercordaie'* above and *'Gratia'* below. Mercy and grace. Hywel's mind flew back to that snatched conversation with Myfanwy as they had prepared to leave Valle Crucis. Her pigs! He smiled to himself. Was that the only thing he had remembered from what she had said? That she had called her pigs Mercy and Grace? No, there had been more. She had spoken of the cross and she had made it all sound so simple. Forgiveness.

Hywel's mind went back again to Cenred, as he had lain on his deathbed, reaching out to him and offering him absolution. He had gone then with the priest and made confession and had made confession many times after that. Still the guilt remained.

After he had offended Rhodri and Julian he had also done what had been asked of him. He had joined this pilgrimage. But still he carried the burden, still it weighed heavily on him, whatever he had tried to do to shift it. He looked up at the crucifix again, stepping even closer to run his fingers over the word painted in blood red below the nail-pierced feet of the figure of Christ. *Gratia.* Grace.

That's what the cross means. He recalled Myfanwy's words. *Jesus took the punishment that I deserved for all that I have done wrong – that's the mercy bit. And then, because of that, God gifted me with full and free forgiveness – that's the grace bit. … I just had to put my guilt burden down and ask for God's forgiveness in return.*

Was it really that simple? My sin for His forgiveness? It didn't seem like a fair exchange. Surely it should cost Hywel more to earn the freedom he craved?

'It cost Me this.'

The voice startled him and he spun around, but he was still alone. Hywel could feel his heart pounding. He swallowed and closed his eyes to steady himself, holding on to the edge of the table. He listened keenly but could hear nothing more than the sound of the wind in the trees outside and the cry of seabirds beyond. He breathed deeply and let out a deep sigh, not daring to open his eyes.

'It cost Me this.' This time it was a whisper, and it sounded inside his head. All at once Hywel knew it was no human voice. He opened his eyes and looked up at the depiction of the crucified Christ above him, the hands spread wide, nail-pierced and bleeding. The twisted legs, the spear-wounded side, the thorn-crowned head bowed in agony. It was only a lifeless, silent carving and yet it spoke more than a thousand words could have in that moment. A life surrendered, a death embraced, a punishment borne. For him.

'Why should I require you to pay for what already cost Me everything?'
The voice again.

'Lord?' Hywel spoke out loud into the quiet space. He desired with every fibre of his being to hear God speak more, longed to encounter Him. He was tired. Tired of pretending to be what he wasn't, tired of not understanding, tired of carrying such weight. He would even step from this world into the next in order to be free of it all, if that was what was required. He had been ready to do that before. But then he knew that he would have to face God as his judge, still carrying the weight of all he had done, and the thought terrified him. He found himself on his knees.

'Are You here, Lord? I need to know You are here.'

'Fear not, for I have redeemed you; I have called you by your name; You are Mine.' [21]

Familiar words from the Scriptures; he had heard them read out loud before. Now it was as if God Himself whispered them, and for the first time his heart and not just his ears heard them.

As he knelt there, his head resting on the rough wood of the simple altar, other words he had read not so long ago came to mind. He did not have his Psalter with him, but as he opened his mouth to whisper, the words came unbidden. And as the words left his tongue the tears began again, wetting his cheeks with their saltiness and falling unhindered onto the herb-scented rushes beneath him: 'Have mercy upon me, O God, According to Your lovingkindness; According to the multitude of Your tender mercies, Blot out my transgressions.' [22]

And then his heart whispered to the One who had drawn near.

According to Your lovingkindness? Do You really love me? Will Your mercy extend to me?

Hywel felt the weight of divine love cloaking him. He knew what he needed to do now, and the words of the psalm were there to guide him.

---

[21] Isaiah 43:1, NKJV.
[22] Psalm 51:1, NKJV.

'Wash me thoroughly from my iniquity, And cleanse me from my sin. For I acknowledge my transgressions, And my sin is always before me. Against You, You only, have I sinned.'[23]

God. I am so sorry. Thank You for Your mercy and grace. Thank You for the cross. Wash me. Make me clean, God. I submit myself to You, and lay my burden at Your feet.

'Create in me a clean heart, O God, And renew a steadfast spirit within me. Do not cast me away from Your presence, And do not take Your Holy Spirit from me. Restore to me the joy of Your salvation.'[24]

Stay here with me, God. Let me feel Your grace. Change me, restore me, forgive me. I am Yours.

Hywel felt inexplicable peace descend and wash over him, until the very air around him seemed to be saturated with it.

'It is finished!'[25] God's voice, not his.

And then all was quiet. The voice, his mind, his lips. Just the heavy peace that engulfed him, and as he knelt there, Hywel became aware of something else. The weight had gone completely. The whole burden of guilt and shame had been lifted off him. He could not even find it by looking for it. In its place came a joy, bubbling up from deep within him, so that even though tears still fell, his heart wanted to sing.

He did not leave that place until it grew dark outside. And God did not leave him, until at last Hywel got up from that tear-dampened floor and walked out of that little church in Pistyll, leaving his burden behind him at the foot of His Saviour's cross.

[23] Psalm 51:2-4, NKJV.
[24] Psalm 51:10-12, NKJV.
[25] John 19:30, NKJV.

God, give me mercy from your fountain of

forgiveness!

I know your abundant love is enough to wash away

my guilt.

Because your compassion is so great,

take away this shameful guilt of sin.

Forgive the full extent of my rebellious ways,

and erase this deep stain on my conscience.

For I'm so ashamed.

I feel such pain and anguish within me.

I can't get away from the sting of my sin against

you, Lord!

Everything I did, I did right in front of you, for you

saw it all.

Against you, and you above all, have I sinned.

Everything you say to me is infallibly true

and your judgment conquers me.

Lord, I have been a sinner from birth,

from the moment my mother conceived me.

I know that you delight to set your truth deep in my

spirit.

So come into the hidden places of my heart

and teach me wisdom.

Purify my conscience! Make this leper clean again!

Wash me in your love until I am pure in heart.

Satisfy me in your sweetness, and my song of joy

will return.

Psalm 51:1-8, TPT

18
The Sea

The joy and the peace hadn't left him when he woke the following morning, and along with those feelings was one of excitement. An excitement that was contagious, it seemed. They were about to complete the last stage of their pilgrimage. Another few miles and they would reach the far end of the peninsula and the holy island beyond. It would involve a short sea crossing, and that Hywel was choosing not to think about. He wasn't going to let anything steal the smile from his face.

Whether the transformation in him was evident, he wasn't sure, but his good humour seemed to be catching nonetheless. Even Madoc seemed in a good mood as they packed up to leave – although that might have been on account of the hearty meal the others had been served the evening before and the bags of provisions the farmer's wife had pushed into their hands to sustain them on their journey. It seemed that even with Hywel's absence the pilgrims had been well fed in his honour. Hywel felt sorry to have missed out, but he would hold the memory of his encounter with God at Pistyll dear to his heart forever.

I'm free! The realisation hit him afresh. Hywel still felt sad when he thought of what had passed, but the weight of the guilt of it was gone. God had taken it from him and he wasn't looking to take it back. He was so thankful he wanted to sing out loud, but restrained himself for the horse's sake if nothing else. Brenin seemed strangely content beneath him, as if he too felt the burden he carried was somehow lighter.

Rhys was singing for them all, and Myfanwy joined him as they rode along, the sea a constant presence to their right. Even the cooler feel to the air and the low cloud didn't seem to dampen their spirits. Their journey's end was in sight; if not quite literally, it would be visible soon enough.

As they travelled they passed marker stones, spaced along the pilgrim route at regular intervals, each engraved with representations of Christ's cross. As he passed each one, Hywel closed his eyes briefly and whispered his thanks again. They could have stopped at the small church and healing well at Edern, and again at the church at Llangwynadl, both of which sites attracted pilgrims, but the mountain of Y Anelog that rose up before them was calling them on. They stopped only to water the horses and make a meal out of the provisions they had been gifted.

Only Tomos seemed unenthusiastic to be on their way. He had lain with his eyes closed on damp grass as the others had eaten, and could not even be persuaded to eat. Hywel assumed he had not slept so well, or perhaps was apprehensive about what lay at the end of the journey.

They arrived at Aberdaron late in the afternoon, having made good time. As expected, there were other groups of pilgrims already there, but there was overnight accommodation on offer in more than one place. No one was going to be making the crossing to the island that evening. The clouds had thickened and loomed dark above them, and rain threatened. The wind was also strengthening. Madoc turned to them as they pulled up in the village.

'I have stabling arranged for the horses but wondered if you would like one last ride up the mountain before we settle them for the night? The best view of the Island of the Saints is from up there.'

Hywel was keen, and so was Rhys. Tomos shook his head and winced.

'Not me, Madoc, I am too tired, and would rather find a bed and sleep.' With that he half-slid from his horse's back and landed heavily on his feet, barely able to stand upright.

'Then I will stay,' Rhys said, starting to dismount from his own horse.

'No!' Tomos spoke more harshly than Hywel had ever heard him. 'You go on. I will be well enough here.'

'I'll stay with him. I too am weary to my bones, and Tomos and I can keep each other company.' Myfanwy held Rhys' gaze until the man nodded his silent agreement.

The horses took them most of the way up the steep mountain path of Y Anelog, but eventually they had to dismount. The wind whipped around, almost taking their feet from under them, but Madoc had been right. It was worth the climb. From their vantage point at the top of the headland they could see the wide expanse of sea both to their right and to their left. And then ahead of them, just visible out of the descending cloud, was the small-peaked Island of the Saints, alone at what felt like the end of the world.

Hywel wished the skies were clearer and the horizon visible, as the grey sea seemed to go on forever, merging into the sky. It made him feel small, somehow, and yet almost as if he could reach out and touch heaven from that high ground, as if the line between heaven and earth were as blurred as the line between sea and sky. The fact that the sea surrounded them on three sides, the land of the peninsula stretching back behind them, gave the mountain the feel of an island itself, standing proud and almost detached from the rest of the world. It was soul-stirringly beautiful.

Hywel stood, his legs braced against the wind, and held his hands out sideways, lifting his face in praise to the One who had brought him on this pilgrimage, not caring what it looked like, just overawed with the wonder of all God had done, and the joy of being alive. The free freshness of the place echoed the free, fresh feeling he carried within. And he could see the end prize now. Tomorrow they would step onto the holy ground of the Island of the Saints. Hywel's heart swelled with anticipation at the thought. Would he encounter God there also? He hoped so. He had so much more to ask Him.

Later, as they stabled the horses, Hywel remembered Tomos.

'Is Tomos unwell?' he turned to ask a quiet Rhys.

'He has not had another episode since we left St Winefride's, if that is why you are asking. And he had been well, yes, thank you, brother.'

'Just tired, then?'

'I am not sure. It is not like him. He did complain of a slight pain in his head this morning and a tiredness behind his eyes. Strangely, he also asked me if I could see a rainbow around the mountain earlier, as he swore he could see colours in the clouds. I saw only shades of grey.'

Hywel touched the other man's arm gently. 'Well, let's pray he is settled, and a good night's sleep will aid him.'

'Yes, I am sure it will,' Rhys answered. Yet he didn't sound confident.

The stone church at Aberdaron stood almost on the beach. The pilgrims, minus Tomos, who had indeed taken to his bed, attended evening Mass there together. There were perhaps two score other pilgrims there, a good number of whom had already been to the island and had returned to start their long journey home. Hywel watched them for clues of what they might have encountered there, but in the dim, candle-lit church it was hard to read their faces.

Madoc was already planning for the day ahead.

'We will go on foot to meet the boat that will take us across the sound to the island.' He spoke quietly to his companions as they made their way back to their lodgings. 'We will leave the horses here on the morrow and they will kindly tend to them for us in the stables here. If Brenin does not disgrace himself, that is.'

'I will pray for them especially,' Hywel laughed. 'Will the weather permit us to cross tomorrow?'

The wind had not died at all, and there were definite spots of rain in the air.

'That will depend on the boatman. I am keen we get to the island tomorrow, or we might be stuck here for some days. Those who know how to read the skies here tell me that there may be a lull tomorrow morning, but then the storm winds will come back with a vengeance and may last several days. We must be ready to leave at dawn and trust ourselves to those who know these waters better than anyone. You aren't afraid, are you, brother?'

'No, of course not,' Hywel answered, knowing it was not the full truth. He wasn't afraid, exactly, more wary. And that was healthy, surely? After all, the sea crossing to the island was notoriously dangerous. He could swim, and was well used to inland water. But his experience of sea travel was limited, and he had seen the way the waves swirled and crashed around the rocky shores of both the headland and the island.

As he lay down to rest his head later, he did think for a moment that perhaps he was a little afraid. Especially as he heard the sound of the rain come and pound heavily on the roof above him, louder even than Tomos' snores.

He awoke from a restless sleep to the sounds of people moving about. Mercifully, the rain seemed to have stopped, and sometime during the night Tomos' snoring had also stopped. Hywel rose from his bed and automatically rolled it all together, ensuring the Psalter was well wrapped in its oilskin coverings and packed deep among his other belongings, to protect it against the sea and rain. It had to go with him to the end of the pilgrimage. It had become very precious to him.

'I can't wake him!'

The voice was urgent and edged with panic.

'Brother Hywel! Madoc! I can't wake Tomos!'

They made their way to where Rhys was crouched over the still form of his brother. Madoc knelt down and put his ear to Tomos' chest.

'He breathes, and I hear his heart beating. Maybe he is just deeply asleep?'

'No. This is different. He does sleep deeply, but I can always wake him with a good shake, or a gentle kick in the ribs. Not today. Neither has worked. Brother, what can we do?'

Hywel knelt down and laid his hand to Tomos' chest, feeling its rise and fall, and prayed earnestly for the young man to awaken.

'I have seen this before.' It was Madoc speaking. 'Men injured in fights who have slept so deeply as to be unrousable, sometimes for hours, and sometimes for days.'

'I have seen it before also. Tomos slept for three days after he fell from the tree, but then he woke. He came back to us that time.'

Hywel had seen it too. A flash of a memory of standing by his mother's bedside, seeing her pale face and hearing her ragged breath, but not getting a response to his cries for her attention. Memories of being dragged away from that bedside and never hearing his mother's voice again. He closed his eyes to the memory and prayed more earnestly for Tomos, and for his brother stood trembling by his side.

Madoc had gone to the door and was looking up at the lightening sky. The clouds were still spinning across, but the wind did seem to have lessened and there was no rain.

'We need to make a decision as to whether we go to the boat and across to the island, or stay here. If we do not leave now, we will miss the opportune moment to make our sea voyage and may never get to the island.' He thought for a moment. 'We could divide. Brother, you and Myfanwy go on ahead and I will stay here with Rhys and Tomos, in the hope that he wakes and we can join you in a few days.'

No one moved or said a word. The thought of not reaching the end of the journey together, having already lost Matthew, did not sit well. The thought of not reaching the island at all was a disappointment none of them dared to face.

Eventually Rhys spoke. 'We all go and we all go now. Can we not find a cart or a litter? If we can get Tomos to the island I am sure he will be well. I know he would not want any one of us not to complete this pilgrimage on his account. Can we not carry him there between us?' Rhys was close to tears in his earnestness.

Madoc paused only for a moment before darting away, and within a short time returned with a simple wooden cart pulled by a small, stocky pony. The decision had been agreed without contention, and between them Madoc, Hywel and Rhys lifted the dead weight of Tomos onto the back of the cart.

Hywel expected the boatman to refuse to take Tomos, but seemingly it wasn't the first time he had carried the sick and dying across to the island, and he readily accepted the extra coin proffered to make room in the small boat for Tomos' lifeless bulk. They had to wade into the water to lift him in and then begin to clamber in themselves, clasping their few belongings to their chests.

It was a very small boat, Hywel realised with dismay, made yet smaller by the fact that it carried a man lying insensible. Rhys positioned himself in the bow of the boat, so that he could cradle his brother's head in his lap. Madoc helped Myfanwy in and she sat at the stern end, Madoc plonking himself next to her. Hywel hesitated, watching the boat rise and fall with the movement of the waves, aware that the seawater was working its way gradually higher up his soaking habit. He steeled himself to step into the boat, stumbling slightly as a wave hit the boat at that exact moment.

'Steady there, brother.' The thickly accented, bearded boatman grabbed hold of him as he lowered himself into the boat to sit at Tomos' feet. He was already wet and cold, and now sat in a seawater puddle in the bottom of the boat.

'Are you sure it is safe to sail today?' He shivered.

'Oh, now, I've done this crossing many times, and in worse weather than this. As long as the winds are in our favour, we'll be there before you know it.'

They were out into open water soon enough. It was then Hywel remembered why he didn't like sea travel, as his stomach lurched up and down in time with the rocking of the boat. Bile rose to his throat and the urge to empty his stomach came like waves. He closed his eyes, willing the feeling to subside, but it did not seem to improve things, so he opened them and focused on the dark rock of the island in the distance. It never seemed to get any closer.

Added to his discomfort, the skies had opened and a steady cold rain was falling. He wasn't sure if it was his imagination but the winds seemed to have picked up as well; the boat was rocking from side to side as well as up and down, and every now and then a wave crashed over the side, soaking them all.

Terror seized him. It did not feel safe. He was not sure he trusted the confidence of the boatman. Perhaps he would never make it to the Island of the Saints. Was this it? Had he come this far in his journey, finally made his peace with God and received a new start, for it all to end here? Hywel had heard of the many who had lost their lives on this sea crossing, only to be buried on the island said to have 20,000 saints laid to rest under its rocky soil.

God, did You save me for this? Is this the end of my pilgrimage? To die and be buried here? Save me from this, get me safe to the other side, God, and the remainder of my life will be truly Yours.

The urge to empty his stomach came with such an intensity that Hywel scrabbled to his feet to lean over the side of the vessel. At the exact same moment the boat hit a wave and lurched violently. Hywel felt himself falling and was surprised when he hit the water, taking in a huge gulp of the sea with his gasp. The cold shock went right through him and, spluttering and disorientated, he floundered for a moment, feeling for the solidness of the boat beneath his feet and not finding it. *I can swim*, his mind reminded him. And he tried, moving his arms and legs mechanically as he knew how to, all the time the boat seeming to be just out of his reach. Soon he could see nothing but grey and white waves rising up and down all around him, and it became evident that any attempts to swim were proving useless. It also became clear that his waterlogged habit was dragging him down faster than he could pound his legs to keep his head above the water.

This was it. He gave up. He could fight the inevitable no longer. He stopped struggling and took one last deep breath, closing his eyes as he sank beneath the waves. A calmness he didn't expect came over him. He was floating towards a bright light, the tightening of his chest the only indication that he was still in the land of the living, when he felt strong hands grab his arms, pulling him roughly back above the surface and into the stormy waves he had only just escaped. His lungs involuntarily took a deep breath and his eyes flew open. He found himself face to face with the concerned faces of Madoc and Rhys as they hung on to his sleeves over the side of the boat.

'We have you, lad, we have you,' Madoc ground out, as they roughly manhandled him back into the boat.

Then it was the boatman's face that appeared above him, his face white with shock.

'It wasn't you I expected to lose on this journey, brother.' He genuflected wildly. 'God forgive me. I did think the sick one might not make it, but not you.'

Hywel struggled to focus on anything other than the relief of feeling wooden slats beneath his sea-soaked body. He was aware that he was shaking with cold, or shock, aware too that the boat was still riding the waves, up and down, but he was too exhausted to care. He just lay there, willing the voyage to end, praying for it to end.

As if God had heard him, the boat suddenly slowed and he felt it hit something solid beneath him, grinding to a stop. He closed his eyes, feeling rather than seeing the hands that pulled the boat up the beach. He kept his head down as he was helped up and out of the boat, feeling a heavy cloak thrown around his shoulders and warm arms holding him, someone trying to rub warmth back into his skin. But as his feet hit the solid stones he knew he was done. He fell hard on to his knees with exhaustion, and then remembered nothing else.

The floods have lifted up, O LORD,

The floods have lifted up their voice;

The floods lift up their waves.

The LORD on high is mightier

Than the noise of many waters,

Than the mighty waves of the sea.

Psalm 93:3-4, NKJV

19

Island of the Saints

'See to the horses, Hal.' It was Cenred, and he was beaming and slapping him on the shoulder. Hywel wanted to spin around and grab hold of him. Hold on, and explain that he had made his peace with God, to say that he was truly sorry, and that he understood about forgiveness now. But as he reached out, Cenred was gone.

'See to the horses, Hal.' He spun around in the other direction. It was his father's voice. Sir Robert was dismounting. Beside him stood Hal's brother, Robert, grinning broadly at him, holding the reins of his horse, Flight, in his hand. He stepped towards them, longing to embrace them, wanting to tell them he was at peace with his past and ready for his future; that he trusted God to show him the way now, not his own ambition. But as he approached them, they, too, faded from view.

'See to the horses, Hywel.' Prior Gwrgenau appeared, speaking in his calm, measured way. He paused, locking eyes with him. Hywel saw such kindness there that it made him long to be back with his brothers at Cwmhir. Gwrgenau moved to one side and behind him stood Rhodri and Julian, arms linked. There was no animosity on their faces. Julian lifted a hand and beckoned to him to come. Hywel was ready to follow, to find his way back to his abbey home, and to his future there. He wanted them to hear how God had dealt with him, for them to see that he was a changed man, and so ready to embrace all that God had for him, whatever that looked like.

'See to the horses, Hywel.' The voice was familiar, but Hywel couldn't quite place it. The monks had gone and in their place a light so bright that Hywel had to shield his eyes. He could see the silhouetted form of a man, but could not make out His features. The voice terrified him, and yet at the same time filled him with a strange warmth.

'Who are You?' he whispered. And then again, a little louder. 'Who are You?'

'Who am I? Brother, it's Myfanwy! Do you not know me?'

'Myfanwy?' His voice came out like a croak. He opened his eyes and tried to focus, but the bright sunlight streaming from a high window opposite him was shining straight into his eyes.

'I have been praying so hard that you would wake and speak again, but now it seems that you are awake but have lost your faculties. Oh dear, how much more tragedy must we endure? God have mercy!'

He could see it was Myfanwy now, in outline at least, although there was something different about her. In his half-awake state he couldn't quite work out quite what. She was speaking again, and offering him a cup.

'Here take a sup of this, brother.'

He groggily lifted his head enough to take a sip. It was milk, warm and sweetened. And so very good for his parched throat. He levered himself over on to his side, half-sitting, half-lying, so at least the sunlight didn't bother him any more. He could see he was in a long, wide room, with high windows and beds lining the walls. His head was thick and every part of his body seemed to ache.

'Thank you,' he managed, before taking another drink.

'Oh, Brother Hywel, you have come back to us! Praise be to God.' She jiggled about with excitement.

'How long… have I slept?'

'A whole night has passed since we arrived here, and it is now almost noon. So a good few hours. At least you did not develop a fever, as we feared. It must have just been the fright of near-drowning and the fight you put up to save yourself that exhausted you. I have sat vigil for the last hour; we pilgrims have taken turns, along with the good brothers here, of course. We could not lose you too.'

'Lose me? Who else is lost? You refer to Matthew?'

'No! Oh dear no, you would not know. I speak of our dear friend Tomos, brother. I am grieved to be the one to tell you, but he never woke, you see. He was carried here, as you were, into this infirmary. And tended to and prayed for. But he slipped away from us, and is being buried in this holy ground as we speak.' She raised a hand to her cheek and wiped away a solitary tear.

Hywel had a vague memory then of waking while it was still dark, thinking it was the bell for Vigils that had awoken him, and assuming that the sounds he had heard, the urgent whispers, were brothers rising from their beds to attend prayers. It must have been them tending to Tomos, praying over him, as he left this world for the next. He felt an intense sadness that he could not have been there, and would never see Tomos, or hear his laughter, again.

'Rhys... I must go to him.' He tried to sit upright and the room spun.

'Now then, brother, there is time enough for that. Madoc is with him now. And you need to eat before you rise from your bed. I will see what I can find for you.'

With that she was on her feet and scurrying out of the room.

It was only then that Hywel realised what was different about her. She stood straight! Her back and neck were perfectly in line, and she walked with the grace and agility of a woman half her age. He fell back on his pillow, not quite believing what he had seen.

She was not gone long, returning with a bowl of something steaming and a hunk of bread. He took pains to look at her hands, as she offered the meal to him. Her fingers were no longer awkwardly bent, her joints of normal size.

She must have been watching his face, because when he looked up at her she was smiling broadly, her eyes twinkling.

'So you have noticed, then, brother, that I have had my miracle?'

'When did this happen?'

'Well, at St Winefride's of course. You were there.'

She was teasing him, surely?

'Oh, you mean this?' She straightened all ten fingers and thumbs dramatically, and pulled her shoulders upright, turning her neck easily from side to side, like she was doing her own little celebratory dance. 'Well, I knew in my heart that He had healed me, but it took a few days for my body to catch up, 'tis all.' She was actually laughing now. 'If you could see the look on your face, brother! You'd have thought you had never seen a miracle before!'

'To be truthful, I don't believe I ever have. I doubted, Myfanwy. Forgive me, I doubted your certainty about the healing you had received. I thought your faith misplaced. There is no doubting now.'

'No, now you can rejoice with me! And praise God for it too.'

'Tell me, please, how it came about.' The simple meal was doing him good. His head was clearing and his mind anxious to understand. He sat finishing the broth with his back resting against the cool stone wall as she told her tale.

'It was something that Madoc said as we left the monastery church after prayers last night. I knew he had come here on his own personal pilgrimage and he told me a bit of the story of it. The thing he said that struck me was how long it had taken him to forgive himself. Long after God had forgiven him, he had held on to his own self-loathing, and had originally started coming to the island as an act of self-abasement. And how that had not helped his peace of mind and soul. Now he has forgiven himself and comes just for the memories.'

Her explanation was raising all sorts of questions for him about Madoc that he longed to have the answers for, but they could wait. This was about Myfanwy.

'Well, I took what he said to heart. I realised that I too was still punishing myself, in my mind at least. I knew God had forgiven me, but I had not been able to forgive myself, brother. That is what weighed me down. As I laid down to sleep I prayed earnestly that God would give me the grace to forgive myself, and to perhaps see myself as worthy to be loved by Him. I asked Him to take away that final part of the burden that I was still choosing to carry.

'I do believe something happened at the holy well; I felt it, brother. It is hard to explain. I just knew something had changed. And the pain went, but not the disfigurement. I was content with that, and praised God anyway. But He had more to give me, it seems. I woke this morning as you see me. Restored and made whole. No longer bowed over or burdened.'

Hywel understood the power of an encounter with God; he had experienced his own life-changing moment at Pistyll. He also believed God was almighty. And here before him was the evidence that God healed miraculously. Myfanwy stood before him completely free – from her affliction, and in her soul, it seemed. The joy shone from her eyes, and he rejoiced with her. But what had such a sweet lady ever done to create such a guilt burden? He understood the gravity of his failings, but could not comprehend how she could have so sinned.

'I killed a man.' She had sat on a stool beside him. 'This is not a confession, brother, the absolution is already mine. I just felt as if God wanted me to tell you my story in the hope it might help you.'

She had his attention. *Murder? Surely not.*

'Oh, now, I didn't take a knife to his heart, or even slip poison into his soup, but in a way I hastened his death. In my own mind, at least, I was guilty of killing him.' She looked over at him and he reached out and squeezed her hand, encouraging her to continue.

'My husband was a bad man, Brother Hywel. When we first married, and I was young and fair, he was sweet enough. But as the years went on and I became more and more crippled, he became more and more cruel towards me. He hated me for not giving him children, but he didn't hate me enough to do away with me. He needed someone to feed his belly, mend his clothes and warm his bed. He was often angry, and always harsh with his tongue and ready with his fist. He would not let me leave the farm without him. I had no friends. My only relief was attending Mass once a week. Even then, he would escort me to the church and wait outside to take me home, so that I had no time to speak to anyone, or even share more than a quick smile with my neighbours.

'I was trapped in my nightmare of a life and dreamt of escape. I dreamt especially of seeing the world, of travelling somewhere new, going on a journey like this one. I was never free to do so.' She paused to wipe away a stray tear, a sadness remembered. But her face was composed, and she smiled at him reassuringly before continuing. 'One day last summer he fell, and caught his leg on a sharp rock. The cut was deep and ragged, but he would not let me leave him to find a healer. He made me care for him, and I did the best I could. But I had limited knowledge of the healing arts, and the wound began to fester.

'I watched as the days passed and his leg began to swell and darken. If he was in pain, he dulled it with the ready source of ale he demanded I bring him. Finally he fell into a stupor. He was burning with fever and a rash had appeared all over his body. That was my chance, brother, to go and find help for him, to fetch a herbalist, the midwife, the priest even, to pray for him. But I did nothing. I closed the door and left him there, choosing to sleep with the animals in the barn, preferring their stink to his.

'When I returned the following morning, his breathing was laboured and he was insensible. This time I decided I would go. I knew in my heart he was beyond physical help, so I went directly for the priest. We arrived back too late. He had died alone without chance of making confession or receiving God's forgiveness. And I had allowed that to happen.'

Some would say he got what he deserved. Hywel thought it, but did not say it. He was no man's judge. He looked at the woman sitting by him, who had only ever displayed the sweetest of natures, who had been kindness personified throughout their journey, and his heart broke for the years of suffering she had endured. But now she was free, in every sense. He wondered what she would do with that freedom.

'What will you do now? When we leave here to make our journey back?'

She smiled up at him. 'Oh, I think I shall return to the abbey at Llanllugan and the sisters there. I want to be of some use to God and give Him back the life He has given to me. I loved the small community there, and Mother Gracia was grace itself. I think I will find a welcome place there to live out my days.'

Hywel smiled in return. 'They will be honoured to have you.'

He must have dozed again, because when he awoke she was gone and a small, round monk dressed in black stood over him.

'Ah, brother, can I assist you in any way? I am Brother Ignatius and I run the infirmary here, among other things. I am also extraordinarily good at lighting fires – it's how I got my name,' he added with a strange little laugh.

'My thanks, brother. I think I need to get up out of this bed and get moving. Will you help me?' Hywel lifted the blanket to see he was clothed in a simple linen tunic. 'It seems I need some clothes.'

'Oh, your habit is cleaned and dry here for you.' Brother Ignatius gestured over to a small table where Hywel could see his clothes neatly folded. A small oil-skinned package sat neatly on the top of the pile. Its familiarity cheered him.

'Oh, my Psalter. I was worried it had been lost.'

'No, no. It seems to have survived the boat trip better than you did, brother.' Brother Ignatius laughed again. 'It is safe and dry inside. Here…' He handed the pile of things to Hywel, who, after quickly inspecting the inside of the oilskins and the visible edges of the book, confirmed that the Psalter was seemingly miraculously undamaged. He quickly divested himself of the borrowed tunic, welcoming the rough, familiar feel of his woollen habit. His sandals too were there and soon he was properly shod. All the while the monk hovered, jumping from one foot to the other. He seemed a jolly sort, if a little odd.

'Can you tell me where I might find Rhys? The tall one whose brother you carried to his grave this morning.'

'Ah, he is in the graveyard still, I believe. Come, come, I will show you the way.'

It wasn't a long walk. Nothing was, it seemed, on the island. The monastery buildings took up much of the available level ground. Sheep grazed on the slopes of the small mountain that made up the rest of the island's land mass. Behind the monastery church there stretched an unenclosed area, uneven and rocky in places but with line upon line of simple grave markers. Hywel could see the evidence of freshly dug graves, and also signs of more ancient burials.

'They say thousands of saints are buried on our small island. I don't know about that. But we have certainly buried hundreds in the years I have lived here. We mourn, of course, praying for each soul we lay into the ground, but we also celebrate that they have found their rest in this holy place, where many long to be buried among so many other faithful souls.

'There…' He stopped abruptly and pointed to a heap of freshly turned soil that marked a newly filled grave. Rhys and Madoc were sitting by it, in deep conversation.

'Thank you, brother.' Hywel turned to his companion, but the monk had already left his side, skittering his way back towards the infirmary.

They must have seen his approach as Madoc rose to come towards him, reaching out his hands to grab Hywel's arms warmly.

'It is very good to see you upright, my friend.' And he said it like he meant it. 'Rhys, too, will be pleased to see you have recovered. It was a bit of a shock you gave us, diving out of the boat as you did. Praise God the boatman was quick to turn the boat about before you were swept away out of our reach – and that we were able to grab hold of you. You had us scared a second time when you collapsed on the beach. But it seems all is well.' He was looking him up and down to satisfy himself of the fact.

'How is he?' Hywel nodded towards the lone figure still sat by the grave.

'Better than you might expect. It was as if he knew that he would lose his brother one way or another on this journey. Tomos had apparently spoken of staying on the island and joining the community here. Well, he got his wish in a way, I suppose. Go to him. He will appreciate your company, I'm sure.'

Hywel walked over to where Rhys sat. The storm that had plagued their journey had seemingly blown over more quickly than expected as there were growing patches of blue sky among the clouds, and the breeze blowing in from the sea was pleasantly warm.

''Tis good to see you, brother.' Rhys greeted him with a sad smile.

Hywel lowered himself down gingerly, his muscles still complaining from his battle with the waves. He rested his hand on Rhys' shoulder.

'I was sorry to hear Tomos did not wake. And for your loss, my friend.'

'It is strange to me still, that he is not sitting here with us even now. Yet he is, in a manner of speaking.' He touched the soil heaped beside him. 'I will miss him. He always knew how to make me laugh, however I was feeling. He would be making a joke at my expense, probably.'

'He was good company, indeed.'

'I am sad that he is gone, brother, but I am not as sad as I thought I would be. I think perhaps God prepared my heart for it, if that makes sense to you. Tomos loved God, I know that. He had a simple faith and a hope-filled outlook. I think he learned that from our mother.'

'Your mother has been gone from your lives a while, I understand… And please, Rhys, call me Hywel.'

'Yes. She had a hard life and it was a kind of mercy when she went to be with God. Did Madoc tell you about her?'

'Not in any great detail.'

'She was a very special person, Hywel. She had suffered so much at the hands of men, but still was not embittered. First a nobleman's son wooed her and promised her the earth, before leaving her with child and marrying one of his own class. He was my father.'

Hywel shifted uncomfortably. That tale was a little close to home. But Rhys continued.

'My mother was lovely, but she was also resourceful. She posed as a widow, and with me as an infant she moved to another village to find work on a farm. The farmer took a liking to her, and one day took it too far, forcing himself on her. He was Tomos' father.

'So you see, both of us were conceived in pain. But she loved us nonetheless. We were raised to understand right from wrong, and to treat others with kindness. She worked so hard to give us the food on our table and the clothes on our backs; and there was always just enough. But her greatest gift to us was her devotion to God. I think if things had been different for her, she might have ended up in a convent herself.

'Tomos adored her, and felt her loss greatly, but I knew when it was her time to go. She was ready, and God took her. I felt the same about Tomos, a strange peace, if you like. His affliction, like the reputation my mother bore, was always going to mark him as different, outcast, less than who he truly was. I had hopes for this pilgrimage, that he would find healing on it. And it seemed as if he had. He was so thankful to God for what he believed had happened to him that he was going to see if he could stay and serve Him here.'

'So I understand. He would have been an asset to this community, I'm sure.'

'Well, now he can lie in rest here in this beautiful place. And he won't be afflicted in heaven, will he?'

'No, I don't believe he will.'

'And he will be with Mother, and that is good.'

Rhys paused there. It was more words than Hywel had ever heard him speak, and he seemed done in. There was one more thing Hywel wanted to ask him, because the realisation had come that not only had Tomos' death freed him from his affliction, but it had also freed his brother.

'Rhys, you told me that you had vowed to protect and care for your brother. It bound you to him. We saw that. We marvelled at your devotion to him. But now that vow is ended, so what will you do?'

Rhys smiled to himself then. 'I was just talking with Madoc about that. I've never really thought about myself and what I want out of life. But you are right. I am free now to choose. I will return with Madoc to Rhaeadr Gwy, and I will see if our little house still stands where I left it. Our small flock I left in the care of a friend.' He smiled rather sheepishly then. 'If Gwenllian will have me, I think I will ask her to be my wife. I am a simple man, Hywel, and want nothing more than that – the chance to be a husband, a father, even, and to live in peace with animals and green hills around me.'

'That is a worthy desire, my friend. And I pray you will find all as you wish it to be on your return.'

Hywel shifted himself again, this time owing to the pain in his leg muscles and the ache in his back.

'Now I think I must get up from this damp ground and go and rest some more. I feel like I fought the sea and only just won.'

'With a little help from your friends, perhaps? Here, let me help you up, and we can walk back together.'

Rhys stood and reached down to him. Hywel was glad for his strong support as they held on to one another for the brief walk back. He realised, too, that in height and colouring, the two looked more like brothers than Rhys and Tomos ever had. He thought of his own flesh brother, Robert; he loved and missed him. He knew Rhys would miss Tomas too.

But God had shown him that brotherhood relied on far more than blood ties. In Christ, men of different parentage, different social status, different backgrounds, could find themselves as close as brothers. Like the man by his side, a simple man he would have likely passed by unnoticed before taking this journey. It didn't matter to him any more that he was a nobleman's son and Rhys a poor shepherd. In every aspect that mattered they were equal, brothers, sharing a mutual respect and love for one another. He thanked God for the revelation, and that it had humbled him.

Hear my cry, O God;

Attend to my prayer.

From the end of the earth I will cry to You,

When my heart is overwhelmed;

Lead me to the rock that is higher than I.

Psalm 61:1-2, NKJV

I called on the LORD in distress;

The LORD answered me and set me in a broad place.

Psalm 118:5, NKJV

20
Journey's End

Madoc seemed in no hurry to leave the island. He disappeared off by himself for hours, but was always there to join them for meals, and seemed relaxed and happy, ready with a smile, and more at peace than Hywel had seen him before. Maybe it was having fulfilled his responsibilities in getting them to the end point of their pilgrimage; he could now enjoy his freedom before leading them back on their return journey. He had confided in him that his decision to stay a few more days was to give Hywel time to regain his strength and for Rhys to have more time to grieve. But Hywel secretly thought it was also Madoc who needed the time to rest and receive what the island offered.

It was a beautiful place. Sometimes it felt wild, when the wind whipped off the sea and the waves crashed against the rocky shore. The fact that it was surrounded by the sea didn't comfort Hywel much. Still, the separation from the mainland gave it an unearthly feel, and it was true what he had been told, it felt closer to heaven there. The prayers and devotion of so many pilgrims and sojourners over the centuries had left a tangible legacy in the atmosphere around them and in the ground beneath their feet.

Hywel had removed himself from the infirmary and into the simple guest accommodation, sharing a space with Madoc and Rhys. He had felt a fraud lying with the sick, and he had also endured Myfanwy's devoted ministrations long enough. She was still there in the infirmary, using her new-found health and strength to assist the brothers in caring for others. They were blessed to have her.

Rhys seemed to be doing well enough. There were moments when he appeared with tell-tale signs of weeping, but mostly he carried a quiet peace about him. He still sang; quiet, melodious songs rather than loud, joyous ones. And more than once Hywel had seen him turn to his side at the meal table, as if to share something with his brother, and look in surprise to find him gone.

Six days after they had landed on the island, Hywel woke to a clear blue sky. The weather had been unpredictable, changing by the hour some days. They had experienced more high winds and driving rain, and sat under low mists that hid the mainland from their view. And then they had been blessed with mornings like this one, where the sun held court in the sky, the birds sang with joy and the grass smelt fresh and green.

The weather had also made the coming and going of pilgrims unpredictable. More had come, and some had left, the boatman busying himself back and forth across the sound. Hywel wondered, as he stepped outside the door and saw Madoc coming purposely towards him, if today was the day they would book their places on that boat. He wasn't sure he was ready – either to trust himself to the waves again or to leave this place.

'Good morrow, Hywel. Are you well this morning?'

'I am, Madoc. I trust you are well also.'

'What say you to a little climb today?' Madoc indicated the tall peak standing high at the far end of the little island. 'Are you fit for it?'

Hywel felt a moment of relief. Not sailing today, then? That was good. Climbing he could definitely do.

'I would love to join you, my friend, but perhaps we could break fast first.' His stomach grumbled noisily.

'No need – I brought provisions, and there are plenty of fresh water springs on the way.' He thrust a small loaf in Hywel's direction and indicated the bag slung across his back.

Hywel thought he must have raided the monastery kitchen, by the look of its bulging weight.

It was early, and there were few signs of human life, although Hywel imagined the brothers had been at their prayers for hours already. The two of them set out at a brisk pace, crossing the small isthmus of land that separated the main island from the mountain. The grass beneath their feet had been close-cropped by the sheep that wandered freely, and the golden gorse and purple heather stood beautifully backdropped by the lush green. Large seabirds played in the air currents above them, smaller birds scuttered around pecking for worms, and the sheep grazed lazily, unconcerned by their nearness.

Hywel followed close behind Madoc, the other man saying little, but moving at a fair pace for an older man. Hywel found himself breathing with effort, especially as they began their upward climb. He had to concentrate more on where he put his sandalled feet, too, all the time Madoc's reassuring back going ahead of him.

They stopped about halfway up, by one of the promised streams. Hywel was grateful for the rest, and for the sweet fresh water they scooped into their hands and drank greedily. He was enjoying this walk immensely, if chiding himself for not being fitter. Too many hours in the saddle and not enough hours doing honest hard work, perhaps. That would change when he got back to the abbey. The thought did not worry him; he felt ready to go back home to Cwmhir now.

He had just begun to breathe comfortably again, taking a lungful of the cool, clean air, and he wondered if perhaps he should say something to Madoc, start up a conversation. But the man was already on his feet and ready to go on. Hywel fell in behind him, wondering why he had actually been invited to come, when Madoc seemed happy enough with his own company and was obviously familiar with the narrow path.

It was only as they breathlessly reached the very top that Madoc turned to him with a smile.

'Look, Hywel.'

Hywel raised himself upright up from where he had bent over with his hands on his knees to catch his breath after the last demanding slog up the steep slope. He held on to a pile of rocks that seemed to have been formed into an ancient cairn, and looked around him. It was stunning. He could see the mainland with its green fields and forests and the vast range of the Welsh mountains in the far distance. He could see sea, blue and calm, stretching out in all directions, meeting a clear blue horizon. He could see shadows of other land forms in the distance too. More of Wales in one direction, Ireland in the other, maybe. He could see the island coming to life below him, people moving about, a boat approaching the shore. And all around them were birds, of incredible variety of size and colour, nesting in rocky holes, swooping in with food for their young, squawking and screeching at their intrusion.

'It is… hard to put into words. Thank you for bringing me up here, Madoc. I will never forget this place, these views. I feel as if I could reach my hand up from here and touch the clouds, touch heaven, even.'

Madoc laughed softly. 'There are very many days when the clouds descend low enough to touch you here, believe me. But I know what you mean about feeling closer to heaven. It is why I come here. I wanted to share it with you, brother. And share this, too.' He was running his hand over one of the stones set into the cairn. 'Look here.'

Hywel bent down to look at the stone. On it was inscribed what looked like a name and a date. He traced his fingers over the marks: they spelled out the name 'Elin'.

'Elin?'

'My daughter.' It was spoken softly.

The date was harder to make out.

'She has lain here for many years, brother. At rest on this island.'

'So this is why you come? It really is a very personal pilgrimage?'

255

'I love coming to this, her resting place, yes. And I do feel closer to her here. But I come on pilgrimage also out of thankfulness to God, for what He has done in the past, and for what He continues to do for me. I no longer come to grieve, or to punish myself. I come now to remember and give thanks.'

Madoc moved and sat down with his back against the stones, out of the light wind that was definitely cooler here. He opened the bag of provisions and offered cheese, bread and an apple to Hywel.

'Sit with me for a while, brother. I started us out early and pushed us hard in the climb in the hope we would have undisturbed time to talk.'

Hywel lowered himself down to sit beside him and took the food thankfully.

'I didn't like you much at first, you know.'

'I did get that impression.' Hywel laughed good-naturedly. 'I didn't like myself much, either.'

'You were like so many young men of a certain class I have had the good fortune to encounter. Proud, entitled, ambitious, and all the time living in pretence. Yet I could see you also carried a tremendous burden on your young shoulders, and that I could equate with. I also began to see that you weren't all that bad. You showed kindness and genuinely acted with good intentions, even when you got it wrong. And you put up with me telling you what to do! I have seen you change further as we have journeyed together. Am I right in saying that God has been dealing with you, perhaps?'

'Yes. God has been gracious to me, and taught me many things. I have heard His voice, even, Madoc.'

'At Pistyll?'

He nodded.

'I thought so. You seemed a different man as we rode away from there. You put your burden down, I think?'

'I believe so, yes. God showed me His great mercy and His love for me. I laid down my guilt and exchanged it for His forgiveness. And I am so thankful to Him.'

They sat in silence for a while. It was worth contemplating – the gloriousness of what God had done for him. He was pleased that Madoc had noticed the change in him.

'So do you like me a bit better now?' Hywel asked with a grin.

Madoc smiled back at him. 'Question is, do you like yourself better now?'

That *was* a good question. Hywel had to think about that. He did think he was a better version of himself now, but did he really like himself? He knew God had forgiven him, but the fact remained that it was his choices and his behaviour that had caused so much grief and pain for others. He was not sure he could ever forget that. He had thought himself a good person before Hild, before he gave into his base passions. Now he had to live with the knowledge that within him was the potential to behave cruelly towards others. He had proved that again in his outburst at Cwmhir, the hurt he had caused his brothers there.

'I don't have a very high opinion of myself, no.' It was good to admit it.

'Hmm. And yet God loves you as you are, and has freely forgiven you? My guess is that you have not yet forgiven yourself. I know a bit about that, as I have been on a similar journey to you, Hywel. You confided in me that you loved and lost a woman and a child. I guess, then, that you bore the guilt of her death and that of her child?'

'Yes.' Hywel allowed his mind to go back. It still pained him, but like a lifeline he could cling to, he felt God's peace soften the memories. 'She was another man's wife, and that man was my friend and mentor. He and I shared a love of horses.'

'And he taught you your horse-handling skills?'

Hywel nodded. ' His name was Cenred. I betrayed him, and in doing so betrayed my family's trust, and put my vocation into doubt also. Hild died birthing our child, and I entered Orders a broken man, yet proud enough to believe I could somehow earn back my father's good opinion – earn favour with God, even – and with the mistaken belief that I could work my way into some place of prominence in the Church. I am not a bad man, Madoc. Well, I wasn't a bad man. But I made bad choices and then tried to repair the damage I had done, by myself. I think God has used this pilgrimage to show me that was not possible. Cenred tried to tell me himself. He told me both to accept God's forgiveness and to forgive myself, so that I could walk free, but I didn't know how to at the time.'

'Let me tell you my story. Perhaps it might help?'

Hywel settled back to hear it, aware he was being allowed into a confidence not lightly given.

'I am no man of God, brother. I am a soldier. I have seen and done things that would make you shudder. And yet now, perhaps, I understand that being a man of God is not always about wearing a habit and shaving your head. Now I consider myself a friend of God, at least.

'But when I was younger, I was headstrong and proud, as you were. I was full of ambition too, and ready to prove myself. I served Prince Llewellyn, and the powerful princes of Powys before him, fighting in battles and skirmishes all over Wales, and even over the border at times. I loved the life; the comradeship, the excitement, the rewards – which were many in terms of women, fine food and drink, coin and reputation. I soon became well known for my fearlessness, my recklessness, even.

'I was at the height of what I had hoped to be when I met Aelwen. She was a serving woman in the court of Magared, Llewellyn's mother. Small and delicate, but with the most lovely of faces, I thought I could just have her. Women tended to throw themselves in my path in those days, if you can believe it. But she was different. She wouldn't come to my bed without being joined before a priest. It didn't mean that much to me at the time; I didn't see how being married would change the way I chose to behave. After all, we were away for weeks at a time, and what I did when I wasn't with her she need never know about. So we wed, and I bedded her. I still don't know why she gave herself to me. She must have loved me, I suppose. If she did, I did not appreciate it. I was fond of her, but then there had been others I had been just as fond of. She was sweet and I was happy to return to her bed every time we were at court, but I did not treat her as she deserved. I deeply regret that now.

'I did not treat her much better when our child arrived. It was not that I was cruel. I tried to be loving in my own way, but it wasn't enough. The child was small and weak, and a girl, and I was disappointed. I threw myself back into my work and left them abandoned for weeks on end. Weeks that turned into months.

'One day I returned to court to find them gone. I was angry at first, but also relieved. They were a responsibility that I wasn't ready to commit to. I heard that Aelwen had taken the child to the nuns at Gwytherin. I assumed she had stayed with them there also. To my shame, I didn't go looking for them. Over the years I gave them little thought. It was only as I reached my middle years that I began to wonder about them. I saw men of my age with families, children, grandchildren, even, and I began to yearn for what I had thrown away in my youth.

'So I travelled to Gwytherin to enquire after them. I first met Sister Gracia there, in the years before she moved on to Llanllugan. It was she who told me that my wife had died many years earlier, when Elin was still a small child. Elin had been brought up with the nuns and had chosen to take novitiate vows when she reached her fourteenth year. Gracia had been her friend growing up at Gwytherin, had become as an older sister to her.

'I suddenly desperately wanted to meet the child, the young woman as she would have been then, to get to know her. But I was too late. She had decided to undertake a pilgrimage, very like the one we have just completed, before taking her final vows. She had never been in good health, and living among the nuns she had suffered further deprivation. They had practised rigid self-denial and she had been a little too severe in her own practices. Gracia told me that she had been a sweet-natured girl, and other-worldly in her ways, not caring about her own well-being, serving God and others self-sacrificially, to her own detriment. She had never returned from that pilgrimage. Like many before her, she came here to die, and lies buried among the saints.

'I cannot tell you how that tore into my soul, Hywel. The pain at losing a daughter that I had never got the chance to know. The realisation that I had squandered that chance through my own selfish choices. The guilt I took on, knowing I had abandoned her mother and my child, without a second thought, to pursue my own selfish desires. The weight of it hit me hard. Broke me.

'I vowed to make the pilgrimage to this island every year as a kind of penance. I hoped that somehow I would find some kind of absolution that way. But it just became an exercise in self-flagellation, every time I came, for those first few years. I would leave feeling worse, having been reminded each time how much I had betrayed them. How I had caused suffering to two sweet, innocent women.

'It was Gracia who became my saving grace, and your Prior Gwrgenau, whom I had known from my days in Powys. Both offered me godly wisdom and pointed me to the only way I could deal with my guilt. Gracia demonstrated the grace of God to me in her acceptance of me in my brokenness; she never once blamed me for my part in the loss of her friend. Rather, she only showed selfless care and concern for me and now has become like a daughter to me. Gwrgenau led me to the cross of Christ, and I learned what you have about God's mercy. That He is more than able to take the burden of our sin and disgrace.

'In time, I chose to leave Llewellyn's guard and to spend my remaining days guiding others on their pilgrimages. Each time I have seen God do extraordinary things in the lives of people, and I thank Him afresh for what He did for me.'

'And you have forgiven yourself?'

'Yes. That took a little longer, but yes, I have. God brought me here to this mountaintop one time, and met with me here. I dreamt I saw the figure of Christ, and by His side stood my wife and my daughter. All three were smiling and looking at me with such love, that I just knew I had to be kinder to myself, for their sake. If my life was to count for anything, in their honour, I had to let my self-loathing go. It was making me angry and bitter. That particular burden I think I left here, where I carved Elin's name in the rock. If ever I am tempted to punish myself again, I remember the love in her eyes and the love of my Saviour in dying for me.'

Madoc was moved by the telling of his tale. His cheeks were wet, but his eyes were bright.

'And now, brother...' The old gruff Madoc was back. 'You will keep what you have heard here, and the tears you have seen, as a memory for yourself alone and not as a tale to be retold.'

'Have no fear. Your secrets are safe. Thank you for honouring me with them.'

Hywel knew he had more business to do with God, and there was time to do that later. For now he appreciated the company of the man beside him as they made their descent of the mountain. This time they took it at a more leisurely pace.

'We must leave here soon.'

Hywel knew it was an inevitability they could not put off forever. The boat trip back was all that really concerned him.

'When?'

'The early boat tomorrow, I think, if the others agree. I have talked with them, and both appear eager to return for different reasons. Myfanwy feels called by God, and Rhys by love, it seems. And what of you, brother? Do you look forward to what lies ahead of you? I think perhaps you are better equipped to pursue position within the Order now, with a clear conscience at least.'

Hywel thought on his words, but he already thought he knew the answer to that question. 'I am not so sure that position and status is the path God has for me, now. Yes, I want to return to Cwmhir, and I will not break my vows. But I have made other more personally binding vows now.'

Save me from this, get me safe to the other side, God, and the remainder of my life will be truly Yours.

'My father had ambition for me to rise through the ranks of the Church, and I inherited that ambition, wanting to prove myself to him and to the world. But I saw from the monks at Basingwerk that leading can be through example, and that serving one another in God's love is the way of Christ. I want to serve God with the rest of my life, and serve others as He directs. That might be as a leader in the Church, but it might not be, and I am content with that. I get the sense that, like you, that God has called me to be a guide of sorts to other lost souls. Although I have much yet to learn, and I must remain humble before Him to do so.'

Madoc was looking at him with what looked distinctly like admiration, and it was making Hywel feel distinctly uncomfortable. He turned away and kept talking to hide his discomfort.

'I think I might have heard God again. In a dream I had the other night. I think He told me what He wants me to do.'

He continued to relate the dream to Madoc, who seemed unfazed by the conclusions Hywel had drawn from it.

'"See to the horses, Hywel," is what the voice said. I think that was my instruction, and it sits well with me. In fact, it makes me feel both excited and content all at once. I love horses, and He has given me a gift in handling them, of that there is no doubt. That He might be calling me to serve Him and others by doing something I love is a wondrous thing to me. And a calling I can embrace wholeheartedly.'

Madoc smiled then.

'I am pleased for you, brother. Now let's get back and see if there is some warm food on offer. We have fed our souls here, I believe, and now our bodies need feeding.'

With my whole heart, with my whole life,
and with my innermost being,
I bow in wonder and love before you, the holy God!
Yahweh, you are my soul's celebration.
How could I ever forget the miracles of kindness
you've done for me?
You kissed my heart with forgiveness, in spite of all I've done.
You've healed me inside and out from every disease.
You've rescued me from hell and saved my life.
You've crowned me with love and mercy.
You satisfy my every desire with good things.
You've supercharged my life so that I soar again
like a flying eagle in the sky!
You're a God who makes things right,
giving justice to the defenseless.
You unveiled to Moses your plans
and showed Israel's sons what you could do.
Lord, you're so kind and tenderhearted
and so patient with people who fail you!
Your love is like a flooding river
overflowing its banks with kindness.
You don't look at us only to find our faults,
just so that you can hold a grudge against us.
You may discipline us for our many sins,
but never as much as we really deserve.
Nor do you get even with us for what we've done.
Higher than the highest heavens –
that's how high your tender mercy extends!
Greater than the grandeur of heaven above
is the greatness of your loyal love, towering over all
who fear you and bow down before you!
Farther than from a sunrise to a sunset –

that's how far you've removed our guilt from us.
The same way a loving father feels toward his children –
that's but a sample of your tender feelings toward us,
your beloved children, who live in awe of you.
You know all about us, inside and out.
You are mindful that we're made from dust.
Our days are so few, and our momentary beauty
so swiftly fades away!
Then all of a sudden we're gone,
like grass clippings blown away in a gust of wind,
taken away to our appointment with death,
leaving nothing to show that we were here.
But Lord, your endless love stretches
from one eternity to the other,
unbroken and unrelenting toward those who fear you
and those who bow facedown in awe before you.
Your faithfulness to keep every gracious promise you've made
passes from parents, to children, to grandchildren, and beyond.
You are faithful to all those who follow your ways
and keep your word.
Yahweh has established his throne in heaven;
his kingdom rules the entire universe.
So bless the Lord, all his messengers of power,
for you are his mighty heroes who listen intently
to the voice of his word to do it.
Bless and praise the Lord, you mighty warriors,
ministers who serve him well and fulfill his desires.
I will bless and praise the Lord with my whole heart!
Let all his works throughout the earth,
wherever his dominion stretches –
let everything bless the Lord!
Psalm 103, TPT

Epilogue

1231
Abbaye Grand Selve, France

Hywel stood over the sleeping form of the man in the bed before him. The sleep was not peaceful. After Hywel had pulled the wounded knight from that muddy ditch and brought him here to the abbey, they had tended him and watched him fight for his life. Physically he was doing well enough now; the danger seemed to have passed. But he was not safe yet. Hywel recognised the tell-tale signs of trauma and despair. He knew this man had a few more battles ahead of him, and yet he was strangely drawn to stay close to him, through whatever difficult days would come. He should have left for Wales with his horses days ago, but here he still was. And now he stood clutching his precious Psalter with the realisation that it was not going to be his much longer.

What had Titus and Jean-Pierre told him? That this was a gift that one day he would be required to pass on. He had kept it close for years, but now he felt the unmistakeable nudge from God that this was the time, and here was the soul who needed it more than he did. He laid it gently down on the table by the man's bed, moving the tallow candle so that the wax did not drip on the cover. He remembered how it had felt when he had first held the lovely book in his hands, and how much of a lifeline the words it contained had become to him. He prayed they would do the same for its new owner.

His mind took him back to the memories of that life-changing pilgrimage, and he smiled in the remembrance. He had made good friends on that journey, and kept contact with them over the years. Myfanwy had ended her days peacefully at Llanllugan, and had become a mother to many young girls trying to find their place there. Madoc had led more of his pilgrimages, before deciding on the last one not to leave his beloved island, or his beloved daughter, and made his home permanently with the saints, in life and eventually in death. Rhys had married Gwenllian and they now had an abundance of children, grandchildren and sheep in their care. He was still singing, the last time Hywel had seen him.

He thought fondly of Tomos, and of Matthew too, of whom he had heard nothing more.

Julian and Rhodri, of course, had welcomed him back like a long-lost brother, and were still his closest friends even all these years later. Well, second only to the horses, maybe! He had been so blessed to stay doing a job he loved, and it hadn't seemed to disappoint his family that he had not been promoted into position. God had used him, over and over again, to help others on their journeys, and the joy and peace he carried within him were no longer a pretence.

Looking down at the man in the bed, he knew that he had been called by God once more – to lead by example, to serve, to love and to guide a broken soul as they walked a pilgrimage journey of their own.

Historical Note

Brampton Barre is based on a real castle, whose ruins still stand in the village of Brampton Bryan in Herefordshire. It was founded and built, originally as a wooden motte and bailey structure, sometime in the late eleventh century. By the time of my story, the family that resided there had taken their name Brampton from the fortress, and had built the stone keep tower. They were indeed subtenants of the more powerful Mortimers of Wigmore. A far as I am aware there was no Sir Robert Brampton with a son named Robert; I created them for my own means. But Sir Roger Mortimer of Wigmore was a real man, a powerful Marcher Lord, who did indeed patronise Abbey Cwmhir.

King John had a troubled history with both his barons and with Llewellyn the Great. He did indeed give his daughter, Joan, to be the Welsh prince's wife, she being one of many of the king of England's illegitimate offspring, and it enabled an uneasy truce to exist between them. Llewellyn based his court in Abergwyngregyn, Gwynedd, and brought his new English bride back there to live.

Abbey Cwmhir was founded in 1178 and colonised by Cistercian monks from Whitland Abbey. Its stone-built church claimed to house the longest nave in Europe at the time. Few ruins remain, but the valley after which the abbey is named (Long Valley) is still worth a visit for its peaceful, affecting beauty. The period this story is set in was at the height of the Cistercian expansion in Britain, and I have tried to illustrate this with the building and founding of the great abbeys our pilgrims visit on their route.

The pilgrim route our travellers took is now known as the North Wales Pilgrim Route. The island of Bardsey (Ynys Enlli in Welsh) was simply known as the 'Island of the Saints' (Ynys y Saint) in the early medieval period. It was said that to complete three visits to Bardsey was the equivalent of a pilgrimage to Rome, and so it became a very popular medieval pilgrim route, with established stops along the way. I could have had my pilgrims travel west from Abbey Cwmhir in Powys towards the Lleyn Peninsula in the far north-west of Wales, but the pilgrim route to Bardsey traditionally started at Basingwerk Abbey and St Winefride's Well at Holywell. So my pilgrims had to head north before they travelled west, extending their journey. They would have received a pilgrim's 'badge' at every holy site they visited en route.

As always, apart from a few verifiable facts, my imagination is responsible for much of the historic content and character portrayals in this book. My apologies if I have corrupted or misrepresented people, places or customs in my attempts to add authenticity to my tale.

Acknowledgements

My thanks go to the team at Instant Apostle for believing in my writing and making this second book possible. As before, your care and professionalism have made this a great publishing experience.

Thank you to everyone who read and responded to *The Healing*, and whose encouragement made me keep writing. I hope you won't be disappointed with this follow-up offering.

Thank you to my brilliant writer friends, most of whom I have yet to meet in person, but whose encouragement and wisdom has been invaluable. Thank you especially to the Association of Christian Writers, Wordy Chat, FabChow, History Writers and, of course, to The Priceless Ladies (all fabulously supportive and hilariously funny Instant Apostle authors).

Special mention to Joy Velykorodnyy whose beta reading was exemplary, and whose prayerful Zoom friendship has helped keep me going through some tricky patches! Thank you too, to Joanna Watson, for stirring my faith with her own writing.

Of course, my family deserve a mention. Tim, my husband, my chief supporter, for giving me the time and space to do what I love. My parents, parents-in-law, siblings and kids for their ongoing love and support. And my grandson, Judah, for being an excellent distraction. Also, my dear friends and church family. I have so very much to be grateful for, with the people God has chosen to surround me with.

Three of my friends have to have their names in print because, as promised, their monk creations appear in this story. Thank you to Esther Wintringham for Brother Titus (renamed from Timothy for my husband's sake). Thank you to Katie Blow for Brother Jean-Pierre – I so loved writing him in! And thank you to Sarah Sansbury for Brother Ignatius, who perhaps deserved a bigger part.

My chief thanks always and forever, go to God. For His mercy and grace towards me, and for this gift He has given me in order to declare His goodness and faithfulness. This is all for Him.

If you have enjoyed *The Pilgrim*, check out *The Healing*, where Brother Hywel reappears.

Driven to despair by heart-breaking betrayal, nobleman Philip de Braose has lost faith in God and man. Working as a soldier for hire, he recklessly seeks death and is brutally injured, only for rescue to come in the unlikely form of a Cistercian monk.

This joy-filled, kind and compassionate man walks alongside Philip as his body slowly recovers and he is forced to confront the more painful wounds within. As they travel from France to an Abbey deep in his Welsh homeland, Philip disguises himself as a Cistercian and begins to rediscover the man God always intended him to be.

But when his past invades the present, his newly awakened faith is challenged by long-buried dreams and he must decide if he can live a life devoted to God outside the Abbey's walls.

'A feel-good exploration of forgotten times that leaves a final lump in the throat.'
Ian Hampson, Lay Reader, Church in Wales, and student of Welsh ecclesiastical history

'Impossible to read without encountering hope.'
Billy Doey – Senior Pastor (Retired), Welcome Evangelical Church, Witney